PRAISE FOR KATI HIEKKAPELTO

'An edgy and insightful chiller with a raw and brooding narrative. Skilfully plotted and beautifully written, Hiekkapelto has given us an excellent and suspenseful crime novel' Craig Robertson

'Kati Hiekkapelto deserves her growing reputation, as her individual writing identity is subtly unlike that of her colleagues … her socially committed style acquires more polish with each successive book' Barry Forshaw

'Seriously good! The taut elegance of the writing brilliantly contrasts the grit of the subject matter. Kati Hiekkapelto is the real deal' Anya Lipska

'There is something fresh and slightly subversive about Hiekkapelto's writing … that makes the novel stand out from the pack' Doug Johnstone, *The Big Issue*

'Crisp and refreshing, with a rawness that comes from a writer willing to take risks with her work' Sarah Ward, CrimePieces

'A gripping slice of Scandi Noir' Raven Crime Reads

'Hiekkapelto's particular type of crime genre is deeply intertwined with social critique, as was already evident in *The Defenceless*. This is a happy marriage, and she manages to discuss touchy and topical issues such as immigration without succumbing into the dangers of holier-than-thou territory. For me, however, this was a book about Anna' One Day I Will Read

'Chilling, disturbing and terrifyingly believable, *The Defenceless* is an extraordinary, vivid and g[...] one of the most exciting new voices in crime

'Kati Hiekkapelto's second novel has fully delivered on all of the promise of her first. *The Defenceless* is a gritty crime novel with a pulsing vein of social realism. It is entertainment with a conscience, fiction with heart-rending insight into the real lives of people on the fringes of our own societies' Live Many Lives

'From the outset *The Defenceless* ticks so many of the boxes that Scandinavian crime fiction lovers look for in their favourite crime sub-genre, and here's why … The real stand-out feature of this book is the strength and balance of Hiekkapelto's plotting. A gripping slice of Scandi-noir' Raven Crime Reads

'In her follow-up novel, Kati Hiekkapelto weaves a complex, multi-layered narrative that forces the reader to re-evaluate long-standing opinions. More strident than its predecessor, the book uses the crime fiction genre to shine a torch on to under-reported social problems.' Andy Lawrence, Crime Time

'With *The Defenceless* you're so caught up in the characters, the sub plots and the hunt for what appears to be a brutal killer that when the killer's identity and motive are revealed it comes like a bolt from the blue. It brings to (my) mind the reveal in Håkan Nesser's *The Unlucky Lottery*. The translation – by David Hackston – should also receive the strongest nod of approval; at no point in reading *The Defenceless* was there any indication that this was anything other than the language the novel was written in, and the deft translation ensures that the novel's momentum and feel flows uninterpreted across the language transition' Tony Hill, Mumbling About Music

'*The Defenceless* is a powerful read, tackling illegal immigration and the role of gang members in exacerbating the desperation of migrant workers. Hiekkapelto is unflinching in her chilling descriptions and, once more, it is her police investigator protagonist, Anna Fekete, who dominates the narrative' Sarah J. Ward, Crime Pieces

The Exiled

ABOUT THE AUTHOR

KATI HIEKKAPELTO was born in 1970 in Oulu, Finland. She wrote her first stories at the age of two and recorded them on cassette tapes. Kati has studied Fine Arts in Liminka Art School and Special Education at the University of Jyväskylä. The subject of her final thesis/dissertation was racist bullying in Finnish schools. She went on to work as a special-needs teacher for immigrant children. Today Kati is an international crime writer, punk singer and performance artist. Her books, *The Hummingbird* and *The Defenceless* have been translated into ten languages. *The Hummingbird* was shortlisted for the Petrona Award in the UK in 2015 and *The Defenceless* won the prize for the best Finnish Crime Novel of the Year 2014, and has been shortlisted for the prestigious Glass Key. She lives and writes in her 200-year-old farmhouse in Hailuoto, an island in the Gulf of Bothnia, North Finland. In her free time she rehearses with her band, runs, hunts, picks berries and mushrooms, and gardens. During long, dark winter months she chops wood to heat her house, shovels snow and skis. Writing seems fairly easy, after all that. Follow her on Twitter @HiekkapeltoKati or visit *www.katihiekkapelto.com*.

ABOUT THE TRANSLATOR

DAVID HACKSTON is a British translator of Finnish and Swedish literature and drama. He graduated from University College London in 1999 with a degree in Scandinavian Studies and now lives in Helsinki, where he works as a freelance translator. Notable publications include *The Dedalus Book of Finnish Fantasy*, Maria Peura's coming-of-age novel *At the Edge of Light*, Johanna Sinisalo's eco-thriller *Birdbrain* and two crime novels by Matti Joensuu. His drama translations include three plays by Heini Junkkaala, most recently *Play it, Billy!* (2012) about the life and times of jazz pianist Billy Tipton. David is also a regular contributor to *Books from Finland*. In 2007 he was awarded the Finnish State Prize for Translation.

The Exiled

KATI HIEKKAPELTO

Translated from the Finnish by
David Hackston

Orenda Books
16 Carson Road
West Dulwich
London SE21 8HU
www.orendabooks.co.uk

First published in the United Kingdom by Orenda Books 2016
Originally published by Otava, Finland, as *Tumma*, 2016

Published in the English language by arrangement with Otava Group Agency, Helsinki

A catalogue record for this book is available from the British Library.

ISBN 978-1-910633-51-9

Typeset in Garamond by MacGuru Ltd
Printed and bound by CPI Group (UK) Ltd, Croydon CRO 4YY

Orenda Books is grateful for the financial support of FILI, who provided a translation grant for this project.

SALES & DISTRIBUTION

In the UK and elsewhere in Europe:
Turnaround Publisher Services
Unit 3, Olympia Trading Estate
Coburg Road, Wood Green
London N22 6TZ
www.turnaround-uk.com

In the USA and Canada:
Trafalgar Square Publishing
Independent Publishers Group
814 North Franklin Street
Chicago, IL 60610
USA
www.ipgbook.com

In Australia and New Zealand:
Affirm Press
28 Thistlethwaite Street
South Melbourne VIC 3205
Australia
www.affirmpress.com.au

For details of other territories, please contact *info@orendabooks.co.uk*

To my mother

JUNE 19th

Droplets of blood on the light-green wallpaper, like overgrown poppies along the verge.

Here, where the hazy grey sky swallows the edges of the immense wheat fields, where you can sense the Tisza, the river flowing past, even when you can't see it. The river is always present, always on the move, arriving, leaving. It flows like a giant artery through the poisoned fields, where weeds, poppies, cornflowers and dandelions are stifled and beaten back, past this small town where life feels unchanged, where time seems to have stopped while the country around it changes name, fights wars, languishes on the precipice of economic collapse, harbours its war criminals, ashamed of itself but too proud to admit its own mistakes. That country contains dozens of identities, nationalities, minorities, majorities, languages. It has signed the UN Declaration of Human Rights but doesn't uphold its contents.

The river will come into blossom any day now. People are saying it will be the biggest flowering in living memory. Perhaps right now millions of mayfly larvae are beginning to hatch and dig their way out of the mud on the riverbank. Soon they will swarm above the river like a giant, beautiful cloud of flying flowers; they will mate, lay eggs and die. People gather along the riverbank to celebrate, many taking their boats out on the water, in among the insects, so they can feel the delicate beating of their wings and the touch of the insects' rubbery bodies on their skin. The flowering is a wondrous carnival of life and death, an event the town eagerly awaits and that people celebrate with great verve. Nothing like this happens anywhere else in the world – only at this bend in the river, at the centre of this town. As though the town was special, blessed.

Droplets of blood. They converge on the light-green wallpaper into a large, blackening pattern, a giant amoeba. The wall is around two-and-a-half metres high, five metres in length, and behind it is one of the house's two bedrooms. The wall is bare – no paintings, no mirrors. Only plain, light-green wallpaper, and now that pattern in the middle, the amoeba, the poppy field.

A moment earlier a figure cast a shadow as he sat down at the antique desk by the window. The desk was bare; it had just been cleared, its drawers emptied. From outside came the sound of footsteps, the happy laughter of children walking past, laughter that seemed out of place in the atmosphere of the room.

A road leads directly past this house. In this part of town all the houses are built like this, snuggly against one another and so close to the road that they form a wall along the narrow pavement. A cherry tree can be seen through the window. It stands on a small strip of grass between the road and the pavement, its leafy branches shading the house so well that the occupants rarely need to lower the blinds, though the afternoon sun shines mercilessly on this side of the building. The blinds in this window are drawn last of all, in a futile attempt to hold back the heat when the summer outside is so sweltering, so oppressive that it penetrates everything. The branches are heavy with cherries – dark-red, juicy globes, ripe and ready to be plucked. Will anyone pick them this summer, preserve them in syrup, organise the jars in rows on the shelves in the pantry behind the kitchen?

A moment longer after he sat down, then his head and body worked together. The sturdy barrel of the pistol was placed squarely beneath his jaw, at such an angle that the bullet would go right through his skull and not just injure his face, leaving him alive but in pain. The pistol was loaded, his hand wasn't trembling in the slightest, his body was steady and prepared. With one exception, his head always had perfect control over his hand and pistol.

A shot, and before that a single thought: hell is here. Right now.

JUNE 3rd

THERE WAS A SMALL WINE FESTIVAL going on in the park outside the town hall. To Anna the word 'park' seemed a bit over the top for the green but rather underwhelming strip of land, bordered to the south by the town hall and to the east by the road running between Horgos and Törökkanizsa, which pared off a chunk of the town. At the northern end of the park was the main shopping boulevard, and to the west rose the beautiful belfry of the Orthodox cathedral. The area was barely a quarter of a hectare in size, nothing but a stretch of lawn shaded by the chestnut trees right in the centre of Kanizsa. In the summer people sat in the shade of the trees watching the passers-by, keeping an eye on their playing children and exchanging gossip. In the evenings the place was filled with youngsters. Fine, call it a park, thought Anna. After all, it even had the obligatory statues – busts of two local artists and a monument to commemorate the Second World War. *Za slobodu*, it read in Serbian. *In the Name of Freedom.* The park was as tenuous as the freedom that existed in this country. A semi-park. A semi-freedom. Anna wondered how she might translate those words into Hungarian. She couldn't think of anything. Word play worked better in Finnish, and in Finland the notion of freedom seemed to grow more absurd by the day.

The evening had grown dusky. Light bulbs dangling from the trees like strings of pearls lit the asphalted path running through the park. The path was lined with wine-tasting stalls, tables and chairs. People crowded around them, drinking and laughing. Acquaintances and half-acquaintances, and even some complete strangers, who must have been friends of Anna's mother, stopped as they saw Anna and greeted her with smacking kisses on both her cheeks. Anna could smell the wine and tobacco on their breath as they went through the list of compulsory questions, excited and apparently with genuine curiosity. How are you doing? When did you arrive? How long will you be staying? Did you fly into Budapest? How long is the flight? I'm sorry about your grandmother. She was a good woman. Oh, you didn't make it to the funeral? Your brother has been here for a while now. How is he getting on? And how is your mother keeping? You must come and visit one day, any time you like. Finally they whispered to Anna, almost apologetically, that last year's fair had attracted many more people. What a shame it's so quiet this year. It's started straight away, thought Anna: the apologising. Had people apologised like this back in Tito's day? Or had it only started after the war that led to the break-up of Yugoslavia? It seemed that a sense of inferiority had descended over Kanizsa like a veil, a layer of dust in an abandoned house. But the locals barely noticed it. Here, complaining about things and belittling themselves were an integral part of communication, and nobody thought of the effect this had on the atmosphere and on people's confidence and self-respect. People were slowly but surely giving up. Anna had sensed this in the past too.

Anna thought there were a surprising number of people at the fair. After the scorching daytime heat the evening was still warm, and a hint of approaching rain hung in the air. People weaved around one another and the atmosphere was almost jubilant. On a stage erected at one end of the path a band struck up and started playing covers of Hungarian hit songs; the music was so loud it could probably be heard on the other side of town. Inferiority complex or not, at least people here knew how to celebrate, how to live in the moment, and the following morning nobody, not even the grumpiest old codgers in town, would complain about being kept awake by the noise. They were all probably enjoying the party too, asking their grandchildren to bring them little tasters of the different wines.

In front of the stage a group of youngsters were slouching around, bottles of beer in their hands, and more people were arriving all the while. Anna felt tired. To tell the truth, she'd wanted to go to sleep a long time ago, or at least to withdraw into the peace and quiet of her bedroom. All the greetings, the shrieks of excitement, the kisses on the cheek and the questions about how she was doing had quickly got on her nerves. In Finland she forgot all about the inquisitiveness of the people of Kanizsa, so gushing it was almost overwhelming, and after the first few days of her holiday it always managed to exhaust her. She instantly started making comparisons in her mind: in Finland people do this and that instead. It annoyed her. It was as though she was constantly awarding each place plusses and minuses, as though this would help her decide where she belonged. As though she had to make a choice. But she didn't. Fate had made that decision for her long ago.

Anna had arrived in Kanizsa late in the afternoon. After a bad night's sleep she had set off ridiculously early from her one-bedroom rented apartment in Koivuharju, taken a cab to the airport, flown south to Helsinki and caught a connecting flight to Budapest. There she had jumped into a hire car – a white Fiat Punto with automatic gears and with such efficient air conditioning that she could still feel the chill in her shoulders – and driven a few hundred kilometres directly south. She crossed the border at Röszke, taking a deep breath once she arrived on the other side, where the Hungarian steppe, the *puszta*, stretched out on both sides of the road like the open sea. A few kilometres later she turned right at the intersection leading to Horgos, where the houses looked like they might fall down at any minute, and then to Magyarkanizsa, which the locals referred to simply as Kanizsa.

The transition was too quick. It was like this every time. When a plane shoots into the sky and hurtles through the air at hundreds of kilometres per hour, carrying people from one city and one country to another, the soul has no time to catch up. Its habit is to unwind itself slowly, at its own pace. Anna knew this perfectly well, but she never seemed able to protect herself against the shock; she always went straight to Kanizsa to visit friends as soon as she'd arrived. Instantly she became so agitated that she almost hated the place, regretted ever coming back and felt as though she was suffocating inside her own soulless body, as though it was the soul – the innermost being – that defined the extremities of our body and protected it from outside attacks. It was a strange feeling but one that would soon pass. She knew that too.

They sat down in front of a stall belonging to the Nagy-Sagmeister vineyard and bought three bottles of wine and one of mineral water. Anna was with friends she had known since they were at nursery school together: Tibor, Nóra, Ernő and Véra. Réka hadn't joined them. She'd been feeling ill all day, and she and Anna had agreed to meet up tomorrow. Anna's mouth felt bone dry after the long journey, and she downed a large glass of water. Her friends handed her a glass of white wine – *furmint* – which the local vineyard had bottled the previous autumn. This stuff's fantastic, top notch, they assured her. You won't find anything better in Hungary either. This producer – a Kanizsa local – was set to bring Serbian wine culture to new heights, they proudly proclaimed. Anna sipped the wine. It was good. She watched the people walking past and noticed a man standing at another stall with a glass in his hand, looking over at her. For a moment Anna looked elsewhere and nodded at Tibor's stories as if she were actually listening to him, then she cautiously glanced back at the man. Yes. Now he was openly staring at her. Anna awkwardly looked down at her wine glass.

'Don't look now, but who is that man over there on the left? The one with the bespoke suit and the grey hair,' Anna asked Nóra.

Nóra peered over Anna's shoulder. The man was engaged in conversation with the owner of the wine stall.

'That's Remete Mihály. He sits on the local council. He's a big fish. Apparently he's going to run for parliament at the next election.'

Again the man looked over at Anna.

'He's staring at me,' said Anna and felt an uncomfortable tingling sensation in her back.

'Mihály likes younger women. It's an open secret round the town,' said Tibor and gave Anna a teasing nudge on the shoulder.

'He's old enough to be my father,' Anna scoffed.

The man paid for his wine and began walking towards their table.

'Damn it, he's coming this way,' Anna whispered.

'*Jó estét kívánok, Remete Mihály vagyok.*' The man stood smiling in front of Anna and held out his hand.

Anna shook his hand and introduced herself. The man had several thick golden rings on his fingers.

'I know who you are,' he said 'I knew your father well. He was a good man.'

Of course, thought Anna. Everybody had known her father. Back here she would always be her father's daughter. This defined her position in a society to which she no longer belonged, but to which she was eternally bound. Her grandfather, grandmother and great-grandfather were roots, and her mother and father the trunk from which her own branch grew. She could almost see that branch appearing like a speech bubble in a cartoon as the local man tried to place her in the right bough of the right tree in the arboretum called Kanizsa. A sense of relief flashed across their faces when they found the correct tree, the correct branch. Good. You're not an outsider. We know you. We know how to treat you.

How ludicrously wrong they were.

'Are you here on holiday?' asked Remete Mihály.

Anna repeated the same things again, answered the same questions, smiled and raised her wine glass when the man decided to make a toast to her father.

'Come and visit me some day,' he said. 'I could show you a few photographs of your father from when we were young. You might be surprised. We were a pair of tearaways.' At that he gave a hollow chuckle, bade the group good evening and went to the next stall to get another glass of wine.

'Nice guy,' said Ernő. 'I voted for him last time.'

Anna could hear Ernő beginning to slur his words. Nóra wanted to take the obligatory selfie with Anna and their glasses of wine and upload it to Facebook straight away. Anna put on a smile and posed for the photo: cheek-to-cheek with Nóra, *cheese*; and with our glasses raised, *cheese*; now with the guys. The prodigal daughter has returned, Nóra typed and tagged them in the photograph. She giggled at her own inventiveness and wondered out loud why Anna still wasn't on Facebook. Anna explained – for the umpteenth time – that she simply didn't want to. Eventually she said she might consider it in order to keep in closer contact with her old friends, but only because Nóra's effusive Facebook sermon started to make her feel pressured.

The guys' conversation had shifted to local politics, a subject about which they both seemed to have trenchant views, while the women chatted about their work and what they had cooked for dinner earlier that day, yesterday, last week. Anna tried to engage in her friends' conversations but couldn't get a grip on the rhythms, couldn't deploy appropriate words at the appropriate moment, and didn't really know what to say about either subject. After a while she gave up and listened to the buzz of chatter, punctuated with bursts of laughter. Before long she'd given up on that too. She drifted into her own thoughts, sensed the dizzying smell of the *hársfa* in her nostrils, closed her eyes for a moment and slowly began to relax. Things will be fine, she thought. I can soon go to bed, they'll understand I'm tired. Tomorrow this will all feel much nicer, much cosier, and I'll see Réka for the first time in ages. We can go for a walk across the *járás*.

Just then Anna felt a violent shove at her back. She was buffeted against the table – so hard that Tibor's wine glass toppled over. Golden-yellow *furmint* trickled over the edge of the table on to the ground and splashed on Anna's trousers. Tibor leapt to his feet and shouted something, and it was then that Anna noticed her handbag had disappeared from the chair next to her.

'My handbag!' she shouted. 'Someone's taken my handbag!'

Tibor and Ernő dashed into the crowd of people.

'Stop! Thief!' Tibor hollered. It sounded almost like a joke, like something straight out of a cartoon strip.

Anna rushed after them. She saw someone running. The figure disappeared into the crowd, reappearing a moment later at the edge of the park. The situation had erupted so unexpectedly that nobody had time to react. Anna barged past people standing in her way, and when she eventually reached the pathway, she caught a glimpse of two people running in different directions: a man, and a little girl in a red skirt, who swiftly slipped away among the high-rise apartment blocks rising up behind the Orthodox cathedral. The man was running towards the school. Each of them carried a bag.

For a fraction of a second Anna considered which of them to run after. She chose the man. Ernő, who was in much poorer physical shape than Tibor – he had put on weight and smoked like a chimney – had run off in the same direction, but there was no chance of him catching up with the thief on foot. Tibor was heading down the main road after the girl.

The man was already running past the school and now disappeared round the side of the building. Anna couldn't see whether the bag in his hands belonged to her. She increased her pace and sped past Ernő, who by now was gasping for breath, ran round the corner of the darkened school and reached the next road. From there she could see the cathedral and as far down as Kőrös, but the fleeing man had disappeared from sight. Anna came to a halt at the intersection and listened. Normally it would have been easy to follow the echo of footsteps in the otherwise quiet town, but now the boom of music from the park drowned out all other sounds. A barn owl leapt from the cathedral copula and glided into a silent hunting flight. Its pale silhouette disappeared behind the tall chestnut trees. Ernő finally caught up with Anna.

'Where did he go?' he asked, panting loudly. He rested his hands against his knees and grimaced.

'I don't know,' Anna replied. 'It's no use standing around wondering about it. I'll go that way, towards Sumadija utca. Go and check round the church, maybe he's hiding somewhere, lying low in the rose bushes round the corner.'

'What shall I do if I find him?' asked Ernő.

'Catch him.'

'How?' Fear flashed across Ernő's eyes. Fear and uncertainty.

Anna didn't answer. This wasn't the time for a lesson in apprehending a suspect. She took off her high-heeled shoes and jogged off briskly – barefoot and almost silent – down Sumadija utca, past the nursery school, hoping she would be the one to find the man and not Ernő. The darkness thickened around her. Small sharp stones pricked the soles of her feet, but Anna didn't care. One of the aims of rigorous exercise was to get used to pain, and Anna was a master of that. Be that as it may, she hoped she didn't step on a broken bottle. Even she had limits.

The sound of the music had died down, or perhaps the band was having a break. Streetlamps were few and far between, and there were no cars in the street. Kőrös looked all but deserted. This area to the north of Kanizsa had once been at the bottom of a lake. Back when the Yugoslav economy was booming, it had been built up into a middle-class residential area with two- and three-storey houses standing tall and silent, each in their own fenced-off garden. The empty, almost ghostlike feeling was heightened by the heavy shutters pulled across the windows, making the buildings look dark and abandoned. What's more, each building had its own garage, so there were no cars parked out on the street. Nowadays few people could afford to keep these enormous houses heated during the winter months. As the price of imported Russian gas had skyrocketed, the upper floors of these apartment blocks were often left unheated all winter, and in a house with six rooms, people sometimes heated only two: the kitchen and the living room.

At the Szent János crossroads Anna again had to make a snap decision about which direction to take. She listened to the silent streets for the space of a long, deep breath. For no logical reason she decided to run towards the Gong restaurant and took the first left on to Szőlö utca. All of a sudden a metallic gate gave a clatter right next to her, as though something was trying to clamber through it. Anna gave a startled shout, and on the other side of the fence a mongrel with a tangled coat ran alongside her barking wildly.

'Quiet!' Anna snapped at the dog, which stood at the corner of the garden barking after her. Now they'll know for sure where I am, she sighed, and at the next crossroads slipped into Tvirnicka utca. She jogged up and down the streets. Small, sharp stones cut into her feet, tore a hole in one of her socks and scratched her heel, but still the thief was nowhere to be found.

When she saw Ernő approaching her on Jesenska utca, Anna came to a halt.

'That bag had my passport and credit cards in it. Everything, *perkele*,' she said, and noticed she was swearing in Finnish.

'What about your phone?' asked Ernő. He was so out of breath he could hardly speak. His cheeks were glowing red and his brow was covered in sweat. You should go for a run more often, Anna found herself thinking meanly.

She tapped her jacket pocket, discovered that her phone was still there and showed it to Ernő with a look of feigned victory on her face.

'Hah, at least they didn't get away with everything.'

'Damn tinkers,' said Ernő.

'How do you know that?' asked Anna, somewhat taken aback. She hadn't seen anything of the thief but the back of his jacket.

'Well, the girl looked … you know. It's obvious.'

'Looked what?'

'You know … untidy.'

'How closely did you get a look at her? I didn't really see the man at all. Height, one hundred and eighty centimetres; average build; dark jacket; but if someone asked me to describe him, I don't think I could do it. I guess he's probably fairly young, thirty at the most.'

'So you didn't get a look at him then? I don't think I'd be able to say anything at all about the girl either.'

'Height? Age?'

'She couldn't be very old because she was quite small. Nothing but a kid. I didn't really see.'

'But you said she looked untidy. In what way?'

'I can't say really. It must have been her hair. Long and tangled.'

'And that automatically makes them Romani, does it?'

Ernő couldn't avoid the irritated tone in Anna's voice.

'Come on, you'd recognise them a mile off,' he said, trying to defend himself.

'The girl was wearing a red skirt,' said Anna.

'Was she?'

Anna hadn't paid the thieves' ethnic background any attention. And if Ernő hadn't noticed the girl's red skirt, how could he possibly have seen whether her hair was untidy? His observation was nothing but prejudiced supposition, thought Anna. Was there a single place on earth where 'gypsy' wasn't a synonym for 'thief'? She swallowed her desire to give Ernő a piece of her mind. After all, he might be right. To Anna the average Romani looked exactly like the average Serb or Hungarian. Over here the Romani women didn't wear frilly blouses and black velvet skirts, and the man didn't wear straight trousers and a jacket like they did in Finland, where they clearly stood out from the crowd. Here they dressed just like everybody else. But still, people here seemed to know just by looking who was a Romani and who wasn't. As if having a skill like that was in any way important.

'They live nearby, don't they?' asked Anna.

'I don't think they were locals.'

'What makes you say that?'

'This is such a small town, the locals have to go thieving elsewhere. Everybody knows everybody else. Almost.'

'Shall we go and take a look?'

'They won't let us in, and we can hardly batter the door down. They'd shoot us first. And if those two have gone that way, they'll be well and truly hidden by now. The most sensible thing is to go straight to the police station and report the theft.'

Anna thought about this for a moment. The idea of snooping round the gypsy quarter by night appealed to her, but still she hesitated. Maybe it really would be best to report the theft at the police station. What a great start to her relaxing holiday. Just then the sound of a dog barking could be heard in the distance. Ernő turned his head and listened closely.

'That's coming from the gypsy quarter,' he said.

'Right, we're going down there.'

'The hell we are, in the middle of the night.'

'Are you afraid?' asked Anna.

'No.'

'Neither am I, so let's go.'

Anna wiped the sand and grit from her feet and put on her shoes. Her socks were torn to shreds and there was a bleeding cut on the ball of her left foot. She tried not to think about the searing pain that was now running up her calf muscle, or that her high heels weren't making it any better.

The clack of Anna's shoes echoed across the deserted street. She was irritated. She'd had to pick these shoes, hadn't she? And tights and a skirt. It meant something, she thought. She was wearing more make-up, more feminine clothes than in Finland. What exactly was she trying to hide? Or reveal?

The dog had stopped barking. The silence was sultry and oppressive.

The town came to an abrupt end at a large brick factory. The edge of the town looked like it had been measured with a ruler. On the final street before the factory stood a white, roughcast, terraced house. The courtyard was on the side facing the factory; the building's run-down façade was half the length of the street and completely concealed the view into the courtyard. The windows were all dark.

Anna went up to the locked gate.

'Is there anyone there?' she shouted. 'Open the gate!'

Tethered to a thick chain, a mongrel that resembled a dachshund appeared from around the corner and growled.

Ernő stood further back, agitatedly glancing around.

'They might have guns,' he whispered.

'Nonsense,' Anna scoffed and rattled the gate. 'Open up!'

The dog started barking, a window near the gate opened up, and a young-looking woman poked her head out.

'Who is it?' she asked.

Anna stepped closer and stood right beneath the window. The

woman's thick, black hair was tied in a bun. Her skin was dark, and she was very beautiful. Her eyes were large and pitch black. And as she looked down, Anna thought they betrayed a sense of caution. There was something else in her expression too. Maybe pride, maybe contempt.

'What do you want? You'll wake up the kids,' the woman snapped.

'We're looking for a young man and a little girl in a red skirt. Have they just come into this house, by any chance?' Anna asked.

'Nobody comes in at this hour. We're all asleep.'

'Mummy, who's there?' came the sound of a sleepy child, a little boy perhaps.

'Back to bed now, there's nothing to worry about,' the woman said gently before turning back to Anna. 'Has something happened?' she asked and looked Anna in the eyes.

Anna felt embarrassed. It was as though the woman could see right through her, as though she knew exactly what had happened and who they were looking for. There was also something very defensive about the woman's demeanour, and Anna couldn't tell whether this was aimed at her personally or the people she represented. She wasn't welcome here; that much was clear. She no longer wanted to disturb the peace in their house.

'We're probably in the wrong place. Sorry to disturb you,' said Anna, then turned and nodded to Ernő as if to say it would be best if they left.

They had only walked a few metres when the woman's voice echoed across the stone walls of the houses.

'*Tiszavirág*,' the woman shouted in a voice that made Anna shudder. The flowering of the Tisza – when the river's long-tailed mayflies all hatched and mated in the space of a few short days.

Anna and Ernő stopped and turned around, but the window had already closed behind them. The cut in Anna's foot was throbbing painfully.

'What on earth was that about?' asked Anna.

'I don't know, but I know that woman.'

'Really? Who is she?'

'Her name's Judit. She's an organiser for the local Romani community group. She runs camps for the kids, that sort of stuff.'

'But that sounds great,' said Anna.

'Well, they probably get money from the council for it,' Ernő replied. 'Let's call Tibor. Maybe he caught the girl.'

Ernő took out his phone and exchanged a few quick words with Tibor. He shook his head at Anna. The girl had disappeared. Tibor and the others were going home for the night and didn't feel like partying any more.

'Let's stop by the police station. It's best to report the theft immediately rather than tomorrow,' said Ernő after he'd finished his phone call. 'What a crap start to your holiday. Never mind, we'll make up for it.'

DZSENIFER CREPT BACK towards the town. Branches tore at her already tangled hair and her little feet were soaked from the muddy earth, where even the smallest depressions had captured water from the flooding Tisza. She had crouched by the riverbank until it was light, to make sure the monster had disappeared. She had gone down to the water's edge to take a look at her brother. Then she'd picked up the passport and the credit card, which lay in the mud, and stuffed them in her pocket. She lifted her gaunt face to the sun and tried to forget everything that had happened that night. That's what she'd done when Mother had died, and it had helped then too. But that was so long ago that Dzsenifer couldn't really remember what she'd done or thought.

She walked towards the town centre and sat down near the bus station. She felt as though she blended into the group of people loitering around there, people whose skin and hair was as dark as hers. She didn't know who they were, where they had come from or why. But she knew that her brother had had some dealings with them. Business, he'd always said. For Dzsenifer business meant bread and meat, milk and *burek*. When her brother's business was doing well, she could eat until her tummy was full, and when business was slow they were hungry. That's when she snuck round to the neighbours' house. The tables next door weren't exactly overflowing with treats either, but Dzsenifer didn't expect them to be. The neighbours gave her bread and lard. When your stomach was howling with hunger that was a treat above all others.

This summer her brother had had plenty of business, and Dzsenifer couldn't remember the last time she'd gone hungry. Now she felt a pinch at the bottom of her stomach. She started to cry as the image of her brother lying by the banks of the Tisza forced itself into her mind. Perhaps her brother would wake up and find her later. Maybe he'd just been sleeping more soundly than usual. Maybe the horrible man who'd attacked him had only appeared in Dzsenifer's nightmares. She often had nightmares. That's why she was afraid of going to sleep. That's what must have happened.

Her brother would come home later.

Dzsenifer knew what to do with the passport and the credit card. She knew where to take them. All those people who had wandered here from places she didn't know and who spoke strange languages and who seemed to fill every bit of the town, they were in the same place she was going. One of them would buy the passport. Then Dzsenifer would be able to buy lots of bread.

The bus jolted to the stop, its exhaust sputtering. The driver stepped out to smoke a cigarette, looked at the crowd of people and shook his head. Dzsenifer felt like darting into the bus, but she waited until the driver had smoked his cigarette, thrown it to the ground and stamped it beneath his shoe. Then she stepped calmly up to the driver's booth, bought a ticket and went to sit on the back seat. Neither Dzsenifer nor anyone else paid any attention to the grey-haired man sitting in a car parked in front of the Venezia pizzeria and watching her leave.

JUNE 4th

A CLATTER COULD BE HEARD from the kitchen. Anna opened her eyes a fraction. The blinds in the upstairs room were pulled so tight, the light only came through in tiny bright spots, like pinpricks in a black window. As her eyes grew accustomed to the darkness, she began to make out the contours of the familiar furniture: the desk beneath the window, the small bookcase in the corner and the armchair with her clothes thrown over the back.

Once Anna had turned eighteen, her mother had returned to their former homeland. This used to be Anna's room as a girl. The toys had long since been packed away and taken up to the attic, or given to relatives with young children. There were no posters or photographs on the walls, because that phase of Anna's life had only begun once they arrived in Finland. It hadn't really taken off there, though; unlike all the other teenage girls at school, Anna had never been head over heels about any particular band or actor. She'd taped a few posters to the wall of her room in Koivuharju, but only so that she didn't seem like a total freak if one of her classmates visited. She couldn't even remember which bands they were. She did remember that guests at their house were few and far between.

'*Kértek a pálinkát?*' Anna could hear the creak of the pantry door, the sounds of her mother fussing round the kitchen. Anna looked at her phone. Ten o'clock. That meant it was actually nine o'clock, because her phone hadn't automatically changed to local time. *Pálinka* at nine in the morning – home-brewed fruit liquor that was stronger than vodka, thought Anna, and smiled. Welcome home.

She changed the time settings on her phone and listened to the agitated chatter from downstairs. She truly didn't want to get out of bed yet. It must have something to do with yesterday's handbag theft, she thought as she gently stroked her stomach. She made out the words 'gypsy' and 'thief'. Maybe they'd caught up with the culprit. Maybe she wouldn't have to get up just yet, have a shower, call Ernő and Tibor, go back to the police station and try to establish a chain of events while her friends interpreted. Most of the local police officers were Serbs and Anna's grasp of the language wasn't up to scratch. Some of those who had worked in Kanizsa for years spoke Hungarian too, but the young duty officer who had been there the night before had been so monolingual that Anna suspected he might have been from Kosovo. It was ironic that here, in her so-called homeland, she had to rely on her friends' interpreting skills to deal with the police. The duty officer had sat smoking in his Plexiglas booth, logged the event in his computer and encouraged them to come back in the morning when there would be more staff around.

No police stations on holiday, thank you. No interviews, eye witnesses, uniforms, investigations – Anna didn't want to remember that such things even existed. She wanted to lie in, drink Turkish coffee with her breakfast, let her mother make a pleasant fuss and wait on her. She wanted to buy warm white bread from the local bakery run by the Albanians, walk along the banks of the Tisza with Réka, talking about everything, sweat in the heat, and eat cherries straight from the tree. She would have time to do all those things before the holiday was over: if the weather remained this warm, the first cherries would ripen at the end of June. But of all the bags to steal, someone had stolen hers. Could she have had any worse luck? Anna thought, rubbing her eyes and stretching her arms.

Réka hadn't joined them last night. They had messaged back and forth throughout the day and Réka had said she'd been working in Szabadka, the nearest large city on the Serbian side, which in Serbian was called Subotica. Eventually Réka had said she'd felt so ill all day that she didn't want to drive all the way to Kanizsa. Anna was disappointed because Réka normally joined her as soon as she arrived. Feeling ill sounded like an excuse. Réka has something going on, something more important than me, Anna thought, almost jealous. But her other friends had been waiting for her at the house, and she'd hardly had time to eat or exchange news with her mother before they rushed her off into town. Then her handbag had been stolen and she'd forgotten all about Réka.

Anna reluctantly swung her legs out of bed and placed her feet on the brown, patterned carpet, the kind that were popular when the house was built in the seventies. It's so handy not to have to take rugs out and air them, her mother used to say. Nobody thought then of the dust and dirt that became ingrained in them over the years – she wasn't sure they thought of it nowadays either. In a country where people still smoked indoors, the dirt clinging to fitted carpets wasn't a particular concern. Anna went into the bathroom and noticed that the voices in the kitchen had fallen silent. An unpleasant sensation pressed down sharply on her chest, the same way a mother feels when she realises the sound of her child playing has stopped: something has happened.

Anna quickly pulled on her clothes, didn't bother brushing her teeth or combing her hair, and went downstairs.

A man and two women were sitting in the kitchen. As Anna appeared in the doorway, they turned to look at her but didn't smile or greet her in the normal, cheery fashion.

'Your bag has been found,' said her mother.

Anna was puzzled at the subdued atmosphere.

'That's great, isn't it? Let's drink to that,' she said. She walked over to the kitchen cabinet, took out a glass, ran water from the tap in a hopeless attempt to cool it, then took a long gulp of lukewarm water and looked at the assembled group of people, none of whom raised their glasses of fruit liquor to their lips.

'This is Kovács Gábor, his wife and their neighbour, Gulyás Katalin,' said her mother. 'You've met them before. Gábor was a policeman at the same time as your father, though he's been retired for a while. How long is it now, Gábor?'

'Seven years since I left the force,' the man replied in a low, pleasant voice. The hair across his brow was grey and silvered, he wore a thick moustache, and his eyes were brown and alert.

'Is it so long?' said her mother, almost to herself, and shook her head.

'Where did they find my bag?' asked Anna.

Only once she'd spoken did she realise that she hadn't rolled out the usual formal greetings and pleasantries. One of the women, the policeman's wife, seemed to turn her nose up. She probably thought Anna was an impolite brat. Anna had felt this same awkwardness countless times before, particularly around older women – the barely hidden rejection that began to seep from them like frost from an opened freezer the minute Anna forgot to use the right words in just the right way. She would never be a *hölgy*, never be considered an *úriasszony*, a lady, a woman who understood the rules of etiquette, her family life in impeccable shape and her cupboards in order. This fact she had to face every time she met her mother and her mother's friends.

'Some way along the banks of the river, down towards Törökkanizsa,' said Kovács Gábor.

'Was my wallet still there?'

'Yes. But we'll have to establish whether anything's been taken from it. Do you have a credit card?'

'Yes, a Visa card.'

'Well, that wasn't there.'

'I cancelled it last night, so it'll be no use to anyone.'

'Good. Did you have much cash with you?'

'A few thousand dinars. I only arrived yesterday, so I hadn't had time to change any more.'

'There were only a few coins in your wallet. The notes had been taken.'

'Of course. What about my passport?'

'Gone, I'm afraid.'

'Brilliant,' Anna said, disappointed. The loss of her passport meant she'd have to contact the embassy in Belgrade and fill out who knows how much paperwork. Fucking hell, she cursed to herself.

'Isn't it just bushes down that way?' she asked. 'Do you know how the bag ended up there? Did you catch the thief?'

'We've got the thief,' said Kovács Gábor.

'Who is he?'

Her mother cast a worried look at the elderly policeman, and he nodded at her almost imperceptibly.

'*Was* he…' her mother said quietly. 'He was lying next to your bag. Dead.'

'What?' Anna gasped.

'We don't know who he was,' Gábor explained. 'But he wasn't from round here. He'd drowned. It appears he stumbled into the water and got himself caught on some tree roots spreading out into the river; they stopped him from being washed away with the current. Your bag was on the shore right next to him.'

'*Úr Isten!*'

'The man might have gone into the bushes to clean out the bag and slipped into the river – the ground round there is muddy and slippery, and the bank is quite steep. Naturally, the police will conduct a thorough investigation. You'll have to come down to the station as soon as you can and tell us everything that happened last night. We'd like to speak to your friends too. The police will need witness statements from everyone who was present at the time of the theft; even the smallest detail might be of use in the investigation.'

'I know,' said Anna and looked out of the window. The morning sun shone enticingly, promising another scorching day. 'I'm a criminal investigator too, in the Violent Crimes Unit.'

'Your mother told us. As you see, I still help out at the department. I can't seem to keep away.'

'Were you there when they found the thief?'

'No. I leave crawling around in the undergrowth to the younger ones. But I went to the station as soon as I heard the news. And we all agreed it's a good idea to have a Hungarian officer helping you sort this out. Our younger colleagues are almost all Serbs.'

Helping me: Anna repeated Gábor's words to herself. Sounds as if I'll have to spend my holiday assisting the police. Great.

'That's kind,' she said out loud.

'I'm sure we don't have the same kind of resources as the Finnish police, but you can be sure we do our job as well as we can. I imagine you'll be fascinated to see how we work round here. You're your father's daughter,' said Gábor.

'You look just like him,' the policeman's wife added and attempted a smile.

I guess I do, and I suppose I am, thought Anna. And my holiday is ruined.

'*Voi vittu perkele*,' she swore in Finnish and smiled.

'What does that mean?' Gábor's wife asked, suddenly curious. Anna's mother shot her a look that was sharper than a dagger.

'"How interesting",' Anna replied and headed for the shower.

THE POLICE STATION in Magyarkanizsa looked like a desolate apartment block. The giant yellow box was situated on a quiet side street on the edge of the town centre, right next to the tangled woodland that continued all the way to the riverside. Somewhere down there Anna's handbag and the dead thief had been found.

Anna waited for Ernő and Tibor in front of the station. In the small courtyard was a statue in memory of local policemen who had died during the Yugoslav war – a little monument engraved with officers' names. A painful memory momentarily punched the air from Anna's lungs, and tears welled in her eyes. Her eldest brother, Áron, hadn't been a policeman. He hadn't had the chance to be anything other than a wild young man, whose studies, and eventually his whole life, were cut short by the war. Ákos still carried inside him the pain of losing his older brother; they'd been very close, almost the same age, and always together. Anna swallowed her tears. It was hard to bring Áron fully to mind, Anna's memory of him had faded so much. His face, his body – now they were familiar only from photographs. Anna could no longer truly remember his voice, the way he walked, his gestures or expressions. And yet the pain of losing him was like a heavy weight hanging from her shoulders. What must it feel like for Mum? she wondered. Her mother never spoke of Áron. Or of her father.

'*Szia!*'

Anna heard the cheery greeting from across the street and looked up from the monument, where someone had lain a wreath woven from red flowers. She waved to Ernő and Tibor. Ernő looked the worse for wear.

'*Sziasztok!*'

They walked inside the station and explained who they were to the young officer on duty, who, to Anna's surprise, was a Hungarian. And quite good-looking. The man asked them to sit down on the brown, metal-legged chairs and wait for the detective.

'It seems there are Hungarians working here after all,' Anna said to Ernő and nodded towards the man sitting in the booth at the entrance. The man looked back at her, not even trying to hide his interest. Anna could feel the blood rushing to her cheeks and she quickly looked away again.

'Sure, there are a few. Why wouldn't there be?'

'I was told most of the police officers were Serbs nowadays.'

'Well, they're in the majority, like they are in the border patrol. But as far as I know there has to be a quota of Hungarians, so some of them must be our lot. The nearest Hungarian-speaking high school is in Törökkanizsa, although that's mostly a Serbian-speaking town.'

'What's that got to do with it?' asked Anna.

'Think about it, you're a smart woman,' Ernő scoffed and didn't look like he was going to explain any further.

'Just tell me.'

'The government is using deliberate political decisions like that to drive our language and culture into the ground. They're just trying to make our lives difficult. Sure, it looks great that there's a Hungarian-speaking high school, but why isn't it here in Kanizsa? Why did they have to locate it in a neighbouring town where there aren't many Hungarians?'

Ernő's tirade was interrupted by the arrival of a tall, authoritative-looking, grey-haired man in a uniform laden with medals. The chief of police himself had come to meet her. Anna was rather taken aback. The man introduced himself and apologised in awkward Hungarian that he wouldn't be able to deal with the case in Anna's native language. His former colleague, Kovács Gábor, had kindly agreed to assist them. Anna nodded. I know, she answered in Serbian. She knew a few words and phrases, thanks to Ákos's old friends – Zoran in particular.

The chief of police led them to his office on the second floor, where Gábor was waiting for them. The chief picked up the phone on his desk, made a call, and a moment later there came a knock at the door and an officer in uniform brought in Anna's handbag. The officer was wearing gloves and the handbag had been placed in a transparent plastic bag.

'Could you inspect it to see what is missing,' said Gábor.

Anna looked at the chief of police and nodded. She carefully removed the bag from its protective covering. It felt strangely light. Pens, junk, receipts, her diary, eyeliner, a compact, a lighter, a tub of pastilles, chewing gum. A condom. The old men's stares embarrassed Anna as she placed the small, square plastic package on the tabletop with her other belongings. She could sense Ernő and Tibor's smirks on her neck and began to feel like a blushing teenager.

Her wallet was made of black, worn leather. She'd had it for years, never having the heart to replace it with a new one, even though it was old and tattered and the seam was unravelling at one corner. Anna looked inside. Driving licence, ID card, all the thousands of customer loyalty cards, but no credit card and no cash.

'Everything seems to be here except my passport and credit card,' she said.

'Then you'll have to contact the consulate and your bank, as you probably know already,' said the chief of police. Gábor interpreted, though Anna understood the chief well enough.

'Well, I've already cancelled the credit card. How can I contact the consulate? Do you have a phone number for them?'

The men glanced at each other.

'There must be information online,' said Gábor. 'When are you going back to Finland?'

'June the twenty-fifth.'

'There's plenty of time, though I'd advise you to take care of this sooner rather than later, to make sure you get your travel documents in order before you leave. You never know how long these things can take.'

The chief of police cast his eyes across everyone in the room before speaking.

'I need you all to tell me exactly what happened last night. Each of you in turn. Let's start with the boys; Anna, you can go last.'

'Can I say something first?' Anna asked.

'What?'

Anna noticed a hint of irritation on the chief's face. She had spoken in the full knowledge that it was inappropriate to challenge the order that he had specified. From the very moment he had walked into the foyer in his shiny cap, Anna sensed he didn't take her seriously. She wanted to show him that nobody walked over her. She wanted to needle him.

'I'd like to see the body,' she said.

'I'm afraid that's impossible. Besides, it isn't here. We have no facilities to store bodies,' said the chief, Kovács Gábor duly interpreting.

'Where is it then?'

'The body will be transferred to the coroner's office in Novi Sad as soon as possible, once our own technicians have conducted an external examination. This should happen in the next few days, if not sooner.'

'Yes, but where is the body *now*? Where will the examination take place?' Neither of the policemen responded.

'Are you leading this investigation?' asked Anna.

'No.'

'Who is, then?'

'He'll contact you later.'

Really? thought Anna.

'I want to see the body,' she repeated.

'Why?' asked Gábor.

'Wouldn't it make sense to be sure this is the same man who stole my handbag? I think I'm the only reliable witness. Admittedly, I only saw him from behind, but I noted his size and what clothes he was wearing.'

'He was found lying next to your bag,' said the chief of police.

'And if he'd been found next to a boat, would that automatically make him a fisherman? Or if he was near a church would you assume he was a priest? Or behind a hospital—'

'Very well, you're right,' said the chief. 'I'll try and arrange something.'

'Thank you, that would be excellent. And what about the little girl?'

'What little girl?'

'Last night at the wine fair. She was involved in the theft, the whole sequence of events. They've probably done things like this before, it all happened so smoothly. I'm not sure which one of them shoved me, but they both ran off immediately afterwards and headed in different directions. And both of them seemed to be carrying a bag.'

'We know nothing about a girl, but I'll make sure to tell the team working on the case. This could be important,' said the chief. 'One thing we can be sure about is that the boy – well, he was a grown man – wasn't a local.'

'How do you know that? Surely you don't know every resident of Kanizsa. This isn't that small a town,' said Anna.

'Of course we don't know everybody, but local people don't steal handbags in front of dozens of witnesses. We have enough experience of these things that we're quite sure about it. And, for that matter, the local gypsies are generally decent folk.'

Anna could feel the irritation bubbling up inside her. Again they'd pulled out the gypsy card. Unbelievably prejudiced.

'Fine, I trust your experience. But the man must have been lying low somewhere and, wherever it is, the girl is still there. Shouldn't we be looking for her? Maybe she knows what happened to the man.'

'Anna,' Kovács Gábor interrupted. 'This is only a stolen handbag. At the end of the day you've only lost your passport and your credit card.'

'Only a stolen handbag! A young man died soon after he and a little girl stole my bag. This is about quite a bit more than just my handbag.'

Kovács Gábor and the chief of police exchanged glances. Anna saw in their expressions all the thoughts they weren't saying out loud. Does this woman think she knows better than us? Is this woman going to get difficult? Woman, woman, woman. Worse still, a woman who had grown up abroad. The men's faces said more than a thousand words.

'Say something, then,' Anna snapped to Ernő and Tibor.

'We … I … Anna, listen, it was just some nameless gypsy,' Ernő said, almost under his breath.

'Some nameless gypsy? Why do you keep on using the word gypsy over and over? Don't you know it's an offensive term? They are Romani. And what the hell difference does it make what ethnic group he belonged to? They are human beings, and a human being is dead!'

Anna forced herself to swallow her anger. She was only too aware how people treated the Roma here and throughout Eastern Europe, but people's attitudes still shocked and angered her. She had often thought that, despite their difficulties, Finnish Roma were lucky compared to their southern brethren.

'To be honest, we can't be sure the thief was a gypsy. Whole gangs of people have started appearing round here lately,' said the chief of police. 'But it goes without saying that we will look into this death thoroughly.'

'He'd clearly slipped and stumbled into the water while he was rummaging through your bag, grabbed on to the tree trunk and drowned,' Gábor added. 'Your things were strewn across the ground.'

'Have you seen the photographs from the scene?'

Gábor nodded.

'I want to see them too.'

'I'll try and arrange that,' said the chief. 'But I can't promise anything. If I'm honest, I don't think it will be possible. There are strict regulations regarding our work, as I'm sure there are in Finland too.'

'I could identify the thief from those photographs. Don't you realise I'm a witness?'

'We will call you as a witness if the investigation requires it,' said the chief of police in a voice that didn't allow any room for argument.

'Where exactly was he found?' Anna asked in just as firm a voice. 'I want to see the location of the body.'

'It's quite hard to get there. There is thick vegetation and the ground is muddy.'

'I don't mind. I clamber through plenty of mud in my job. I want to look at the scene. What if my passport and credit card are still in the bushes? Was the surrounding area thoroughly inspected? Who found the body?'

Anna was surprised at her own words. This was exactly the kind of thing that only this morning she'd sworn not to get involved with. Now she felt she had no other option. Holiday or not, she didn't trust this man decked out in medals and a shiny cap.

'Calm down, miss,' the chief of police boomed. 'A fisherman saw the body lying by the shore from his boat early this morning. The area has been inspected. Two items of value to you are missing. You'll have time to get another passport before going back to Finland.'

'So where are these two items? If they weren't found at the site, the man must have gone through my bag before he got there and given or sold my valuables to someone else. Either that or the fisherman has taken them.'

'The fisherman didn't even get out of his boat. He called us from the middle of the Tisza and went back to his business. He is a local, professional fisherman, a good man; and he's found drowned bodies before. I can assure you he hasn't taken your passport.'

'Can I have his name?'

'I'm afraid he's asked to remain anonymous. He just wants to be left to fish the river in peace. He is afraid.'

'Of what?'

'Smugglers – the mafia. They move around on the river and hide out on the shore. No upstanding citizens want to stand up to them.'

Anna thought for a moment. 'Perhaps the girl has my passport and credit card. We have to find her.'

'If a young girl is somehow involved in this case, she will already have left Kanizsa, you can be sure of that.'

'Why on earth would the thief rummage through my bag among the bushes in the pitch dark if he had already passed on my money, passport and Visa card? This isn't as straightforward as you're trying to suggest.'

'Anna, dear,' said Gábor.

'I'm not your dear,' she snapped.

Ernő gently frowned at Anna. Tibor guffawed and tried to cover his laughter in a pretend coughing fit.

'Listen to me, Anna,' Gábor continued, smiling, fatherly and patient.

Anna took a deep breath and tried to hold her tongue.

'I know this might sound terrible, cruel even, but there's an endless stream of Syrians, Iranians, Somalis, Iraqis, Kosovan gypsies and people from who knows where being smuggled through here into the EU all the time. It's becoming a real problem for us. Every now and then we find unidentified bodies drowned in the river. We don't have the resources to investigate every case individually. Besides, it's Hungary and the EU that should be taking on these cases; that's where these refugees are heading. We don't get a penny from the EU, and yet they expect us to serve as some kind of buffer. You're right to say this is about something far greater than your handbag and travel documents. This is about how the EU responds to the people smuggling taking place along the river and the escalating refugee crisis in Serbia. They all come here and wait for any opportunity to slip across the border. You should see the camps near Szabadka. Believe me, Anna dear, this is such an enormous problem, you won't be able to do anything about it, not even with your Finnish education. And that is the end of the matter. Get yourself a new passport, enjoy your holiday and forget all about it. Of course, the boy's death is very unfortunate, but let us worry about that.'

The chief of police sat next to Gábor and nodded. So you understand Hungarian after all, thought Anna, again swallowing her irritation. She gave her official statement about the events of the previous night, took her bag and its plastic cover from the table, put her things back inside it and turned to leave. The policemen stood up, hurried to open the door for her, and asked Ernő and

Tibor to stay behind to give their own statements about what they had seen.

'I'll wait for you outside,' Anna told them.

'Give your mother and Ákos my greetings,' said Gábor.

'Remember, I want to see the body or at least the photographs from the scene,' Anna told the chief in Serbian, though she wasn't entirely sure whether the word *body* was masculine or feminine. To hell with the grammar, Anna thought, indignant. I want this man to realise I understand his language too. Though not nearly well enough.

The chief of police nodded.

'Why don't we schedule a time now?' Anna continued.

'I'll do my best to make it happen,' the chief responded but looked as though he wasn't planning on lifting a finger to do anything of the sort, and that he'd had enough of Anna's nagging. 'The detective will contact you if we have any further questions,' he continued and closed the door.

Anna stood in the corridor and tried to listen through the door to the men's discussion, straining to hear what Ernő and Tibor were saying about the event. But the door was thick and the noise from the adjacent staffroom smothered everything else.

Less than five minutes later the men stepped out of the room. That was thorough, thought Anna derisively.

Anna, Tibor and Ernő took the stairs down to the foyer, where a handful of people were sitting around, queuing with papers and documents, just like they would at any police station in the world. The young police officer was still sitting in his booth, but had been joined by a colleague – an attractive female officer in uniform, her dark hair tied in a tight plait and an officious but friendly expression on her face.

On the spur of the moment Anna walked up to the hatch and began playing the ignorant tourist, asking what to do now that she had lost her passport. The man – Vajda Péter, Anna read on the small metallic badge on his jacket – smiled contentedly as he looked up the contact details for the Finnish Embassy in Belgrade and handed Anna the information on a post-it note. He then filled out a form officially registering the loss of the passport and encouraged Anna to take this with her to Belgrade. Anna thanked him, a little too enthusiastically, perhaps, gave him the most charming smile she could muster and almost imperceptibly winked at him as she turned away from the hatch. The officer stood staring at Anna. If Anna had eyes in the back of her head, she would have seen the female officer poke the man teasingly in the ribs.

Once they were outside, Ernő and Tibor lit cigarettes. Anna had to fight the desire to ask for one.

'What was that all about?' asked Tibor as he drew the Marlboro smoke into his lungs.

'What was what?'

'That ridiculous flirting.'

'Hah. Jealous, are you?'

'Of course.'

'Don't you worry, dear,' said Anna. 'I'm a bit of a restless soul, but you're still the only one for me.'

'Good. For a moment there I was worried,' said Tibor.

'Let's see what those guys come up with,' said Anna nodding back at the police station. 'There's something funny about all this.'

'You've been trained to think like that.'

'You bet I was, and that's precisely why I know something's not quite right.'

'The guy drowned by accident.'

'Probably,' Anna admitted. 'But the matter still deserves to be investigated thoroughly. That's what would happen in Finland. What did they ask you?'

'Nothing much. What time the theft happened, who else might have seen it, that kind of stuff.'

'Did you tell them we paid a visit to the house in the Romani quarter?'

Ernő hesitated for a moment.

'Yes,' he said eventually. 'I mean, I told them we ran after the thief and looked around Kőrös for him. The guy with the medals asked if we'd seen anything in the gypsy quarter. I told him we were there but we didn't see anything in particular.'

Anna thought about this. There was something very strange going on.

'Hey, let's grab a cup of coffee,' said Tibor.

'I need a beer,' said Ernő and seemed to perk up. 'But I have to be home for lunch at two. Véra will throw a fit if the food gets cold.'

'You two go. I'm meeting Réka. We'll talk soon!' said Anna and walked off briskly towards her mother's house. Réka, her oldest and closest friend, might be waiting there already.

Anna smiled. For the first time in a long while something approaching happiness flickered in her chest.

THE SUN WAS LIKE AN ENORMOUS, glowing eye looking down omnisciently on the *járás*. Somewhere in the distance came the mooing of cows. During the daytime the cows roamed freely across the *járás*, nibbling at the sparse nourishment they could find – thin, yellowed hay and chewy flowers – as the shepherd and dogs followed behind them, keeping them in check and guarding the herd. In the evenings the cows wandered home across the fields in long, lowing lines, to their barns and shelters to be milked and fed; they knew their own farms, slipping in through the gates and into their own stalls just as they had done the previous evening, and waiting for someone to relieve the pressure they could already feel in their udders. The sheep spent the night outdoors, their freedom guarded only by the dogs.

The sun would soon set behind the shimmering horizon. White speckled butterflies danced around tiny flowers; the terrain was rough, dotted with struggling grass, clusters of wild mint here and there. Réka plucked bunches of mint that hadn't yet flowered. It makes good tea, she said. Anna knew this. As children they had picked mint when their families had gone on picnics together. Anna's mother had dried the herbs on clothes pegs and boiled them to make tea on winter evenings.

Anna took another sandwich. Réka had brought wine too, but because she didn't want to drink any, Anna poured herself some juice and they decided not to open the bottle. They had already caught up on all of each other's news; at least, almost all of it. There were some things Anna didn't want to talk about, not even to Réka. The kilometres and the years between them were like a river without a bridge. They were like Bácska and Bánát, the regions between which the dark waters of the Tisza flowed. Yet, despite all of that, this was her best friend. Anna took a closer look at Réka. She looked tired; she'd aged. People down here seem to age more quickly, thought Anna.

Was it to do with the sun? Réka had put on weight too. Her cheeks were rounder and her breasts, which had been full before, looked swollen. Yet Réka seemed happy, just as full of smiles as she always had been. She had finally found a boyfriend. Anna told herself that she didn't feel a single pang of jealousy at this. She was genuinely thrilled at her friend's happiness. At least, she wanted to be.

The western sky had started to swallow the sun now and the air was cooling quickly. Apart from the bottle of wine, their picnic basket was empty.

'Should we be getting back?' asked Anna.

'Yes, let's go.'

'That visit to the police station is really bugging me,' said Anna as they walked back to the car parked at the side of the narrow, bumpy country lane.

'Why?'

'I don't really know. There's something about it I can't put my finger on.'

'Maybe it's just that the police do things differently round here,' Réka suggested.

'Maybe. But they didn't seem at all interested in the little girl. They completely dismissed the idea. It's odd, because the girl must know the identity of the dead thief.'

'They'll talk to the Romanies. Everything will work out.'

'What use will that be if the thieves weren't from round here or if they weren't even Romanies? That's what the police kept repeating: they're not from round here, not from Kanizsa.'

'Surely they must have a reason for saying that? They probably know the local pickpockets better than they do their own families.'

'If the man wasn't a local, how on earth did he ever find that spot down by the Tisza that even the locals don't know exists?'

'I don't know. I imagine he was looking for a hiding place.'

'Maybe, but it stills seems odd.'

'Just forget about it.'

'I asked to see the body, but they clearly don't want me to see it.

They should have automatically asked me to identify the thief. Why didn't they?'

'Because you didn't get a proper look at him.'

'I saw what size he was, saw his clothes, the colour of his hair.'

'Anna, dear!'

'That's what my father's former colleague kept calling me. Damn chauvinists.'

'That's what it's like round here. No point letting it get to you.'

'It's as if the whole incident is dangling in front of my eyes like a piece of thread crying out for me to grab it and start winding it in. I just want some answers.'

'It's only natural the whole thing is bugging you. Your belongings have been stolen and it looks like the thief is now dead. It would be weird if it didn't affect you. But it doesn't necessarily mean there's something fishy going on. I think you're letting your emotions cloud your professional judgement. Have you ever had to deal with something like this as a civilian? As yourself?'

'No.'

'There you go.'

Réka was right, but her words only served to confuse Anna all the more. What was she as a civilian other than a police officer? Was there such a thing as an off-duty Anna? Perhaps she should follow Réka's advice, forget all about it and enjoy what was left of her holiday. I might even find the person hiding within this police officer's body, she thought. Is finding the real Anna the thing I'm trying so hard to escape?

'Give the bottle of wine to your mum,' said Réka, as she opened the boot of her car and put the picnic basket and blanket inside.

'Okay, thanks.'

'Why didn't you have any? You're not pregnant, are you?' Réka laughed and tapped her stomach.

And before Anna could think of a way to reply, Réka continued. 'Anna, I've got to tell you: I am.'

She looked at Anna, radiant.

'Réka, that's wonderful,' said Anna and hugged her friend, trying to force a note of happiness into her voice.

'I'm still only in the early stages, but I've already put on a few kilos. *Jebiga*, I'm hungry all the time!'

'When's it due?'

'At the beginning of December. József and I are going to have a Christmas baby.'

'From now on, I'm going to call you Mary.'

Again Réka chuckled. Her laugh sounded just as it had when she was a little girl. All of a sudden Anna thought of the rooms in their nursery school, the noise, the laughter, the large windows covered with paper flowers the children had made. Réka had stopped at Anna's house every morning and they had walked to the nursery hand in hand. How small could they have been? Four or five, maybe. It's a wonder we were allowed to walk all that distance by ourselves, thought Anna.

'Did we ever have an adult with us when we walked to nursery?'

'What? I'll never get used to the way your thoughts bounce around. What made you think of that?'

'But did we?'

'When we were really small, our home help used to come with us. If I remember right, we were allowed to go by ourselves when we were about five.'

'Five? Goodness.'

'Anna, we lived right next to the nursery.'

'Still. Would you let your Christmas baby out alone at the age of five?'

'We were always together. And Kanizsa is a safe place. You're right, though, I don't know how to answer that. We'll see when the time comes.'

'How's it been going, the pregnancy?'

'Fine, except that I felt like being sick all day yesterday. But it's all right. It's wonderful.'

'I'm really happy for you,' said Anna.

I am happy, I really am, Anna tried to convince herself.

'Thank you, you really are a good friend. You've got to meet József as soon as possible. Let's go to Szabadka together.'

'Sounds good. I want to meet the lucky man.'

Réka smiled. Then she hugged Anna again.

'It's so nice you're here. I've missed you terribly. I hope you come again over Christmas; you'll get to meet our baby. I wonder whether it's a boy or a girl. Mum wants a boy, but József and I really don't care. As long as it's healthy. Even that doesn't really matter. As long as it's … a baby.'

Anna stared at the shimmering sun as it dipped beneath the horizon. She didn't want to continue this conversation. Not now. Not yet.

'I wonder who the fisherman was. The one that found the body,' she said.

'There you go again, your mind won't let up. It could have been anyone. You can't buy fish in the supermarkets, so everybody fishes for their own.'

'The police said it was an elderly man, a former professional fisherman.'

'Ah, in that case it must be Nagy Béla.'

'Should I speak to him?'

'Absolutely not. I want to spend as much time with you as possible. I don't want you to spend the whole of June crawling around in the bushes, investigating something that doesn't even really concern you. Forget all about it; promise me?'

Anna hesitated but acquiesced. 'Okay.'

'Good. Let's go, it's getting late,' said Réka.

They drove back into town in Réka's old Zastrava, thick, stinking smoke sputtering from the exhaust pipe. There were always spare parts for these cars and people knew how to repair them without looking things up online. Réka liked that sort of thing. She liked everything to be old-fashioned, collected antiques and old furniture.

She wanted to buy an old house that she and József could renovate in the traditional style. Nobody else understood why she would want to do such a thing, but Réka didn't care. She had always gone her own way – studied journalism in Belgrade and dreamed of working abroad, or as a conflict correspondent at a large newspaper. She'd lived by herself for a long time too. We've got a lot in common, thought Anna. And still it feels as though we've become strangers to one another.

Darkness descended quickly, revealing a star-lit sky, the lights of the local farmsteads too few to ruin it. As they approached the town the amount of light increased and the twinkle of the stars faded away. Yet Anna liked the moderate lighting in Kanizsa; it was as though the town respected the night. The Finnish summer nights, when you could sit outside and read a book without the lights on, had a special atmosphere all of their own, but Anna loved the dark, warm summer nights in the south, the chirping of the crickets and the gurgling of the frogs, the thunderstorms that lit up the dark night sky after the heat of the afternoon.

Réka dropped Anna off at the gate of her mother's house and sped off in a cloud of exhaust fumes.

A clamour of loud voices drifted over from the beer garden outside the Gong. Anna delicately pulled her keys out of her bag. This bag, her very own handbag, now hanging on her shoulder as innocent and innocuous as it had before, had only yesterday been with a man who was now dead. The thought made her shudder. She would need to be very careful how she handled it from now on.

JUNE 5th

'ANYU!' Anna called to her mother, who was busying herself in the kitchen.

'Are you up already, child? Come into the kitchen, I've baked a walnut pie.'

Anna pulled a dressing gown over her nightdress and put on her *papucsok*, the pair of slippers she'd picked from the basket beneath the coat rail as soon as she'd arrived. She took her mother's green leather gloves, which she'd used to take her handbag to her room upstairs the previous night, went downstairs, put the gloves back in their place and went into the kitchen.

Ákos was there. He looked happy, healthy and content. Anna felt an overwhelming sense of joy spreading through her body, the same sensation she'd experienced as a child when Ákos had picked her up from school and her classmates had stared, envious and maybe a little afraid, at her big brother with the Mohican and two safety pins through his cheek. Nobody else had a brother as cool as hers. The riskiest their brothers got was a leather jacket and a pair of army boots, but nobody else had a Mohican or safety pins. Now there were only scars on Ákos's cheeks. Someone had ripped the safety pins out without opening them. He might even have done it himself.

'Hiya,' Anna said to her brother in Finnish and gave him a hug. Ákos smelled good.

'Hi there. How's my little sister doing?'

'You've probably already heard.'

'Yes, Mum told me. Shit, that was bad luck. You'll need to call the consulate about a new passport.'

'No, I'll have to go to the embassy in Belgrade. *A kurva életbe*. I was at the police station yesterday.'

Ákos started to laugh. 'You can't help yourself, can you? Even on holiday you can't keep away.'

'Tell me about it, *saatana*,' Anna said in Finnish.

'Watch your language,' her mother snapped but didn't sound all that shocked.

'Where have you been?' Anna asked her brother.

'I've been in Szeged for a few days visiting János and Berci. Do you remember them?'

'No.'

'We were all in the same class at school. They both live and work in Hungary these days. Have you seen Réka yet?'

'We went out to the *járás* yesterday for a picnic. It's so beautiful out there.'

'I know, it's nice. We should go out there fishing some day, in the canal. You know the place?'

Anna's mother put water in the *dzsezva* to boil for the coffee and set the table with plates, cups and spoons. The morning sun shining into the kitchen was so warm that Ákos opened the door leading out to the patio.

'I got the impression the police weren't interested in investigating the theft properly,' Anna said. 'It's odd – surely they can't just turn a blind eye when a body turns up?'

'Did they say they didn't want to investigate it?' her mother asked, her voice tight. Anna knew that her mother couldn't bear hearing anything that might be interpreted as criticism of Kanizsa. And if that criticism touched on something with which her husband had once been involved – be it how to brew proper *pálinka*, how to look after the fruit trees or how the police conducted themselves – she had a tendency to get really angry. So it was as though Anna's comment was intended as a reproach aimed directly at Kanizsa, her father and, indirectly, at her mother.

'They didn't say as much, but they don't want me to see the body.

They wouldn't even tell me where they found it. And they returned a very important piece of evidence to me straight away – my handbag. I wonder if I should fingerprint it myself.'

'Good idea,' Ákos said in a teasing voice.

Anna gave him a smirk. 'It's probably far too late, but I've got to do something.'

'If they didn't say they *weren't* going to investigate it, then sure enough they *will* investigate it,' scolded her mother. 'You'll just have to trust that the police round here know how to do their job too.'

'It's not that, Mum. I know the police here are as good at their job as police anywhere else.'

'Who found the body?' asked Ákos.

'Some fisherman. Réka said she thought it might be Nagy Béla.'

'He's an old family friend,' said her mother.

'You should call him,' Ákos suggested.

'You'll do no such thing,' said her mother, shocked.

'Give him a call. He'll tell you where he found the man and your bag,' said Ákos.

Anna stood up to fetch the old Kanizsa phone book from the cupboard beneath the phone.

Her mother followed her into the hallway. 'Let this go,' she said in a pained voice.

'Why?'

'Dear child. This is a different world from the one you're used to. There are some situations to which the normal rules don't apply. Thank God, you don't know anything about this kind of place.'

'What's that supposed to mean?'

'I mean that, if you got the impression the police don't want to investigate this properly, they probably have a good reason.'

'Such as what?'

'How should I know? The first thing that comes to mind is that this might have something to do with the mafia, with politics, big money, something like that.'

'And what if the reason is quite simply that the death of a Romani or a refugee isn't worth investigating because it's not considered all that important?'

'That might be the case, dear. And if they don't consider it important, then it's almost certainly linked in some way to politics or the mafia, and with them there's always money at stake. Keep out of this. Please. I don't want anything to happen to you.'

Anna thought about this for a moment. She couldn't dismiss her mother's words all that easily. She knew that, more than anything, her mother was afraid of losing yet another family member. She put the phone book back in the cupboard, gave her mother a hug and went back into the kitchen. The coffee was ready and it smelled wonderful. Ákos had cut thick slices of walnut pie for everyone, put milk and sugar on the table and stood smiling.

'Well, Ákos, aren't you going to tell your sister about Kata?'

A chill gripped the bottom of Anna's stomach. She tried to hide it in a look of curiosity but she saw that Ákos had noticed.

'Ákos has been dating Kiss Katalin. Do you remember her?'

'No. It seems I don't remember anyone,' said Anna and forced herself to smile. 'Who is she?'

'The Kiss family lives nearby. Katalin was a year behind Ákos at school. Nowadays she lives in Szeged and works as a nurse at a private clinic.'

'Mum, wasn't I supposed to tell her that?' said Ákos with a smile.

Now Anna understood why Ákos hadn't come back to Finland after their grandmother's funeral and his spell at the rehab clinic. Katalin Kiss. Anna couldn't think of anybody by that name. She had no memory of the girl at all.

'We've been on a few dates. It's nothing serious, not yet anyway,' said Ákos. He looked as content and excited as only a young man in love can.

'A few times! You almost live in Szeged these days,' said her mother. She sounded every bit as enthralled as Ákos as she described his new girlfriend. 'Kata has two children. She divorced three years ago. She's a lovely, sweet girl.'

Anna had the impression that their mother had already accepted that her grandchildren might not be her own flesh and blood.

Should I tell her the truth about Ákos's life in Finland? Anna thought, but rejected the idea as soon as it came to her. Her mother knew some of the truth. After all, it was her mother who had taken Ákos to rehab after their grandmother's funeral. Anna thought she should ask him how things had gone at the clinic, but decided this was one subject about which it was best to keep quiet. Besides, Ákos looked radiant. Healthy, happy and upbeat, the complete opposite of the Ákos who lived in the filthy apartment in Koivuharju, who hung out with dodgy people and drank away his benefits as soon as they appeared in his bank account. A sense of panic seemed to clench Anna's chest, a dull hum at the back of her head. She took a deep breath and tried to dispel the thought, but it was no good. Ákos and two children – Jesus Christ. Ákos and a normal, decent woman. A nurse.

But as she watched her handsome brother, who positively glowed as he sat eating his slice of pie, Anna began to calm down and almost felt guilty. Why couldn't she allow her brother happiness like this? Surely nothing could be nicer than Ákos settling down with a family and a life worth living. Why did she always have to assume it would end in disaster? Was it because she was worried that her brother might decide to stay here and not come back to Finland after all? Because yet another of her relatives had succeeded in doing the one thing everyone expected of her – the one thing that she never seemed to get right? Settling down, having a meaningful relationship, a family life. A reason to exist.

'Well, are you going to introduce your little sister to the wonderful Kata?' asked Anna, forcing the bitter thoughts from her mind. She saw the look of nervousness disappear from Ákos's eyes.

'Sure. She's got a few days off at the end of the week. She's coming to visit. The children are going to their father's place. She really wants to meet you too.'

SUNDAY WAS MARKET DAY at the *piac*. The market square was busy long before six in the morning as the locals got together to buy and sell seasonal vegetables and a whole array of other products. Once they'd finished their morning coffee, Anna's mother fetched her basket and asked Anna and Ákos to join her. Ákos said he was going to a friend's place and Anna didn't feel like going with her mother. She wanted to go swimming, but the water level was still high from the spring floods and the river was littered with trash, branches, and sometimes even the bodies of animals, which didn't make the strong current any more appealing.

Instead Anna ran a hot bath and had a long soak, then dried her hair, got dressed and left the house. Outside the morning was fresh. The cloudless sky and the still of the air hinted that the day would warm quickly. If at all possible, I'm going to take my holiday in July and August next year, thought Anna. I want to feel that infernally hot weather. I want to sweat and burn, take refuge in the merciful shade. I want to spend all day in an armchair under the plantain tree and drink ice-cold beer at night.

She walked to the beer garden at the Gong and sat down at a table in the corner, where she could watch the people arriving and nothing could happen behind her back. It was strange, primal behaviour – or was it perhaps the paranoia that came with her job that made her choose a seat like this whenever possible, watching her back even in safe places?

The stale smell of the previous evening's thick tobacco smoke still clung to the cushions and tablecloths. A few years ago a Perspex screen had been built round the garden, and the opaque, wavy wall of plastic meant that fresh air no longer circulated through the terrace and you couldn't watch people walking past. A few regular customers were sitting at the bar – men having their morning coffee. If men could give birth, all Balkan children would be born in cafés, thought Anna. She didn't look out of place, a young woman in a bar by herself, because younger women in particular could finally enjoy a coffee or a beer without the company of men – or without any company at all – but still she felt as though she had transgressed an unspoken law of etiquette. Not that she cared about breaking such rules. Even her mother had stopped nagging about her unashamedly independent behaviour, no longer telling Anna how unbecoming it was for a woman. Perhaps it was because her mother had lived in Finland too. Or maybe because, even in a place like Kanizsa, the world changed eventually.

The waiter arrived and greeted her with a kiss on the cheek, asking how she was doing and seeming genuinely thrilled to see Anna for the first time in ages. For a brief moment Anna felt as though she had settled down in a warm, feather-soft nest, tucked away in the branches of the Kanizsa tree. She ordered a cappuccino and a glass of water. She felt like lighting up a cigarette, but thankfully she hadn't bought any. She had packed her running gear, though. She would go for a jog along the banks of the Tisza that evening. She had planned a relaxed training programme to get her through the holiday, the kind that meant she wouldn't get out of shape but didn't take up too much time or energy. Perhaps she'd learnt something over the years. Perhaps this was even a sign that she might one day be able to treat herself with a little more mercy. Anna smiled. She still had a lot to learn about that.

The coffee was good. Serbia and coffee. The two were so tightly bound together that Anna wondered why the Finns were considered a nation of coffee-drinkers. Finns knocked back cup after cup of watery filtered coffee simply so they didn't get headaches or feel tired. Here coffee was a pleasure, a way of life, one that was generally associated with smoking and good company. The best coffee of all was the Turkish stuff her mother brewed in the *dzsezva*. It was strong and bitter, and the fine grounds sank to the bottom of the cup if you were patient. If not, it left a grainy taste in the mouth.

Someone walked into the bar, greeted Anna and the Serbian man sitting at the next table, ordered a beer and began chatting with the waiter. The Serbian man joined the conversation, shouting out comments of his own. Anna closed her eyes for a moment. The tension in her shoulders began to melt away, the annoyance at losing her passport faded into the piping-hot coffee and the buzz of Serbian chit-chat. The dead thief, the girl in the red skirt and the patronising police officers drifted from her mind, becoming nothing but small specks in the distance before disappearing altogether. I'm going to let the matter go, thought Anna. For once I'm going to be sensible and forget about it.

She opened her eyes and sipped her coffee. Then, from the black leather handbag she'd borrowed from her mother's cupboard without asking, she took a scrap of paper and sighed. Why do I always lie to myself? she wondered.

She looked at the phone number she'd scribbled on the piece of paper. Nagy Béla, the man who had found the body. The man who knew exactly where the body had been lying. I must inspect the scene, thought Anna. I don't want to, but I must. I must, even though my mother will have a fit. I must, even though Réka will tell me I'm silly. If that means I'm a police officer and nothing else, so be it. That's good enough for me. Who says I have to get to know the Anna that's hidden somewhere inside my uniform? What if there's nobody there after all? I'll inspect the scene and try to see the body. I want to make sure, if only for my own peace of mind, that he really is the man who stole my handbag and that he really did drown. Accidentally. That's all I need to know. If I don't find out, the matter will keep bugging me. It's probably exactly as the police said, and it would be crazy to waste their precious resources on an unnecessary investigation.

ANNA AND NAGY BÉLA had agreed to meet at midday on the quayside near the Békavár restaurant. At first the man had sounded irritable and rude, as though he didn't want anything to interfere with his Sunday-afternoon routine, which, over the years, he'd got down to a fine art. But once he realised who Anna was, he started reminiscing about her father, waxing lyrical about what a fine and upstanding man he was, always on our side, always fair and helpful and so on, before finally agreeing – reluctantly and with some hesitation – to deviate from his plans and take Anna to the spot where he'd found the body. But only on the condition that Anna didn't tell anyone about it, that if anyone saw them and asked what they were doing, she told them they were simply looking at the scenery and wondering when the Tisza would come into bloom – bursting out in clouds of insects. Of course, Anna promised.

Anna glanced at her phone and checked the time. Five past twelve. She was used to the fact that, in this corner of the world, being on time was frowned upon almost as much as being late in Finland; but this time she was nervous. What if he didn't show up? What if he'd changed his mind at the last minute?

Seven minutes past. Anna crouched down to test how warm the water was. It was pleasantly cooling as it flowed through her fingers, but didn't feel cold at all. Swimming in this will be fine, she thought, and decided to have a swim as soon as she could.

A couple walked hand-in-hand towards the quayside. Anna didn't know them; they were young, barely eighteen. They stopped and sat down at the end of the quay, kissing each other and not paying her the slightest attention. Anna felt old and embarrassed. She turned away and looked across at Bánát on the opposite shore. I had nobody when I was that age, she thought. Nobody except Zoran, a married man. Had anyone her own age ever been interested in her? She couldn't remember. She'd never looked at anyone else that way, so she probably wouldn't even have noticed any interested glances. What would a therapist say about all this? Serious traumas regarding her father, perhaps even regarding her brothers? Anna sighed. Maybe the day will come when I decide to work out who I am and explain that person to myself, traumas and all. But that time isn't now. Perhaps it'll never come. All this kitchen psychology, digging up the past and agonising over her emotions – what use was it? she wondered. But she knew only too well that her cynical attitude was a form of self-preservation. At least, that's what her headmaster had told her years ago.

Twelve minutes past. Anna looked past the young couple, still engrossed in each other. She scanned the path running down the riverbank towards the quayside and saw an elderly man walking, brisk and upright, towards her. He was speaking on the phone. Rather, he wasn't speaking but listening and nodding as though whoever was at the other end could see his body language. Eventually the man said *hvala, priadno*, ended the conversation, put his phone back in the breast pocket of his threadbare shirt and, reaching Anna on the quayside, shook her hand.

'*Csókolom, Anna vagyok*,' she greeted him.

The man stared at the river as though he was looking for something, then turned to Anna and looked at her keenly and curiously from beneath his wrinkled eyelids. His eyes were blue, his hair and moustache thick and silvery grey.

'You don't half look like your father,' the fisherman said; then, without taking his eyes off her, coughed, spat a lump of phlegm into the water and lit a cigarette.

The man reminded Anna of Esko Niemi, her partner in the Finnish police. That same sense of self-assurance, the life experience, the same arrogance and stubbornness, the same disregard for people's opinions. The same smoker's cough. However, for his age the fisherman looked in good shape, and beneath his sullen demeanour there was a warmth it was hard to find with Esko.

'Best not stand around here if we want to get there today,' said the fisherman. He jumped off the quay and into his boat, which was tethered to a post nearby, and held out his hand to help Anna jump in behind him.

The boat rocked wildly as she climbed in. Anna looked around for a life jacket, but, knowing there wouldn't be one, she decided not to say anything. People round here didn't bother with life jackets, smoke alarms, cycling helmets or safety belts in the back seat of their cars. The number of fatal accidents doubtless reflected that, though Anna hadn't seen any statistics. What she saw was that people didn't worry about trifling things. They didn't think of life as being potentially hazardous, as something you had to watch constantly; and they didn't spend their money insuring everything under the sun. Anna positively admired this attitude, though at the back of her mind her Finnish side was shocked by it.

'We'll have to be quick,' said the fisherman as he started the engine with an assured flick of his hand, reversed away from the quayside and steered the boat with the current in the direction of Törökkanizsa. 'I told the wife I was stopping for a beer and promised I wouldn't be long. Lunch will be ready soon, and she doesn't like having to keep it warm.'

In only a short moment the boat was in another world, as though civilisation had suddenly disappeared into the past and nature had enveloped the whole area, conquering everything in its path. There were no other boats on the river. The heavy, leafy trees and bushes lining the banks leant towards the river, their branches drooping into the water. The sun shone down from the misty-blue sky high above them and warmed Anna's cheeks, though a fresh breeze blew down the middle of the river. A stork leapt into flight from the undergrowth along the shore. Its wings beat in great whooshes, and the bird swooped so close to her head that Anna felt the flow of air against her skin.

After heading south a short distance, the fisherman slowed somewhat, then steered the boat closer to the shore. Glancing around him a few times, he secured the boat in a thicket growing on the riverbank.

'This is it,' he said and switched off the motor.

Anna tried to look at the bank but the bushes were so thick she couldn't make out where the water ended and the shore began.

'How did you manage to see the man? You can't see anything at all in there,' she wondered out loud.

'When you drive past every day like I do, you notice even the smallest things out of place,' the fisherman responded.

'What was out of place on that day?'

The man thought about what to say as he used the oars to guide the boat closer to the riverbank. Anna had to hold back the branches on both sides to stop them hitting her in the face.

'I saw a flash of red,' he said eventually.

'Was the man wearing red clothes?'

'No, black. And dead people don't move. Whatever it was in red was alive.'

'Another person?'

'Probably. What else could it have been? We don't have animals that colour round here,' said the fisherman and chuckled as though he'd told a particularly good joke.

'Did you tell the police this?'

'Of course.'

'What did they say?'

'They said they'd look into it thoroughly.'

Did they now? Anna thought. They didn't say anything to me, though I told them about the little girl in the red skirt.

'Did you get a good look at the red skirt?' Anna asked, unable to hide her agitation.

'I don't know anything about a skirt,' he replied and gave Anna a quizzical look. 'And I didn't see anyone else by the time I got here. Only the man.'

'And he was already dead, yes?'

'I didn't get out of the boat to take a closer look, but he was dead, no doubt about it. He was lying over there, right by the water's edge.'

'What position was he in?'

'With his head down towards the water.'

'Was he lying parallel to the shore?'

'No, his head was pointing towards the water. His legs were up on the verge. His arms were spread out, if I remember right. He was looking up towards the sky.'

'Can I get out of the boat?' asked Anna.

Again the fisherman looked behind him and squinted, allowing his eyes to scan the water as though he was looking for something, but the river was deserted.

'I don't know about that,' he said. 'We shouldn't really be here.'

'Who says so?' asked Anna.

'The police told me not to reveal this place to anyone before they've completed their investigation.'

'You mean on the phone just now, when you arrived at the quayside?'

The fisherman looked at Anna with his blue eyes, another puzzled expression on his face, and nodded.

'Yes. They called me especially to reinforce the point. When I was walking to the quay I was unsure whether I should have come at all. I was already thinking I should call the whole thing off, seeing as my lunch is waiting for me as well, but then the chief of police called me. The boss himself.'

'And?'

The fisherman gave a hearty laugh and spat into the water.

'Then I knew I had to show you the place, even if it meant my lunch getting cold. He wouldn't have called me if there was nothing to hide out here. Don't you think?'

'I think you're right,' said Anna and gave the fisherman a friendly smile. She felt like hugging him, but the boat was rocking so she didn't dare stand up.

'I'll steer this tight up against the shore so you can look at the spot from the boat.'

'I want to inspect the scene as thoroughly as I can.'

'We don't have much time, and I don't think you should go ashore.'

Anna thought about this for a moment. She wanted to argue the point or simply jump out of the boat, but there was something about the man's mood – something about the whole situation – that made her reject the impulse, however tempting it was.

'All right, I suppose it's best if I don't leave any footprints. The police and the crime-scene investigators will be coming back here again.'

The fisherman nodded, lit a cigarette and guided the boat forward until it was touching the riverbank. If someone had been watching them from the river, it would have looked as though the bushes had swallowed them up.

Anna allowed her eyes to wander across the clayey earth covered with last autumn's leaves. If the thief had slipped on the verge, there should be marks leading down towards the water; the weight of his body would have left a deep furrow in the mud, she thought. But there was no such furrow in sight. Instead the ground looked badly trampled and full of large footprints. The police officers must have disturbed the scene when they collected the body. It would be interesting to see the technicians' report.

'Was the water level particularly high that evening?' Anna asked.

'What do you mean?' the fisherman asked, puzzled once again.

'You said the body was partly on the verge when you found it…'

'Yes.'

'Could his head have been under the water earlier in the evening, before the water level fell?'

'It's possibly, in theory, I suppose, but now that the worst of the floods have passed the water level doesn't change very much. So, no, I don't think so. As far as I can remember the river has been at this height for about a week.'

'Would you say it's normal for someone who has drowned in the Tisza to end up on the shore like that?'

The man thought about this for a moment, spat into the water and cleared his throat. 'He drowned, did he?'

'Yes.'

'Well, the bodies I've come across in the past have generally been in the water for some time – they're swollen and the fish have eaten away at them. But it never occurred to me that this man might have drowned. The body looked too normal somehow.'

'The police told me the man had slipped into the water and drowned, that he'd become caught in some tree roots under the water.'

'Well, in that case the tree must have hands of its own, because it would have had to lift him up on to the verge again. There are no trees like that round here, and if there is one, it would probably be able to make itself disappear too.' Nagy Béla chuckled at his own wit.

'So, even if the man had drowned, slipped in, the way the police said, or fallen from a boat, there's no way he could have ended up in the position and location in which you found him?'

'It would be strange if he had,' said the fisherman, then threw his cigarette, which he'd smoked down to the filter, into the water and lit up another.

'Are you certain you've remembered these details correctly?'

Nagy Béla didn't answer. 'We have to leave now,' he said instead.

'Is it possible to get here on foot?'

'Yes, but the path is covered in thicket.'

'Can you show me the way?'

'I only ever come down here by river,' said the fisherman. 'And now we have to leave.'

Anna tried to ask for more details about the body, but Nagy Béla wasn't talking any longer. He was entirely focussed on powering the boat as fast as he could back to the quayside at Békavár.

Once they had docked, he began loudly explaining to the men sitting by the quay that the Tisza would soon come into flower as long as the water level kept low and the air temperature remained this warm, taking pains to point out that he rarely went up and down the river without his nets and fishing gear for the fun of it, but that it was nice for a change. Anna didn't hear the slightest hint of fear in Béla's voice, though his reasons for all the explanations were obvious.

So as not to attract any further attention to herself and their suspicious trip down the river, she quickly thanked the fisherman and headed back to town, dozens of strange and unpleasant questions darting back and forth through her mind.

THERE WERE HUNDREDS OF PEOPLE in the brick factory and in the surrounding woods. To Dzsenifer it seemed like there were millions of them. At school they had counted up to numbers their teacher had said were called millions. On paper they didn't look all that big, but Dzsenifer understood that, if you had a million pieces of chewing gum or a million peaches, there wouldn't be room for anything else in the world. There was no room for any more people at the camp either, but new groups of them kept arriving all the time. Dzsenifer wasn't very good at maths or other things they taught you at school. Other children her age were already in fourth grade, but she never seemed to progress above second. It didn't worry her, though. There was one pupil even older than her in the class, a boy who lived in the same cluster of shacks where she and her brother sometimes lived. Anyhow, Dzsenifer didn't bother going to school very often. Her brother didn't think it was all that important, never chivvying her out of bed or making her pack her bags, and the teachers never asked after her either.

The camp smelled of bonfire smoke, strange spices and tobacco. Thousands of black eyes stared at Dzsenifer as she wound her way along the paths formed between piles of rubbish and people lying on the ground, looking around for a young woman. Everywhere she looked she could see only men. Men staring back at her. Dzsenifer was afraid because she'd never been here by herself. With her brother she always felt much safer.

Outside the brick factory was a parked van with a sign painted on its side: a red cross on a white background. Behind the van stood a woman by herself. A long, noisy queue of people had formed in front of the van. Dzsenifer saw that the people in the van were handing out food and could tell by the movements and expressions of the people queuing that they were hungry. The woman behind the van was spooning soup into her mouth and peering vigilantly around her.

She was wearing a long-sleeved jumper and her head was wrapped in a scarf, despite the heat. Her eyes looked friendly. Dzsenifer stepped out of the dilapidated factory building and plucked up the courage to walk towards her.

The woman wasn't interested in the credit card, but her eyes lit up when she saw the passport. She took a quick look at the photograph, then said something in a language Dzsenifer didn't understand. The woman placed her bowl on the ground – it was still half full of soup, and Dzsenifer could have snatched it if she'd dared – and swiftly led Dzsenifer to one side of the camp and into a set of small bushes buzzing with flies. Dzsenifer could tell the place had been used as a toilet; the smell made her want to retch. Holding back the urge to vomit, she watched as the woman pulled a bunch of banknotes from beneath her clothes and handed it to her. Dzsenifer might not have been good at maths in school but she knew how to count the number of euros in the wad of notes and work out how many dinars this would get her. The sum seemed enormous. She'd never had so much money in her life. First of all she would go to the bakery and buy a pastry full of vanilla cream, then maybe to the thrift shop to find a new skirt or blouse. The thrift shops were cheap and their clothes looked stylish.

The woman thanked her; at least that's what Dzsenifer thought she said. Dzsenifer saw tears in the woman's eyes. Then the woman quickly stuffed the passport back where the money had been and walked off. Dzsenifer watched as the woman disappeared into the woods, and for a fleeting moment she felt the desire to run after her, take her by the hand and become her travelling companion, her little sister. But she realised this was impossible: she too would need a passport. Besides, she was hungry.

Dzsenifer walked back into town, skipping across the cracks in the asphalt. She pretended she wasn't allowed to touch them or a great chasm would appear and swallow her up.

In the town, she went straight to the bakery and ate so many cream cakes and drank so much Coca-Cola that she felt sick.

THE DAY HAD WARMED QUICKLY. The temperature was already almost thirty degrees. Anna took off her jumper and tied it round her hips by the sleeves. She bought a large bunch of yellow gerberas from the florist on the main street, exchanging a few words with the stall keeper, who seemed to know her and her mother but whom Anna couldn't remember at all.

The cemetery was on the other side of town, about a kilometre from the town centre. Anna walked through the streets carrying the bunch of flowers, enjoying the tingle of the sun on her face and arms. Bicycles creaked past her, mostly old women with large backsides, their shopping bags dangling from the handlebars. A group of children ran across the road shouting. A horse-drawn cart rattled along the street, the clatter of its hooves calming and age-old. A group of exhausted-looking men walked towards her, black hair, black beards, black, angry eyes. Refugees. This was the first time she'd seen any in Kanizsa, if she didn't count the Serbian refugees that came here during the war in Bosnia – old men and women who had been relocated here in the north, far away from the conflict.

Anna arrived at the railway station, which had once been a busy hub of activity; nowadays though, the only train that stopped here was the rickety old, silver-grey, single carriage, which passed once or twice a day on the way to Szabadka and back. At this time of day the station was empty.

Anna crossed the tracks, where thick grass sprouted from between the lines. She could already see the high wall surrounding the cemetery and the massive iron gates at the front. The thick trunks and leafy branches of the enormous chestnut and lime trees stood tall along the edge of the wall, forming a shady corridor. Anna slipped through the gate. There was no movement in the cemetery. The place was so empty it felt almost ghostly. The gravestones had been erected one flush to the other, with no space for grass to grow between them.

Even the graves themselves were covered in large stones, which made the cemetery look bleak. In Finland, cemeteries were beautiful, there were trees and the grounds looked almost like national parks. This place was stripped of all vegetation. The bunches of garish flowers on the stony graves only served to heighten the unnatural atmosphere.

Beyond the rows of graves, someone was sweeping the path. Anna couldn't make out whether it was a man or a woman. She headed towards the path that cut straight through the cemetery and passed a large brass bell that the warden sometimes rang. Anna didn't know when, though. Perhaps it was for funerals. She tried to think back to her father's funeral, Áron's funeral, but she didn't recall hearing the tolling of a bell.

Take a left here, then forwards ten metres, Anna thought, remembering the way. She came here every time she visited Kanizsa, yet every time she still had to spend a moment looking for the right spot. The graves all looked so similar, there were no landmarks, and she could never remember the names of the people buried near Áron and her father. But she always found their grave eventually; and here it was. This time another name had been carved into the gravestone.

'Hello, Grandma,' said Anna and put the flowers in a vase standing by the grave. 'Hello, Dad. Hello, Áron.'

An emptiness filled her. She didn't want to cry, didn't feel anxious. She couldn't think of anything, couldn't remember anything. All she could do was stare at the names on the gravestones; the sun warmed her neck, a bee buzzed round the gerberas, the sound of birdsong in the distance. Later she would feel a sense of guilt at her own lack of emotion. It would happen later that evening, just as she was going to bed, just as she was supposed to shut her eyes and let sleep overwhelm her. Perhaps she would cry a little, but even then she wouldn't be sure whether she was crying for her lost relatives or because she was unable to bring herself to cry at their graves. Now she pressed a finger against her stomach, just beneath the jumper tied round her waist, and read out the names engraved into the stone as though they belonged to people she had never met. Through the numbness, she felt an intense desire to drink – lots, any liquor she could get her hands on – to go straight to the nearest bar and drink until she couldn't remember anything. There was a terrible dive just across from the railway station, she recalled, though she'd never been in there.

'Good afternoon.'

Anna gasped out loud and turned round. A strange woman was standing behind her with a child, a little boy.

'Afternoon,' said Anna and realised this was the same woman she had woken up the night she was searching for the thieves. The woman's eyes were red from crying, but she smiled.

'*Orsós Judit vagyok.*'

'Fekete Anna.'

They shook hands. The woman's hand was warm and her handshake firm.

'Are these your relatives?' asked Judit and nodded at the gravestone. The child stood silently beside his mother and stared at Anna.

'Yes,' Anna replied, deciding not to go into detail.

'My condolences. One of them seems to have passed away only recently.'

'Thank you. That was my grandmother.'

They stood for a moment, silently staring at the gravestone. To her surprise, Anna felt a lump in her throat.

'We've met before,' said the woman and looked at Anna as though she could see right through her.

'That's right. It was Friday night; I was looking for a young man and a girl,' said Anna. She swallowed back the sobs rising to the surface and turned to look at the little boy, who stood gripping the woman's hand. The boy's hair was pitch black and cropped short. He was wearing blue tracksuit bottoms and a patterned T-shirt. He didn't avert his eyes when she looked at him.

'Yes, that's what you said. Why were you looking for them?'

'They stole my handbag at the wine fair.'

'That's rotten luck. What made you think they were down our way?'

For a moment Anna wondered what to say. 'I followed the man, and I thought I saw him heading towards your house. The dog in your yard started barking just when the man disappeared.'

Judit laughed. 'He barks every now and then for no good reason. So the thieves were gypsies then?'

'I think so,' Anna replied. She immediately felt compelled to explain that she certainly didn't think ill of all Romanies, that she really was a tolerant, broad-minded person and that she knew that, despite conventional wisdom, most Romanies were decent, upstanding people.

'You don't need to explain anything,' said Judit before Anna had said a word. 'I understand why you thought to come and look for gypsy thieves down our way, no matter what you think of us in general.'

'How did you…?' Anna stammered, but Judit cut her short again.

'Do you live abroad?'

'How did you guess?'

'It's obvious,' said Judit with a cheerful laugh, and Anna glanced at her clothes. An average pair of jeans and a top, the same clothes as everyone else.

'Where? Germany?'

'No, Finland.'

'Finland! Isn't it terribly cold there? Did you hear that, Benedek? This lady lives in Finland, the land of Father Christmas.'

The boy gave a wary smile.

'It's cold during the winter, yes, and sometimes in the summer too. But you get used to it,' said Anna. 'Almost.'

'My husband is in Belgium. He works there.'

'Really? What does he do?'

'All sorts of things. He left at the beginning of May and he'll be back some time in the autumn. Benedek misses him terribly, don't you?'

The boy started wriggling and pulling his mother by the hand.

'Mummy, let's go,' he said.

'Soon, my dear, soon,' Judit told her son, then turned to Anna. 'You should come and visit us some day. It would be nice to chat with you.'

'Sure. What about?' Anna asked.

'I don't really know yet. This might sound strange to you, but I have a feeling about it. I'll have a think and tell you when I see you. Come round sometime – after midday. You know where we live. Right, Benedek, off we go,' said Judit and without another word set off towards the cemetery gates.

Anna stood bemused for a moment. What had just happened? Then a thought occurred to her.

'Why did you shout something about *tiszavirág* on Friday?' she called after them.

Judit stopped and turned to look at Anna, her expression serious.

'I have premonitions sometimes. When I saw you on Friday night I thought that something will happen when the Tisza comes into bloom. Something bad maybe.'

Judit looked pensive for a moment, then smiled in farewell and continued on her way. The boy had wrenched his hand free of his mother's grip and was now skipping happily along the path. At the gate he turned and gave Anna a shy wave. Anna waved back.

Judit seemed pleasant and friendly, though Anna suddenly felt as chilled and sombre as the gravestones standing in front of her. The woman had read her thoughts, it was as if she'd seen inside her. A shiver ran down Anna's back and arms. She took her jumper from round her waist and pulled it over her head, and started walking briskly through the eerie cemetery, where time and the air seemed to stand still, forming an invisible dome around her. But her steps were slow and heavy; it was as though the cemetery didn't want to let her go, as though the edge of the dome reached the top of the wall, leaving her trapped here for ever, buried alive.

She passed the brass bell and noticed that the figure with the broom had disappeared. Was it Judit who had been sweeping the path? Whose grave had she been visiting? Anna felt afraid. Was Judit really able to read my thoughts? Was she a real person at all, or just a figment of my imagination?

Don't be silly, thought Anna as she stepped out of the gate without being stopped by a dome or anything else. The sun warmed her again, the leaves rustled in the gentle breeze, a fancy, gleaming car drove past the cemetery and headed towards the town, two children sitting in the back seat. A woman dressed in black was packing her broom and watering can into the boot of a car parked outside the cemetery. Anna greeted her with a nod. What on earth were you thinking? Anna asked herself. Don't let yourself turn into a paranoid old fool.

-♦♦♦♦♦-

There were plenty of interesting things to rummage through in the attic, a world full of the history of the Fekete family, neatly archived and labelled in boxes and bags. Many of the boxes bore the words 'István's Papers'. Anna felt a mysterious attraction to attics and basements and the dark, fusty things stashed away within them. As a child she had built herself a den of old cardboard boxes in the basement of their apartment block in Koivuharju. She had taken a blanket, a pillow and a torch down there and imagined she was a queen hiding away from bloodthirsty relatives vying for her crown. The elves and fairies had brought her food and taken good care of her. Years later her headmaster had been especially interested in this game and tried to draw conclusions from it that Anna found far more imaginative than her own silly games. But this time Anna had no desire to dig up the past. She needed a paintbrush. After looking for a while she found a plastic basket full of painting tools. The brush she picked out wasn't made of ostrich feathers and wasn't particularly well suited to her needs, but it would have to do. After returning from the cemetery she had popped into the pharmacy, looking for some iron oxide, and thanked her lucky stars that, even in a small town like Kanizsa, the shops were open every day of the week. She'd found potato flour in her mother's kitchen.

Returning to her room with the brush, Anna locked the door behind her and pulled on a pair of latex gloves. She carefully took her handbag out of the cupboard, where she'd hidden it, wrapped in the plastic bag. You don't need a lab to take fingerprints, she thought, satisfied.

JUNE 6th

ANNA WOKE TO THE RING of her alarm clock. She heard her mother getting out of bed with a sigh in the room next door and going downstairs, jangling a set of keys, opening the front door and going out to the gate. The gate creaked as it opened. Before long she heard her mother calling up to her.

'Anna, are you still asleep? Can you come downstairs?'

Anna pulled on a dressing gown over her thin nightgown, slid her feet into her *papucsok* and went down to the kitchen, where her mother was already pouring glasses of *pálinka* for herself and an early guest – Nagy Béla. It was still dark outside.

'Would you like some?' asked her mother.

'*Jézus Mária*, not at this time of the morning,' Anna replied. 'Are you crazy?'

Anna's mother glowered at her. Guests should always be welcomed politely and you should always serve them a little something to drink, no matter what time of day it was.

'How are you keeping?' her mother asked Nagy Béla and tried to stifle a yawn.

'Very well, thank you. And yourself?'

'Yes, very well. It's nice to have both my children at home. I see Anna so rarely these days.'

'I saw Ákos down by the Tisza last week. He wanted to go for a swim.'

'Ákos has been here for over a month now. Can you swim in the Tisza yet?'

'Not yet. The banks are still flooded and the water is cold.'

'Have you heard any predictions about the *tiszavirág*?'

'There's supposed to be a record-breaking flowering this year,' the fisherman replied and downed his glass of *pálinka* in a single gulp. Anna's mother immediately raised the bottle to pour him some more, but Béla raised his hand to show he'd had enough.

'In fact, it's your daughter I've come to see.'

'Really? What's she been up to this time?' her mother asked, though she knew perfectly well what this was about.

'Anna? It was your sons that were always up to no good. Who'd have thought they were the children of a policeman? Anna is a little angel.'

Anna's mother poured herself another draught of fruit liquor. A tight knot had appeared at the corner of her mouth.

'If only she'd find herself a decent man and start a family—'

'Mum!' snapped Anna.

Her mother cast her a judgemental look. 'You're over thirty. Soon nobody will look twice at you.'

Anna could feel her forehead tingling with anger. How dare her mother say something like that? And in front of a guest!

Béla lit a cigarette and looked at Anna with a note of pity in his eyes, or at least that's how Anna interpreted it. Her mother stood up and fetched an ashtray from the cupboard.

'It's actually a private matter I need to discuss with Anna,' said the fisherman.

'Of course it is,' said her mother, sounding slightly offended. 'I warned you, Anna. Why do you never listen to what I say?'

'Mum, I do listen to you, but I just couldn't let this matter go.'

'No, I'm sure you couldn't. Do as you please then, and don't bother thinking about how I feel. It's not as if you've cared about it in the past.'

Her mother placed her glass of *pálinka* on the table and left the room. Anna heard her going up the staircase and slamming her bedroom door shut. Anna sighed.

'I'm sorry I came here so early. And I'm sorry for taking you away from the river so quickly yesterday,' said Béla. 'I know you'd have liked to examine the spot more closely.'

'Yes, I would. There were footprints in the mud.'

'I've brought you a map. If you follow this route you'll be able to get there by foot.'

The fisherman took the map from his pocket, spread it out on the kitchen table. Then he drew his finger along the route he had marked on the flaking surface of the map with a ballpoint pen.

'Go there as soon as possible, as soon as it's a bit lighter. It's best if nobody sees you.'

'Why?'

'When you said the chief of police had told you the body had become tangled in tree roots, the alarm bells started ringing in my head. Ding dong. That and the fact that they called me specifically to tell me not to take anyone down there. A voice in my head told me there's something not right going on. And at times like that it's best to be careful.'

'Okay,' said Anna as a shiver ran the length of her arms.

'And there's something else you might be interested in.'

'Oh yes?'

'I've got a photograph, too.'

'A photograph? Of what?'

'Of the dead guy.'

'What on earth…?'

'Even an old man like me knows how to use new technology,' said the fisherman. He gave her a satisfied smile and took a top-of-the-range smart phone out of his pocket.

'Excellent,' Anna gasped.

'I'll send you the photograph now.'

The fisherman tapped his phone and Anna heard a ping from her own phone as the message arrived.

'There you go.'

Anna opened the message. A young man, late twenties to early thirties, was lying on his back by the waterline, his head almost in the water. His eyes were wide open, his lips slightly parted. His clothes were wet and dirty, and looked as though they were glued to his body. Clumps of clay were caught in his black hair, and dried leaves had snagged on his coat. Anna couldn't estimate the man's size just from the photograph, but it certainly seemed to be the same man who had run off with Anna's handbag at the wine fair. The clothes were the same, dark. Anna tried to zoom in on his face but the image became pixelated and out of focus. Was that a bloody scratch on the man's face? Or was it just a shadow?

'Thank you for this,' said Anna.

'No problem. If you need anything, just come round to the house. Your mother knows where I live.'

'Mum doesn't want me to start digging around this case.'

'That's probably wise,' said Béla and stepped towards the door. 'You promise you'll be careful?'

'Of course. Remember, I'm a police officer too. I know what I'm doing.'

The fisherman said nothing, but Anna could read his thoughts in his expression. Police officer or not, it didn't matter round here.

Grey smoke hung in the kitchen air after Nagy Béla had left. Anna opened the window and cool air fluttered inside. Outside everything was quiet. Even along the busy Szabadka út, which brought traffic in or out of the town, she couldn't hear the sound of cars. It was best to set off straight away, thought Anna. Before the town wakes up.

ANNA STEPPED OUT of the gates and into the street before six, only to note – once again – that the residents of Kanizsa still lived according to age-old agrarian timetables. The town was already awake. Almost awake. People were cycling to work, and the smell of fresh bread wafted from the bakery at the corner of the town square. The most direct route from the house to the Tisza didn't take her through the square, but Anna wanted to look as though she was out for a walk. She didn't want to stroll past the police station, and she certainly didn't want to walk along the highway heading towards Törökkanizsa, where drivers would have paid undue attention to any pedestrians. Neither did she want to take the *töltés*, a pathway constructed along the top of the town's flood defences, winding towards the riverbank like an asphalted corridor. While that would have been the quickest option, taking it would have shown without doubt that she was headed for the banks of the Tisza.

To the south, the town of Kanizsa was bordered by verdant parkland featuring a *fürdő* complete with a hotel and spa complex. It wasn't a place for splashing around but a full-scale health spa, its various pools pumped full of the local healing spring water, rich in sulphur. It provided an incredible variety of physiotherapy, massage and rehabilitation services. The spa's early-morning customers were already out and about in the park with their sticks and walking frames.

Anna decided not to walk directly through the park but wandered instead along its labyrinth of shaded pathways. Flowerbeds and rose bushes were dotted here and there, but the overall impression of the place was shabby. The lawns were overgrown in places and there could have been far more flowerbeds. The park's general state of degradation saddened Anna; years ago the place had been carefully tended and kept beautiful. Situated in the middle of the park, the art nouveau Vigadó building had once served as a hub of activity for the locals, but now its walls were daubed in graffiti and the windows were boarded up. The building's former glory could still be seen in the arches and curves of the architecture. If only a millionaire would decide to renovate the property, invest their money in local culture rather than luxury cars and mansions, thought Anna as she walked past the house.

Attached to the tree trunks throughout the park were posters advertising the forthcoming *Tiszavirág* festival, which would be held when the river came into bloom about a week before the end of June. Anna was thrilled that she'd be able to see the flowering this year. She had vague childhood memories of the festival, when the whole family had rowed up the river, clouds of mayflies buzzing around them. It had frightened her. Anna's father had laughed at her fearfulness, captured one of the yellowish insects in his hand and showed it to her.

'See how gentle it looks,' he'd said, but Anna had been revolted at its translucent wings, its large, beady, black eyes and the two long protrusions that formed its abdomen and that looked like spikes, though they were in fact soft and harmless. She couldn't remember ever picking up one of these Tisza 'flowers' in her hand.

This year she would catch one, for the first time in her life.

The route to the place where the body had been found was extremely difficult going. And wet. Anna found herself wading up to her ankles in pools of muddy water that had collected in the uneven ground after the floods. It took a long time until she found the right place. There were no clearly defined paths through the thicket. After wandering round the area, beating several paths to the riverbank, only to realise each time that she still wasn't in the right place, she finally saw some marks in the mud. They weren't clear. The muddy terrain meant that it was impossible to make out well-defined footprints, but the twisted and snapped branches seemed to indicate a corridor through the undergrowth, leading towards the river. Anna followed this corridor, and before long she was at the spot where the fisherman had brought her in his boat.

Now that Anna had the chance to examine the location in peace, she was all the more convinced that there had been a struggle. The ground was churned up. In some spots, dead leaves were pressed so deep into the mud that only a rough tussle could have planted them there.

She spent several hours examining the scene, trying to be as thorough as she could, despite having no forensic equipment. The results: a few receipts in the bushes about four metres from the water's edge. They were all from her bag: an extortionately expensive coffee and croissant at Helsinki airport; a bar of chocolate at a service station near Kecskemét. She took measurements and photographs of three distinct sets of footprints – two large and one small. The smaller prints were near the receipts and close to where the body had lain. There were two different textile fibres and hairs, too: a few long and black, a few short and dark; many grey hairs. And there was a bus ticket. Of course, all this could have been completely irrelevant, but Anna doubted it. Nobody visited a place like this for fun. This wasn't a spot for a picnic; it was a jungle, almost impenetrable and buzzing with mosquitoes. The only people to visit this place were the man who had stolen her handbag and, later on, the police. And, of course, the person with whom the thief had struggled. And the little girl. The smaller footprints did not belong to an adult. Anna was convinced that the girl in the red skirt had been here by the riverbank and that the long hairs she'd found belonged to her. Had the red-skirted girl witnessed the murder, or, worse still, had she been involved in it? Had she taken the contents of Anna's wallet? Where was she now?

Anna found the bus ticket slightly further away, in the bushes. It was a ticket printed in Serbian, issued by the Subotica Trans company, bought for a 'Subotica–Kanjiza' journey and stamped on June the third. There was no specific time on the stamp. If the thief hadn't lived in Kanizsa, he may have travelled here from Szabadka. Anna carefully picked up the ticket with a pair of pincers and placed it in a small, see-through plastic bag, just as she had done with the hairs and fibres. I'll need to find a microscope or a magnifying glass, she thought. But then she thought, what the hell am I doing collecting pieces of evidence? I wasn't supposed to investigate this case at all.

Anna wiped sweat from her brow, tied her hair in a knot above her head and lay down on the ground in the position the fisherman had described. The dazzling sun filtered through the trees and Anna closed her eyes. The wind rustled through the leaves, the sound of an engine carried across the river then disappeared. A branch suddenly cracked somewhere nearby. Anna looked up but couldn't see anything. She sunk back into her thoughts.

What had happened here? What if the man had drowned after all and someone had pulled him out of the water? The girl? Would she have had the strength?

The riverbank formed a slope, so the blood ran to her head. The mosquitoes whined in her ears, biting every patch of exposed skin. Anna's crown was almost in the water. She felt an irresistible desire to stay there, to let the insects bite her and suck her blood. But when a particularly brazen mosquito decided to bite her on the eyelid, the desire disappeared. She sat up and began flicking through the photographs she'd taken. At the third photo she remembered the selfies Nóra had taken at the wine fair. Perhaps she should look through them too. With luck they might provide a glimpse of the thief while he was still alive. And the girl.

On her way back through the thicket, Anna had the nagging feeling that someone was following her, watching her through the branches, someone who knew she had been rummaging around the crime scene. She glanced over her shoulder but couldn't see anyone.

WET FROM THE MUD, the legs of Anna's jeans had dried, hard and brown, on the way home, leaving lumps of clay on the front step as she bounded straight upstairs and into her room. She stored the plastic bags in the top drawer in her old desk, which she could lock with a little key, then uploaded the photos she'd taken by the riverbank to her iPad and sent Sari an email.

From: Anna Fekete <anna.fekete@poliisi.fi>
To: Sari Jokikokko-Pennanen <sari.jokikokko@poliisi.fi>

Hi Sari,
I've got myself mixed up in a bit of a weird case here (brilliant way to start my holiday, I know!), and because I can't access any of our databases from here, I wonder if you could help me find out a few things. I've attached a photograph and a couple of fingerprints. Could you run them through Interpol and see if they match anyone who's already in the system?

For the moment, I won't tell you any more details. This whole thing might be the product of my overactive cop's imagination, which won't even let me relax on holiday. I hope it's not too much trouble. (Of course, I know it's extra work, but I wouldn't ask if it wasn't really important.)

Anna

P.S. How are you? And is Esko still keeping off the cigarettes?

Anna was just about to have a shower when her mother knocked at the door.

'Why is your door locked?' Her mother's voice sounded like she was in a mood. 'Come down for coffee. Kovács Gábor is here. He wants to talk to you.'

'I have to take a shower before I can see anyone.'

'Nonsense. Where have you been? And what did Béla want?'

'Mum, keep your voice down. I don't want Gábor to hear.'

'He's an old family friend – and police too, for that matter.'

'All the same, Mum, please don't tell anyone about what I've been doing.'

'Very well. But get down here and be quick about it.'

Anna opened the drawer in her desk, put her camera, phone and iPad inside, and locked it again.

This case is making me paranoid, she thought, stuffed the key to the desk beneath her mattress and pulled on shorts and a T-shirt, as the morning had warmed quickly. The forecast predicted temperatures over 30°C.

Downstairs, Kovács Gábor was sitting drinking a cup of coffee. Her mother had laid the table with freshly baked *pogácsa* scones.

'I've just got back from my morning run and haven't had a shower,' said Anna. 'Apologies if I smell.'

Anna could feel her mother's judgement settling on her face. Apparently the smell of sweat wasn't a suitable topic of conversation. I need a list of forbidden subjects, she thought, so that I know when to keep my mouth shut.

'Do you work out often?' asked Gábor.

'Yes!' Anna's mother answered on her behalf, but there was no sense of pride in her voice. 'When she was younger she was always running and training; never did anything else. It seems nothing has changed. Always out running. Always some special diet on the go for a marathon or competition.'

'I haven't run a marathon for years,' Anna replied calmly. 'And I'm not on a special diet any longer.'

'Still. Do you ever have time to see your friends? You're always at work or running about somewhere.'

'Nowadays I only run for fun. I must have been eighteen the last time I did it competitively,' Anna explained to Gábor, ignoring her mother's comments.

'You have to run in our job,' said Gábor. 'And sometimes you have to run fast. Best to keep in shape. It's a good thing I don't have to do it any longer – I don't think I'd be up to it.' He patted his swollen belly. 'Excellent *pogácsa*. Did you bake them yourself?'

'Yes,' came her mother's satisfied reply. Anna looked at Gábor as if to thank him for diverting her mother's attention away from chiding her.

'You'll have to give my wife the recipe. These are delicious.'

Her mother blushed with pride, and Anna felt the urge to say something nasty but decided against it. She wouldn't lower herself to her mother's level and put her down in front of guests. She would talk to her mother about it when they were alone.

'Anyhow, there is a reason for my visit,' said Gábor, putting down his scone. 'I have some news. The fact is the investigation into the theft of your handbag has now been officially concluded.'

'Why?' asked Anna.

'Good,' her mother interrupted. 'Then Anna can let the matter go too, isn't that right, dear?'

Anna raised her eyebrows in disdain.

'The coroner examined the body and concluded that the young man drowned. The body showed no signs of a struggle and there was nothing to suggest this was anything more than a tragic accident.'

'But has he been officially identified and his family notified?' asked Anna.

'Everything is in order. You can forget all about it now and enjoy the rest of your holiday in peace. You have already been in contact with the embassy in Belgrade, haven't you?'

'Yes, of course,' she lied, and swore to herself she would see to it immediately.

'Good. Then there's nothing else to say on the matter.'

'Hang on a minute, there are still plenty of unanswered questions. For instance, why the young man was by the riverbank in the first place. And how the little girl is involved in all this.'

'There are some details we will never be able to establish, but I doubt they are particularly salient. What's most important is that the coroner has done his job and we can breathe a sigh of relief. Of course, the loss of your passport is unfortunate, but replacing it won't be all that much trouble.'

'I want to see the coroner's report.'

'In that case you'll have to speak to the chief of police. I don't have that kind of authority at the station any longer. I just loiter around there making a nuisance of myself.'

'I'll make sure I speak to him. Mark my words.'

'Anna!' her mother shouted. 'Stop it. Stop it this minute! Why do you have to be so stubborn? Can't you simply let the matter drop? Good God, I don't understand you in the slightest. You're like a terrier that bites and bites at people's ankles and refuses to be told. I … I'm ashamed of you, Anna!'

Anna's mother turned and stormed out of the kitchen. The front door slammed behind her. Gábor stared awkwardly at his coffee cup. Anna didn't know what to say. It was possible that she was more ashamed of her mother than her mother was of her.

'Is there any coffee left?' Gábor broke the silence.

Anna jumped up, fetched the *dzsezva* and poured the man another cup of black, bitter coffee.

'I understand you both,' Gábor began. 'I know exactly what it feels like for you – I'm a policeman too, after all. And your mother has experienced a lot – she's lost so much. You have to appreciate that she's only worried, that she loves you and doesn't want anything to happen to you.'

'I know,' said Anna quietly.

'I was the one to break the news of your father's death to her. I'll never forget that moment,' said Gábor, and Anna saw that his eyes were teary. 'It was terrible, absolutely horrific. Your mother simply fell to pieces. And just when it seemed that she'd finally got back on her feet again the war broke out and Áron…'

'I know,' Anna repeated. 'I do understand.'

'But I agree, it would be a good idea for you to read the coroner's report. I can put a word in with the chief of police and suggest he gives you permission to see it. Perhaps it will give you some kind of closure. Shall we do that?'

'Yes, please. Thank you.'

'No trouble at all. Talk to your mother. She only wants the best for you.'

'I know,' Anna said for a third time, feeling like a little girl.

Once Gábor had left, Anna sat by herself in the kitchen for a long time. She listened to the faint sounds of the house, the distant ticking of a clock, the hum of the fridge. Maybe it was best to draw a line under this once and for all, she thought. Once I've read the coroner's report, I'll call it a day. I'm only spoiling my holiday and wasting any chance I have to spend time with my mother, or Ákos, or Réka and my other friends. Here I'm not Detective Inspector Anna. Here I'm just Anna. And that Anna really needs a holiday.

THE JOURNEY TO SZABADKA to meet Réka's boyfriend, József, took them past endless fields of crops. The scenery was the same no matter what direction you took from Kanizsa. Vojvodina, or Vajdaság as they called it in Hungarian, was the granary of Serbia. Fields as far as the eye could see, flat, fertile plains, almost monotonous expanses, the enormity of which made it breathtakingly beautiful. To Anna the landscape resembled the sea. Anna and Réka had chosen a slightly longer route, a narrow road, in places in extremely bad condition, winding its way through the small villages and between the enormous fields. The asphalt was pocked, ancient tractors puffed along the road and the tiny hamlets looked almost lifeless.

The fields were dotted with dilapidated farmhouses, abandoned years ago, places that had once been brimming with life. Réka kept her eyes on the houses as they drove, wondering whether she could buy one of them and renovate it, but Anna barely listened to what her friend was saying.

At one of the farmhouses, Réka asked that they stop the car, wanting to take a closer look at the buildings. A tall walnut tree cast long shadows across the overgrown garden around the sagging house. A stork had built a nest of twigs in the building's broken chimney stack. From deep inside the chimney came the chirping of fledglings. The stork stood up and flapped its wings. It clearly didn't want anyone to disturb the peace in its nest.

'This place is wonderful,' said Réka as they entered the main building, which looked like it might collapse at any moment. 'Look, the walls are basically still in good condition. Imagine what this place would look like once it was tidied up a bit and the roof fixed. We'd probably have to replace the floors and windows. But these window frames are amazing. They're original.'

Anna looked but couldn't imagine anything but the chortling of an old tractor. This house was beyond the scope of even Réka's wonderful József, who was apparently a dab hand at DIY. He worked as an art teacher in a school in Szabadka. Réka had met him while she was writing a piece about art teaching in Hungarian schools for the *Magyar Szó* newspaper. The three of them were supposed to go for dinner today. Anna was nervous about meeting him, which made her feel silly.

'This is exactly the kind of country house we've been looking for. It's near Kanizsa and Szabadka. This would be the perfect location. József would have a short journey to work and the child would be between both sets of grandparents. Look at this, there's an old stove too.'

Anna's phone began to ring.

It was the chief of police. He informed her that the coroner's report was due to arrive from the pathology department in Novi Sad within the hour and he could forward it to Anna's email address.

Anna thanked him, cheerily gave him the address, hung up and followed Réka into the other room. The place smelt of mildew and the floorboards were rotten. A round, whitewashed stove dominated the room. It was certainly beautiful, or rather it would have been, without the black cracks in its walls.

'Who was it?' asked Réka.

'The chief of police. I can read the autopsy report on the handbag thief.'

'That's great. Let's hope it gives you peace of mind.'

'I hope so,' said Anna. 'You'll have to find out who owns this old farm,' she continued, frustrated with herself for not having the courage to tell Réka what she really thought of this run-down shack.

Her friend's eyes were alive and her cheeks red as she planned the kitchen cupboards and the children's playroom.

'We could build a garage out in the yard, and that could be József's studio. Large windows facing north and white walls.'

'Sounds good. You'll definitely need a studio.'

'I'm so happy,' Réka sighed. She dreamily stroked her stomach, even though she wasn't yet showing. 'Isn't it time you settled down too, Anna?'

For Christ's sake, thought Anna.

'I haven't really thought about it,' she said.

'Béci! He's coming to Kanizsa for the weekend – he's been asking about you. Now there's a good man for you. He really fell for you after your little fling at New Year.'

Fucking hell, Anna cursed to herself.

'Why don't we get going? I think we've seen enough of this dump,' she said. 'My clothes are going to smell of mould.'

'Anna! You're not angry, are you? Sorry, I didn't mean anything by it.' Réka seemed visibly distressed.

'Look, this is a good location, but the building is in shit condition. Why don't you just build a new house?'

'We don't want a new house!'

'And I don't want to settle down!'

'But, Anna, that isn't normal. You've become so terribly cynical. Surely you'd like to curl up in someone's arms in the evenings? I'm getting worried about you.'

'Exactly how normal is it to want to take on a run-down dump like this? Have you given a second thought to how much work doing up a place like this will be? You'll spend all your money and free time on the renovations. And you won't be curling up in anyone's arms in the evening; you'll be collapsing into bed half dead, grabbing a couple of hours' sleep before you have to slog your way through another day. Besides, how long have you even known this József? You didn't say a word about him when I was having my little New Years' fling. Is it normal to get pregnant and buy a house with someone you've only known for a few months?'

'Anna!' Réka shouted as she burst into tears and ran out of the house.

Anna clenched her fists. Her heart was racing and her breath was shallow.

A fly was buzzing against the dirty windowpane through which Anna could just make out the walnut tree and Réka sitting by its trunk, her head buried in her arms, which she'd wrapped around her knees, pulling them tight against her chest. The fly became tangled in a spider's web fluttering in a light flow of air like a grey, tightly woven curtain.

What now? thought Anna. What should I do now? The situation had taken her by surprise, and her helplessness made her feel dizzy and weak, as though the power was draining from her limbs. Anna sat down by the stove, leant against its cracked plaster and watched the fly struggle in the spider's web, trying to free itself. The web tore ominously. The spider was nowhere to be seen. It had probably already eaten and was so full that it was too tired to come out to paralyse and wrap up its prey, ready for a rainy day. The fly writhed in the trap, and the web eventually tore free of the window frame. The fly fell on to the windowsill. Its body was impressive, plump, and greenish-black, but its wings were helpless, tied up in the grey, silken web. That creature will never fly again, thought Anna. And there's nothing I can do to help it.

Anna ran her hand along the surface of the stove. Its curves felt smooth and cool against the palm of her hand. In the winter months, when frozen winds blew in across the *puszta*, the flanks of this stove would radiate warmth throughout the small kitchen. Anna understood Réka's dreams. She understood them perfectly well. Even she couldn't deny that traditional farmhouses, with whitewashed walls and verandas running the length of the building, were cosy and beautiful. All too often they were razed to the ground and replaced with ugly, contemporary boxes. If Réka and József were to renovate one of the remaining farmhouses, they would be preserving their culture; so why shouldn't they buy this one? I'm such a bitch, Anna thought, standing up.

She slowly walked out to the walnut tree and gently placed her hand on Réka's shoulder.

'I'm sorry. I was mean to you. Come on, let's get going and I can finally meet this wonderful József of yours.'

Réka wiped the tears from her eyes and said she forgave her, but for the rest of the journey into town she seemed quiet and uneasy.

From: Sari Jokikokko-Pennanen <sari.jokikokko@poliisi.fi>
To: Anna Fekete <anna.fekete@poliisi.fi>

Hi Anna,
What on earth have you got yourself mixed up in over there? Is it sensible? That's all I'm saying.

I'll try and identify the prints ASAP. The best option would be if you could check against local databases, I don't think we'll find anything here. But I'll take a look. I forwarded the photograph to Kirsti – she promised to enlarge it and refocus it as soon as she's got a moment.

Esko has got a nasty case on the go at the moment. I won't give you any of the details – don't want to spoil your holiday, though it seems as if you're perfectly capable of doing that by yourself. Anyway, looks like Esko is still off the cigarettes! By the way, good news: Rauno is coming back to work next week!

My wonderful husband is away on business again for a change; to be honest I'm a bit sick of it. The weather here is awful, it's windy and cold, and yesterday there was even a hail shower. In June! I want to join you in the warmth. It's probably the middle of summer there by now.

Enjoy your break. We need you fresh and relaxed when you get back. My holiday starts on July 1st :) Ah! Can't wait. On the down side, that means we won't see each other until the end of the summer. Still, what's to stop us getting together outside of work? It would be nice to do something once you're back. We could go swimming or go for a beer. Well, I'm more of a cider person. (You see, my thoughts are already running around – anything but work. Thank God the weather's so terrible, otherwise I don't think I'd cope with another day cooped up in here. I need a holiday!!!)

I'll be around almost all of July, because we never travel further than my parents' summer cottage. Apparently my husband gets to do all the travelling in this family. Brilliant. What about me?!

Sari

P.S. Be careful, won't you? Your mail really spooked me.

Anna typed Sari a brief reply: *No need to worry. See you in July.*

She noticed that the chief of police had sent his promised email, but she didn't want to read it. Not yet. Maybe never. She switched off her iPad and listened to the silence of the house around her. Her mother had already gone to bed, Ákos had gone to Szeged. A truck thundered along the street. Another. Then everything was quiet again. Anna unlocked the desk drawer and fingered the plastic bags into which she had carefully placed the hairs and fibres she'd found that morning. What the hell was I thinking digging around in there? I'm not right in the head. Maybe tomorrow I should build a bonfire in the yard, cook some chicken *pörkölt* on the open fire and invite my friends for dinner. I could burn these bags in the fire, she thought, and slammed the drawer shut. She tried to concentrate on other, more pleasant things and move the unpleasant thoughts to the back of her mind.

József was really nice. Of course. Smart, good-looking and funny. And he was clearly head-over-heels in love with Réka. They talked for a long time about the house that she and Réka had visited. Réka had glanced nervously at Anna but relaxed when she realised Anna wasn't going to continue making snide comments. Who was Anna, anyway, to criticise anyone else's hopes and dreams, things she had never had? Réka had remained in Szabadka and Anna had driven herself back through the darkened terrain to Kanizsa.

At Palics she'd come across the body of a dog in the road. As she drove past, the familiar smell of decomposition had come in through the window, the same smell as that given off by a body that had been dead for some time. It felt like an omen.

An indistinct sense of guilt and anxiety wrapped itself around her like a sweaty sheet as she tried to find a comfortable position and get some sleep. Insomnia scared her, it was something that usually struck when she most needed to sleep. She hadn't packed her sleeping pills. It hadn't occurred to her that she might become stressed on holiday. But she remembered that in the pharmacies here you could buy almost anything without a prescription. Tibor told her he sometimes smuggled anabolic steroids to bodybuilders in Hungary. Testosterone supplements. He bought them by the kilo at local pharmacies, and not one of the Serbian pharmacists asked any questions. Anna decided to get some sleeping pills tomorrow, just in case. She switched on her iPad again and flicked through the news.

Eventually she gave up and signed into her email account, clicked open the attachment sent by the chief of police and read the report. It was written in such official Serbian and so full of medical terms that Anna had difficulty understanding it. But with the help of an online dictionary she managed to get the gist of what it was saying. The man who'd stolen her handbag had drowned. His lungs were full of water from the Tisza. This was a case of accidental death; certified by the pathologist's scrawled signature, his name typed clearly and an official stamp.

Anna put her iPad on the floor. Perhaps she would be able to enjoy the rest of her holiday after all – clear her conscience and forget all about this. But the sense of relief never came. Something still didn't seem right. She'd seen the evidence of a struggle on the riverbank with her own eyes, so why was there nothing to indicate that on the body? Who had been fighting on the riverbank if not the thief? And with whom?

JUNE 7th

'*ISTEN HOZOTT!*' Judit welcomed Anna in her low, soft voice. Anna stepped through the front door and straight into the dimly lit kitchen, which also served as the living room. There was a dining table, a sofa, and a shelving unit with a television that was on but with the sound off. Beside the unit was a door leading to the room behind the kitchen and facing on to the street. A colourful curtain was draped in the doorway and Anna couldn't see whether Judit's son or anyone else was in the other room. There were no sounds coming from behind the curtain.

'Would you like something? Coffee? Beer?'

'Coffee, please.'

Judit filled the *dzsezva* with water and put it on the stove to boil, lit a cigarette and offered one to Anna; long, thin, white cigarettes that were probably so mild you had to suck your cheeks in to taste the smoke. In Serbia many women smoked cigarettes like these. They thought they were healthier than normal cigarettes, that they were somehow more feminine.

'Where's your son?' asked Anna.

'At school.'

Of course. The summer holiday in Kanizsa only started after the Finnish midsummer and continued until the beginning of September.

'How old is Benedek?'

'Eight.'

'He's a sweet child. When will your husband be coming back?'

'Not until the autumn. He's working all summer. My mother lives here with us, but she's not here at the moment.'

Anna wondered how they could all fit into such a tiny apartment. She also decided not to enquire further about what Judit's husband was actually doing in Belgium. Probably begging, like almost all Eastern European Romanies in the West. What Anna was curious to know was what Judit wanted to talk to her about, but blurting it out would have sounded impolite. The situation began to feel awkward and Anna didn't know what to say. They were complete strangers and they represented the polar opposites of society, a fact that had far greater significance here than Anna could have imagined. Silence descended between them.

And then, as though she had once again read Anna's thoughts, Judit spoke.

'When we were at the cemetery, I had a strong feeling that I wanted to read for you. Would you mind?'

'What do you mean?'

'Read your cards. Actually, as soon as you came knocking at the door the other night I felt that the cards might have something to tell you.'

'You want to tell my fortune?'

'You could call it that.'

'I don't really believe in any of that,' said Anna. Now would be a good moment to leave, she thought, to thank her host politely and close the door behind her for good. Anna was feeling that same unnerving hollowness she'd experienced at the cemetery.

'You don't have to believe in it. Besides, many things happen around us all the time that we can't perceive or understand. I see things that many people don't. Shall we have a look?'

Anna thought about it. She had no truck with premonitions, telepathy, energy fields or homeopathy, though she'd once tried homeopathic drops for her insomnia. She didn't know whether they'd helped her or whether they had simply been followed by a period of better sleep. The placebo effect, that's what it must have been. Perhaps she could try this too, out of sheer curiosity if nothing else. Perhaps fortune-tellers were like placebos: harmless – they might even help gullible people – and with no side effects. People were free to believe in it all if they wished. But still the thought didn't appeal to her. She felt reluctant, but wasn't sure whether it was through instinct or fear.

'I'm not sure … I don't want to know anything I couldn't find out in the real world.'

'This is very real for lots of people – far more people than you might think. There's no need to be afraid.'

'I'm not afraid but I really don't believe in fortune-telling.'

'This isn't really fortune-telling in the truest sense. The cards might wish to tell you something about the future, but generally they help you to see and understand things that might otherwise skip your attention. Things that already exist in your life, one way or the other, but that you just can't see.'

What things might they be? thought Anna. If you can't see them, they can't be of very great significance. Still, perhaps she could think of this as adding to her list of interesting experiences. A gypsy fortune-teller. That would be a good story to tell people at work. Esko would be amused when he heard.

'Okay then,' Anna finally consented. 'It can't do any harm, I suppose.'

'Definitely not. On the contrary, in fact.'

Judit pulled the curtain across the only window in the already dusky kitchen. Then she locked the door.

'So that nobody can disturb us. Benedek will be back from school soon.'

'Where will he go if the door is locked?'

Judit looked up at Anna, amused. 'Next door, of course. Right, let's start. Place some money on the table, any sum you wish.'

Aha, thought Anna. That's what this was all about. The cards were the woman's way of making a living. She took out a thousand-dinar note, about ten euros, and placed it on the table. Judit's eyes opened almost imperceptibly. A thousand dinars was a lot of money here. With that she would be able to put many meals on the table and Anna would surely get an excellent reading.

'I must ask you whether you want to hear everything the cards tell me. Whatever that may be.'

'Of course,' said Anna, though the thought was chilling and an unnerving fear pinched her stomach again. I don't believe in this, she tried to convince herself. This is stupid, nothing but primitive mumbo jumbo.

Judit shuffled the pack of dirty, dog-eared cards. Then she asked Anna to select several at random. Judit closed her eyes for a moment, took a deep breath and lay the top card on the table. Then the second, the third, the fourth.

'This card signifies love,' said Judit tapping one of the cards with a long nail decorated with glitter. 'But, because it's between these two cards, it means unhappiness in love. Do you have a boyfriend?'

Anna shook her head. Why don't you ask me whether I have a girlfriend? she thought spitefully to herself.

'A girlfriend?'

Anna could barely hide her surprise and shook her head.

'That's what I thought,' said Judit. 'You don't seem like a lesbian. It may be that you'll never have a boyfriend or a lasting relationship. I'm sorry.' She looked up at Anna with pity in her eyes. 'You said I was to tell you everything.'

For crying out loud, thought Anna. Does she really think I'm going to burst into tears at that particular piece of news?

'But there's someone here, a man,' Judit continued. 'Is there someone on your mind after all? Someone you're attracted to?'

'No,' Anna replied.

'Well, in that case, there's someone who has been watching you and wants to get to know you better. Perhaps someone's following you. That's what this card means. He might be a policeman or something similar. And he's interested in you.'

You know I'm a police officer, thought Anna. You've already been asking round the town, who I am, what I'm doing and who my family are, and you know I'm investigating the theft of my handbag.

It must make this line of work much easier when you keep up to date with the town's gossip.

Judit placed more cards on the table and concentrated on them.

'Your finances are in order,' she mumbled.

What a piece of news that is. People round here probably think I'm a millionaire just because I live in Finland.

'This man, this official, he's following you. Look at this card. It means there's a man keeping an eye on you. He must be in love,' said Judit and gave Anna a teasing glance. 'Are you sure you don't know who it might be?'

'I'm sure,' she replied.

'Well, it will doubtless become clear to you in the near future. But there's something strange going on here too. This card represents love, but it's next to this card,' said Judit and once again tapped a card with her acrylic nail. This time the picture on the faded card showed a female figure in a white dress.

'Someone close to you has died. Someone very close and important.'

You don't need cards to tell me that, Anna felt like saying. You saw me at the cemetery. But Anna didn't want to seem rude. She appreciated the fact that Judit hadn't lowered her voice to a dramatic whisper when she mentioned death, and didn't sound at all like a melodramatic diva, the way Anna thought of all fortune-tellers. Judit simply said what she saw or imagined she saw in the cards, to the point and without any histrionics.

'The death of your loved one still plagues you. It's beginning to haunt you.'

Anna wanted to tell her that she was haunted by the death of a complete stranger, the man who'd stolen her handbag, but she didn't want to give Judit the slightest indication that any of her premonitions was even remotely close to the truth.

Another card.

'Death again. I can see a child.'

'What child?' Anna flinched involuntarily. She touched her stomach, and Judit saw it. Calm down, Anna told herself. That woman can't see anything.

'I don't know, perhaps you know better. There's a child affecting your life in some way. Who might that be? Do you have children?'

Judit waited patiently for Anna's response and looked at her with such intense scrutiny that Anna began to feel uncomfortable. Calm down, this is nonsense, Anna kept repeating to herself, trying to look nonchalant. She shook her head and remained silent.

Judit waited a moment longer and then laid another card on the table.

'You're not safe,' Judit said as mundanely as if she'd said Anna would go to the shop that evening. Yet, despite the calm of Judit's voice – or specifically because of it – Anna was beginning to feel anxious. If Judit were to behave like a drama queen, if she gasped in horror and rolled her eyes, it would be easier to dismiss her as a charlatan, to laugh at the whole spectacle. But Judit's matter-of-fact, almost officious manner made the situation all the more believable. Almost believable, Anna corrected herself. Of course, that's precisely the point, she thought, suddenly relieved. This is theatre, and this woman knows exactly how to perform her role. She has years of experience, and this is how she makes a living. That's all there is to it. The knot of anxiety at the bottom of her stomach relaxed and Anna began to calm down.

Judit gathered up the cards and poured herself and Anna a glass of Voda-Voda mineral water. Then she turned to look at Anna.

'Is there anything you'd like to ask?'

Anna hesitated. There were many things she would have liked to ask, yet at the same time she had no desire whatsoever to ask them. But she had to say something so as not to sound rude.

'What do you mean, I'm not safe?' she asked eventually.

'I don't know, I couldn't see it clearly. But I had the same feeling when you visited the other night. It was a strange feeling. As if it had something to do with the blossoming of the Tisza.'

'*Tiszavirág*?'

'Yes. I don't know what it means but it feels bad. Very bad indeed.'

'I still don't believe in any of this,' said Anna.

Judit sighed and lit a cigarette. She looked suddenly tired. 'You don't have to believe. But if you'd like, you can give the cards something in return. Some money, for instance. We'll place a card on top of the money, and it'll be your lucky card.'

Anna placed two hundred dinars on the table. She didn't want to pay anything more for this nonsense but felt she couldn't refuse. Compared to this woman she was rich. Nonsense or not, Judit and her children needed food and clothes, just like anyone else. They had to pay the bills, go to the doctor and buy schoolbooks. Anna laid down another five hundred. Judit nodded in acceptance, shuffled the cards, plucked one out with her acrylic nail, turned it over and placed it on the table.

'A friend. There's a friend who you cannot trust.'

'Who is it?'

'The cards can't tell me that, but your heart will tell you when the time comes.'

'Thank you. This has been fascinating,' Anna said politely.

'You don't believe in it, but it doesn't matter. There exists another reality too. The kind of reality that normal people like you cannot appreciate. I've had a sensitivity to this since I was a child. My mother had it too. It runs in the family.'

Anna tried to think of something friendly to say, perhaps an interested question about Judit's gift, but a knock at the door saved her. Judit pulled back the curtains and opened the door. The June light flooded into the room, so powerful that Anna had to squint her eyes. The sound of a dog barking came from the yard. A small, black-haired boy with a large rucksack on his back was standing at the door, but, seeing Anna, he didn't step inside.

'*Szia, Benedek! Gyere, gyere,* come inside. Look who's come to visit your mother? It's Anna, the lady from Finland. We saw her at the cemetery, do you remember?'

The boy nodded, shrugged off his rucksack and left it by the door. Anna greeted him.

'*Csókolom*,' he said without looking her in the eyes.

'Were you a good boy at school?' asked Judit.

'Yes.'

'Do you have a lot of homework?'

'Yes.'

'Well, have a sandwich and we'll look at it together.'

The boy sat down at the table. Still he didn't dare look at the guest in the room. Anna stood up and made to leave.

'Stay a while,' said Judit. 'Would you like a sandwich too?'

'No, thank you. I'm afraid I have to get going.'

'I try to support Benedek's education in any way I can,' said Judit as she sliced a chunk from a white wheat loaf. 'Education is the only way out of here,' she said, waving her slender hand in a curve through the air. 'But it's hard. The books cost a fortune. Most of us can't afford them – many of the parents can't even read. How can you support your child if you can't read?'

Anna had no answer to this.

'I run a club once a week where the children get a good snack and we help them with their homework. Perhaps you'd like to come and visit us?'

'That would be interesting,' said Anna, and this time she meant it.

'Great. The next club is tomorrow at the library. That's the final meeting before the summer break. I'll see you there, if you can make it. Two o'clock we start.'

'Good. See you then.' Anna paused, thoughtful. 'About last Friday night…' she began, wondering how to phrase things properly.

'Yes?'

'If you hear anything about a girl with a red skirt or a missing Romani man, would you let me know?'

'Of course. Would you like me to ask the cards about them?'

'If you like. Here's my number. I'd be grateful for even the smallest piece of information.'

'I'll let you know as soon as I hear anything.'

Anna said goodbye to Judit and Benedek. The boy had already laid his books out on the table and waved at Anna with a shy smile. What a sweet child. Anna profoundly hoped he never had to travel abroad to beg on the streets.

ANNA WALKED HOME lost in thought. Her mother lived only a few blocks from Judit's house, and yet it could have been a different world altogether. On the way back she stopped by a shop and bought some potatoes and chicken thighs, though she knew her mother didn't want her to stock up the food cupboards. Cars rushed past along Szabadkai út; a spluttering tractor towed a cage-like trailer containing an enormous pig. Anna found the chaotic combination of a bygone age and the modern world charming. Horse-drawn carriages and top-of-the-range BMWs; the clucking of chickens and the braying of a donkey in the yard next to a brand-new luxury house. The square where old ladies sold vegetables from their gardens, while in the cafés around them people fiddled with tablets and smartphones.

Anna opened the gate to the house, locked it after her, watered the roses in the front yard and went to the garage to fetch the *bogrács*, a large, black stewing pot. She placed it above the outdoor hearth built of light-brown bricks, checked there was plenty of wood for the fire and went indoors. She made herself some coffee. Her mother had gone out on an errand. The house was quiet and empty. She took her coffee out to the patio and sat down in one of the soft, upholstered chairs to read her emails. Sari had sent her a message. A shiver ran the length of Anna's arms.

From: Sari Jokikokko-Pennanen <sari.jokikokko@poliisi.fi>
To: Anna Fekete <anna.fekete@poliisi.fi>

Hi, how's it going?
Kirsti enlarged and enhanced the photo you sent. It's still not clearly focussed, but there's something odd about it. I showed it to Linnea too, and she told me to ask whether there's any chance you might be able to look at the body yourself. There's something about the man's eyes that needs closer examination

before we can tell whether he drowned or not. The photograph was taken at such a distance that it's hard to be absolutely sure. If you give her a ring, Linnea can give you a few pointers and tell you what to look for. She's going on holiday next week, though, so you'd better hurry.

The fingerprints on the bag drew a blank. Do you think you could check with local registers and databases? Just promise me you won't do anything stupid, okay?

And now for something completely different: I've got a suspicion Esko might have a woman on the go. He leaves work on time, though he's working on the big case I mentioned, he's stopped smoking (I know! I asked him…) and he smells good too. He's been to the barber and he seems to have a wardrobe of new clothes. He's almost behaving like a normal human being. Can you believe it? I think he's in love. Poor woman :)

Sari

Anna clicked open the attached photographs.

The man was lying on the ground with his head almost in the water. His hair and clothes were wet. She'd seen all this before. The second photograph was a blow-up of the man's head and neck. The technician had managed to get rid of most of the pixelation so that the image now looked almost clear and bright. The man's face was smeared with mud and his black eyes stared into eternity. The third image zoomed in on his eyes, but the zoom was so powerful, the quality was degraded. The man's eyes seemed to be dotted with tiny red specks. Or were they?

Anna stared at the image so long that her coffee grew cold. The longer she looked at the photograph, the more certain she was that the man's eyes were full of haematomas. There were no red specks anywhere else on the man's face, so this couldn't be simply the result of the grainy, pixelated photograph. Marks like this didn't appear in drowning victims. Anna reread the autopsy report she'd received from the chief of police, searching for any mention of the victim's eyes. Nothing. She knew the word for 'eye' in Serbian, but just to be sure she looked up the words 'haematoma', 'discolouration', and all other possible terms that might have been used in reference to the eyes of the man who had stolen her handbag. The report was simple and to the point. There was no mention of the victim's eyes at all.

She tipped her coffee into one of the numerous flowerpots on the patio. I need to come up with a rational plan, she thought. I have a total of two options: either I forget all about the matter once and for all or I start looking into it for real.

If I let the matter go, I can relax and enjoy the rest of my holiday. But then the case could plague me for the rest of my life. Is my holiday more important than getting to the bottom of the death – or murder – of this young man? Will I be sitting in a rocking chair in my old age suffering from a bad conscience while a potential murderer is enjoying retirement? Anna didn't have to give the matter much thought before she knew the answer: she had to investigate the death of the Romani man, no matter what her mother, Réka or anyone else thought about it.

The clouds were beginning to roll back across the sky. Anna felt something tighten in her throat. This wasn't going to be pleasant, and it certainly wouldn't be easy, she thought; but whatever I do, I do to the very best of my abilities.

She needed a plan of action. What would she do if she'd been assigned this case at work? What would Virkkunen ask her to do? Anna went up to her room, unlocked her desk and took out some pens and a notepad.

She taped a sheet of paper to the middle of the wall and wrote a title in large letters: HANDBAG THEFT. She then began to tape other sheets of paper around the first one: crime scene; eyewitnesses from the wine fair; the girl in the red skirt. She sat down on her bed and wiped sweat from her brow – the upper floor of the house was becoming insufferably humid – then looked at the fragments of an investigation now taped to the wall and began to plan her strategy.

I'll have to call Nóra and go through the photographs from the wine fair. I must get access to the body and examine it thoroughly.

The only problem was that the body was in Újvidék and it had already been examined. Anna decided to make an effort to find the contact details for the pathologist and ask him why the red specks on the victim's eyes had been omitted from the report.

She suddenly remembered the bus ticket that she'd found at the scene. If the ticket had belonged to the man, the driver might remember him. That would be a start. And the gypsies. The Romanies, Anna corrected herself. If the man was a Romani, somebody in the local Roma community was bound to know him. She would have to ask around. But that meant she would have to come up with a way of gaining the community's trust; she realised instantly how pathetic and naïve this sounded. She had only a few weeks to unravel the case. Centuries of oppression and rejection would hardly be forgotten the minute Anna told people she wanted to help.

But then Anna recalled the handsome policeman with whom she'd exchanged a few words at the station. And she had Judit on her side too. A plan quickly began to take shape in her mind.

AFTERNOON SUNSHINE seemed to light up the Kanizsa police station, enhancing its yellow, sanded walls and making the place look warm and almost pleasant. Anna stepped into the foyer, where a few people were sitting on plastic chairs, waiting to be seen. There was someone else in the booth this time – the second female officer Anna had seen here. Her large breasts bulged inside her uniform, which was just a little too small for her, her long dark hair was tied in a neat ponytail beneath her cap, her eyes were heavily made up. The embodiment of men's uniform fantasies, thought Anna. How could someone like that survive as a woman here when even Finland, the paragon of equal opportunity, had problems of its own?

'Good afternoon,' Anna began in Serbian.

'*Dobar dan*,' the woman replied and asked how she could help.

'I'm looking for a Hungarian-speaking officer who was on duty here on Saturday morning. Vajda Péter is his name. It's regarding my stolen passport and Visa card,' said Anna but knew straight away there was something wrong with the Serbian sentence.

'I'll look at the rota. Please wait a minute.' The woman disappeared into a room behind the desk and returned a moment later. 'He's still in a meeting,' she said. 'Would you like to wait?' Then the woman said something Anna didn't understand.

'I'll wait,' Anna replied.

She sat down in the foyer and the next customer approached the hatch: a rotund, middle-aged woman, who started complaining at the top of her voice about litter in the park near the bus station. Anna didn't understand half of the tirade, but she could hear from her voice that she too was a Hungarian speaker and that her Serbian wasn't very good either. Once or twice the woman looked over at Anna as though pleading with her to come and help.

'It's a terrible mess every morning,' the woman repeated.

The duty officer nodded and typed this into her computer. 'We'll see what we can do about it,' she said and asked the woman to fill out a wad of forms.

'I'll need someone to help me with these. Can I bring them back tomorrow?'

'That will be fine,' said the officer.

The woman picked up the papers, folded them carefully, put them in her bag and left. At the front door she turned to Anna.

'Damn refugees turning up here, ruining our beautiful town. They camp out by the bus station and by the time they leave the place is a dump. It's us that have to clear it up. There was shit there this morning too, human shit – can you believe it? It's high time the police put a stop to it.'

Anna nodded but didn't want to comment. She'd seen it on the Hungarian news broadcasts. After swarming towards the coastal regions of Italy and Greece, the tsunami of people displaced by war and famine was now surging through the Balkans towards Hungary and the EU border. The newsreader had used those very words: *swarm*, *tsunami*, *surge*. As if these distressed people – and not the warmongers and terrorists – were a force of nature wreaking untold havoc.

'*Jó napot*,' Anna heard a voice say behind her as the woman stormed out of the front door.

Anna turned and stood up to greet the police officer who had appeared in the foyer. '*Jó napot, Fekete Anna vagyok.*'

'*Vajda Péter. Tudok valamiben segíteni?*'

'I don't know if you remember, but I came here on Saturday regarding my lost passport.'

'Yes, I remember you.'

'I thought I'd come and ask whether there's any news on the matter.'

'Not to my knowledge. I assume you heard that the thief was found dead.'

'I know. How awful. Have you been able to identify him yet?'

'No.'

'Has anyone found my belongings?'

'We can check on the computer. Galina! Can you see if this lady's belongings have turned up?'

The curvaceous policewoman began tapping at her computer without asking for Anna's name or social security number. So they knew who she was. A moment later Galina shook her head.

'It seems not, I'm afraid. There's nothing else I can do at the moment,' said Péter. 'Have you been in touch with your embassy?'

'Yes, of course,' Anna lied. She would have to do it immediately. 'I was wondering whether…' Anna paused and took a breath, '… you'd like to have coffee with me. Only if you have time, that is.'

A cautious, complacent smile spread across the man's lips. Had he been expecting this to happen? Anna wondered. Good. That will make things all the easier.

'Right away?'

'Yes, I'm free now. But I understand if you're busy…'

'I'm sure it can be arranged. I just need to pop into my office. I'll be back in a moment. Why don't we drive to Horgos? It's nice and quiet there.'

'That sounds lovely,' said Anna.

THEY TOOK PÉTER'S CAR to Horgos, a small village right on the border with Hungary. Horgos was the site of the largest and most important border crossing between Hungary and Serbia, and was the very place where Anna had passed between the two countries only days earlier.

Péter talked over the car radio, telling Anna all about himself. He was originally from Novi Sad, or Újvidék as the Hungarians called it, where he had entered the police academy. He had moved to Kanizsa six years before and liked both the town and his work very much. He often spent his days off and holidays in Újvidék. He didn't mention a wife or children, but Anna wouldn't have expected him to in a situation like this. He wasn't wearing a ring, though Anna thought she could make out a lightened stretch of skin across the base of his left ring finger. Did you go to your office to take off your ring? Anna wondered.

Péter wasn't surprised when Anna told him she was a police officer, too, and she guessed there had been talk about her at the station. Péter seemed genuinely interested as he asked about Anna's work, and police training and career possibilities in Finland. The short journey passed breezily, and Anna felt light and relaxed. This is going well, she thought.

A single street ran through the village of Horgos. Along that street were a few shops and a bakery, which also served as a café. Péter pulled up outside the bakery, stepped out of the car and opened the door for Anna. The place was surprisingly busy. A long queue of customers were waiting to buy fresh wheat bread, and there was only one free table in the café. Anna ordered a cappuccino and a large slice of sumptuous *rétes*, while Péter took a hearty-looking *burek* and a tub of yoghurt. Lunch, he explained, and said he would have a coffee for dessert. They took everything outside and sat down on the small terrace facing the street. This too was almost entirely full. Péter lit a cigarette and offered one to Anna. She couldn't resist the temptation and took a cigarette from the packet. The first wave of nicotine rushed to her head, making her dizzy.

'Were you born in Finland?' asked Péter.

'No. I'm originally from Kanizsa. I was born at the hospital in Senta, but I've spent most of my life in Finland.'

'What's it like there?'

'It's difficult to sum it up. It's a big country and quite diverse, I suppose.'

'I heard your brother lives there too.'

'Yes. But he's here at the moment as well. What other gossip has there been about me at the station?'

'Not all that much. They said your father was a policeman too.'

'It's like a broken record. You're your father's daughter, blah blah blah.'

Péter laughed. 'My father was a history teacher. He died when I was a teenager.'

'Really? My father is dead too. I was just a child. I can't really remember him properly.'

Péter gave Anna a look of warmth and understanding. To her surprise Anna felt a sudden sense of solidarity with the man. She felt a twinge of her conscience as she remembered why she'd invited him for coffee.

Péter changed the subject. 'I don't think I could take living so far north. It must be dark and cold all the time.'

'Except in the summer. Then it's just cold, but it only lasts three months.'

'*Úr Isten*, and nine months of winter!'

'You could say that.'

'I'd go crazy.'

'Many people do.' Anna pulled a face and squinted her eyes.

Péter laughed out loud.

'Do you visit home often?' he asked.

'You mean Kanizsa?'

'Isn't that your home?'

'I'm not sure. I've been thinking about this a lot these last few months,' said Anna and surprised herself at how natural it sounded.

'Surely a person can have many homes?'

'Physical homes, yes. You feel at home in Kanizsa and Újvidék, don't you? But which are you: a Kanizsa man or an Újvidék man?'

'It doesn't really matter. I don't want to feel anchored in any one place.'

'It doesn't matter to you because Kanizsa and Újvidék are basically the same thing. There's only about a hundred kilometres between them. I guess you've never had to wonder who you really are or where you belong.'

'You're probably right. I've always thought of home as where my nearest and dearest live. Or rather, the place where I can feel comfortable and … at home.'

'In that case I probably don't have a home at all,' Anna said quietly.

'Don't you feel comfortable anywhere?'

'Let's not talk about this. Let's just say I'm on a journey with these things.'

'I get it, though I've never lived abroad. For me it's enough to think of myself as a Hungarian in Serbia. That's plenty to figure out, don't you think?'

'Oh yes, I know. It's funny how there's nowhere we can really call home.'

'I'm at home in myself. This is my home,' said Péter, pointing first at his chest then at his head. 'Remember that every time your negative thoughts get the better of you.'

Anna smiled. 'The last time I was at home was Christmas – my Kanizsa home, that is. There was a time I didn't visit for years, but now I feel as though I want to spend all my holidays here.'

'Are you single?'

Anna was taken aback, almost shocked at Péter's direct question; but she managed to keep a straight face. This is my chance, she thought. To hell with the shyness, the uncertainty, the pangs of guilt.

'Yes. If I'd been taken I wouldn't have invited you for coffee,' she said and smiled, tucked behind her ear a lock of hair that had fallen across her cheek and gazed intensely into Péter's eyes.

Péter gulped. The crack in his confidence only lasted a fraction of a second, but Anna noticed it, and at that moment she knew she had succeeded.

'Aren't you going to ask if I'm single?' he asked.

'No. Does it matter?'

There was a note of relief in Péter's laugh.

They ate their pastries, drank their coffee and continued chatting about police work in Finland and Serbia. They compared working conditions, procedures, criminality and every aspect of their jobs. They talked at length about what it was like to represent a minority within a public office dominated by the majority. Péter was jovial, making Anna genuinely laugh many times, and Anna used all the powers of attraction she could muster.

When they returned to Kanizsa, Anna built up her courage and asked Péter the first favour she had in mind. Could he possibly check a few fingerprints that she'd found on her handbag? Of course, Anna would wholly understand if this was impossible or if Péter didn't want to do it, but it would be a great help, as there were a few little things that had been bugging her, and she just wanted to reassure herself there was nothing to worry about.

Anna was sure he was going to decline politely and would never want to see her again, but Péter agreed to do what he could. He asked for her phone number, gave Anna his own and told her he was free on Thursday evening if she wanted to get together. They agreed to meet at Péter's place.

He dropped her off at her mother's house. After he drove away, Anna remained standing on the steps, bewildered and happy. Péter's empathy, his interest in her and his desire to help seemed almost too good to be true.

THE TISZA SLITHERED PAST the Békavár restaurant, brownish-black, like a gigantic snake. The river was often referred to as *szőke Tisza*, the fair Tisza. The name was misleading, because even on the brightest summer days the water was thick and dark. A water scooter roared across the water, and then another. This was new. Years ago the only things to glide along the river were the fishermen's wooden boats and perhaps the odd barge; never water scooters. Change. Progress. Some people in the country appeared to have more money than they knew what to do with. The rumble of the motors disturbed Anna. It made the presence of the river feel distracting, intrusive.

As always, the fish soup at Békavár was delicious. The broth, dyed red with paprika, and the bony chunks of fish may not have looked very appealing, but they tasted heavenly. They tasted of home. Apart from Anna there were only a few customers in the restaurant. Most people could no longer afford to eat out. Normal people lived in the shadow of the escalating financial crisis – though this was the same in every corner of the world, even in Finland. For Anna the prices at the restaurants in Kanizsa seemed ridiculous. With her Finnish police officer's salary she felt like a millionaire here. Even her friends thought she was a millionaire. She'd tried in vain to explain that Finland was an expensive place to live, that a large percentage of her wages was spent on living expenses alone. Not to mention the cost of food. One night, after much cajoling from her friends, she'd made the mistake of telling them how much she earned, and from that moment on they had seen her as some kind of Croesus. They'd thought her rich long before this, though; for some people living in the West meant you were automatically affluent. The whole thing amused Anna. Nowhere in the world had she seen as many expensive cars and luxury houses as in Serbia. None of her friends were in debt and they all had assets – houses inherited from relatives in and around Vajdaság, apartments in Budapest; more than she would ever have. Affluence, like everything else, is a relative concept, she pondered.

She'd chosen Békavár not only because of the soup but because it was so quiet. She ordered a coffee, looked up the contact details for the Institute of Forensic Medicine in Újvidék and dialled the number. A young and officious-sounding woman answered the phone. Anna introduced herself as 'Valkay Bea' and asked the young woman to put her through to Milan Pešić.

'Who?' asked the woman.

Anna repeated the name on the autopsy report.

'Are you sure you've got the right number?' the woman asked.

Ten minutes later Anna ended the call, utterly puzzled. She turned to put her phone into her bag and noticed there was a man standing behind her. He was wearing a black shirt and trousers, a jacket that had seen better days and a white sun hat, tilted to reveal a strip of grey hair.

'Has something happened?' he asked, concerned.

'No. I was just sorting something out, nothing important,' said Anna, convinced that he had heard the whole conversation.

'Good. You looked a bit startled, that's all. But … is that really Fekete Anna? Good afternoon. Goodness, how you've grown.'

'*Csókolom*,' Anna replied like a little girl as she tried to remember who the man was.

'Do you remember me at all? I'm the priest at the local Reformed Church. I baptised you.'

'Well, that's such a long time ago I'm afraid my memories are a bit sketchy,' Anna said, and the man burst into laughter.

'Molnár László. Just call me Laci. I live over in Totovo Selo, but I often visit Kanizsa to see my parishioners. And I have a small office in town. How are you? Your mother told me you were here on holiday and that Ákos is at home too.'

'I'm very well, thank you. It's nice to be here.'

'There's a service here in Kanizsa next Sunday, do come along. You and your mother could visit us afterwards. Do you have a car while you're here?'

'Yes, I rented one at the airport.'

'Excellent. What kind of car is it?'

What business is it of yours? Anna thought. 'It's a Fiat Punto, an automatic,' she replied eventually. And then thought, why did I have to mention the gears?

'And what colour is it?'

'White. Why do you ask?'

'I was just wondering whether it was that white Punto parked over there, that's all. For some reason I've always been fascinated by what kind of car people drive. I knew your father very well, by the way. We were childhood friends. God bless him.'

How many of her father's old friends had she met in the space of just a few days? At least three. These strangers knew more about her father than she did. They'd spent their childhood and adolescence with him. They shared so much more history with her father than she had. It seemed so profoundly wrong that Anna suddenly felt the urge to say something spiteful to the man. A priest. How odd that he seemed to know her father so well when religion had meant so little to her family. Her father had been a Catholic but not particularly religious. Her mother was a Protestant, and Anna was baptised in the Reformed Church. Religion hadn't been a major part of their lives. They went to church occasionally, the children were taught to say prayers before bedtime, Áron and Ákos had both been confirmed. Normal stuff. Unlike in many Eastern European countries, the churches in Yugoslavia had continued to operate throughout communism, though people tended to look down on overt displays of faith. So she guessed it was fortunate that her family hadn't been ardently religious. What was more, there had been plenty of party informants in the area, spies twitching curtains – not on the same scale as in Hungary or the Soviet Union, but still…

Anna had only learnt about all of this – and many other things besides – much later in life. But if there was so much about her family and homeland that she'd only heard about in passing, how many other things were there, about which she'd never been told anything?

'Well, I think I'm going to order something to eat. I'm frightfully hungry. Hope to see you on Sunday. And do give my regards to your mother.'

Molnár László sat down at the next table, where he began examining the menu. He didn't speak to Anna again.

Anna paid her bill, left the restaurant, lit a cigarette and thought about her phone call to Újvidék. At first the woman at the switchboard had sounded very brusque, but as the call went on she proved to be very helpful. She explained that she'd only started working there six months earlier, and, as Anna held the line, she went through lists of employees from the last few years. She'd even called the equivalent institute in Belgrade, but nowhere was there a pathologist by the name of Milan Pešić. After this the woman had popped up to the laboratory and asked two different doctors, who'd both confirmed that they had never encountered a colleague by that name. One of these doctors had worked at the institute for the last twenty-five years. The woman had been very apologetic about not being able to help Anna and she didn't seem to believe it when Anna said she'd helped more than she knew.

The autopsy report on the bag thief was a forgery; of that there was now no doubt. Anna wondered whether to contact the chief of police or Kovács Gábor but decided to leave the matter for the moment. She had a suspicion that it was best at this point if no official organisations knew that she had realised the report was false. First she would have to get an idea of what forces were at play here – what or who was behind this. She thought of Judit and her premonitions. There were no 'forces' at play, she thought. People do things like this – normal, ruthless criminals and murderers – and when it came to catching criminals she was an expert. But no matter how much she tried to convince herself of that fact, everything felt strangely surreal. It was as though the terrace outside the restaurant had turned its invisible eye on her and whispered: there are many things that you can neither see nor understand.

As she opened her car door, Anna noticed László the priest watching her through the restaurant window.

TIBOR AND NÓRA LIVED right in the centre of Kanizsa in an ugly apartment block with dozens of pigeons nesting among the roof timbers. The building was surrounded by a circle of grey bird droppings, which the determined women in the block, armed with buckets and mops, tried in vain to wash away. Like graffiti on the side of a train, it always returned. The pigeons just didn't want to leave the building, even though all the balconies and landings were kitted out with barbed wire and mesh fencing. They must like high places, thought Anna. This was the tallest building in Kanizsa, and Tibor and Nóra's apartment was on the top floor. Anna hoped the view made up for the inconvenience of not having a lift.

Nóra put on some coffee and Tibor cracked open a bottle of beer as Anna sat down at the kitchen table. Gizella was playing on the living-room floor while cartoons blared out of the television. The air conditioning blew cool air into the apartment.

'How are you both?' asked Anna as she carefully sipped her piping-hot coffee. It was black and devilishly strong, and it would keep her up all night.

'Oh, fine – day-to-day life with a toddler,' said Nóra 'I made *szárma* for dinner. There's plenty left. Are you hungry?'

'No, I'm fine thanks. Listen, I'd like to see the photographs you took at the wine fair on Friday night.'

'Do you think the thief will be in them?'

'I don't know. But it would be helpful if he was. I need a really clear photo of him.'

'Why?'

'I'm going to find out who he was, and I want to find the girl in the red skirt too.'

'Of course. Gizella, don't go in there.' Nóra darted into the living room to pick up her daughter before she clambered into the cupboard in the bottom of the bookcase. 'Tibor, can you make sure those cupboard doors are secured? I'm sick of telling her not to climb in there.'

'Why shouldn't she play in there? Just let her be,' Tibor muttered.

'Because the whole bookcase might topple over, that's why. Bolt it to the wall properly, then I won't need to worry about it.'

'Okay, okay,' said Tibor. He stood up and went off in search of something to fasten the doors.

Gizella started to cry. Nóra pressed a chocolate cookie into her hand and she quietened down at once. When Tibor had fastened the cupboard doors with a piece of string, Nóra put her daughter back on the floor amid the chaos of toys and fetched her phone.

'Wait a minute … here we are. Looks like I snapped quite a few photos that evening.'

'Good,' said Anna. 'Then there's a greater chance we'll find something.'

Anna and Nóra began examining the photographs. Anna noted down all the people she recognised. She could talk to them if necessary. There was a long list of friends and acquaintances. In one picture – of Anna and Nóra raising their glasses, their cheeks pressed against one another – there was a figure standing in the background. Nagy Béla, the fisherman.

'Look,' said Anna. 'Old Béla was there too, but he didn't mention it to me. This was taken just before the theft.'

'And the thief ran up from behind you. He must have been pretty close by when this was taken. Could Béla have seen him?'

'If he did, why didn't he say anything?'

'He must have moved away by the time it happened.'

'Still, he could at least have mentioned he was at the wine fair.'

'You'll have to ask him.'

'I certainly will,' said Anna.

In the next photograph, Tibor and Ernő were pulling faces at the camera and showing off a bottle of *furmint*.

'Who's that?' Nóra asked suddenly, pointing to a dark figure standing behind the men. Anna spread her fingers across the screen to zoom in.

'It's a man. Wait a minute, look who's hiding behind him.'

The man had his back to the camera, but from behind him peered the head of a little girl with black hair. And a red skirt. The photograph was pixelated and unfocussed, but Anna was convinced that this was the girl she was looking for.

In the next photograph the man had turned around and was now looking directly at the camera. Far behind Tibor, Ernő and the bottle of wine stood the man who had stolen her handbag, there in the dusk, surrounded by people, the intense, concentrated look of a predator in his black eyes. The same dark jacket. The same height and build. The same facial features as those of the body by the Tisza. This was the man. A shiver ran along Anna's arms. The girl was no longer to be seen.

'*Úr Isten*,' whispered Nóra. 'Is that him?'

'Would you lend me your phone overnight? I have to upload these photos to my computer so I can enlarge them and print them off.'

'Of course, as long as you return it tomorrow.'

'Absolutely. Thank you.'

Tibor had remained in the living room with his beer. After finishing the bottle he stood up and came into the kitchen.

'I think I'm going to pop down to the Taverna,' he said. 'Want to join me, Anna?'

'No, thanks, I've got stuff to do tonight,' she replied and showed him the phone.

Gizella yanked at the cupboard door and howled with disappointment when it didn't open.

'She's tired,' said Nóra. 'I'll have to put her to bed. Do you have to go, Tibor? Tonight as well?'

'No. But I'm going anyway.'

'As usual,' said Nóra to Tibor as he went into the hall and pulled on his shoes. Anna followed him.

'Good night, Anna,' said Nóra. 'Don't do anything stupid.'

'I won't. Let's get together tomorrow.'

'Great. Let's meet here at lunchtime. *Szárma* gets better with age.'

'Just like us,' said Anna and hugged Nóra, whose eyes were tired and sad.

ANNA AWOKE TO THE SOUND of her phone ringing and cursed out loud that she'd forgotten to put it on silent before going to sleep. The room was pitch dark, only the flashing blue light of the phone's screen gleamed from the pocket of the hoodie she'd thrown across the chair. Anna reluctantly threw back her blankets and looked at the phone. She'd hoped it might be Péter, but this was an unknown number. Anna answered.

An unfamiliar male voice asked if this was Fekete Anna. When Anna replied that it was, the voice asked whether she was looking for information about the Romani man found dead on the riverbank. Anna could hear that the man was trying to mask his voice, muttering in a high-pitched tone. Again Anna said yes. The voice told her that he had important information but that, naturally, it would cost her. Anna listened to the sum of money, which wasn't particularly big, and agreed to meet the man in the town's large park the following day.

The phone went dead. Anna noticed her hands were shaking. She turned on the light, took her notebook out of the drawer, wrote the words ANONYMOUS PHONE CALL on a fresh sheet and attached it to the wall with the other pages. Had Judit found out something? Why hadn't she made the call herself, then? The prospect of a meeting with the anonymous caller didn't appeal to her. It was unsettling. Would she be putting herself in danger if she went? Was it a trap? Anna pulled up the blinds and looked out into the deserted yard. A cat ran across the street and slipped through a gap in the fence into the yard outside the house opposite. The downstairs lights were on in the house, there was a flash of movement at the window. Anna breathed slowly in and out, trying to calm herself down. A murderer wouldn't agree to a meeting in broad daylight, she tried to reason with herself. There will be lots of people out and about in the park, I won't be in any danger. The information probably isn't even that important. Judit has doubtless told someone about me, someone who senses the chance to make a few thousand dinars. That must be it. There's nothing to worry about.

JUNE 8th

THE FIRST BUS FROM SZABADKA arrived in Kanizsa at 6.35 a.m. Anna had gone through the timetables and noted, to her astonishment, that a total of eighteen buses ran between the two towns each weekday and only a slightly smaller number at weekends. Incredible. Granted, Szabadka was a sizeable town – it was even slightly larger than her hometown in Finland – but how many rural villages or towns in Finland were served by eighteen buses a day from the nearest city, with the possible exception of Helsinki? None at all. In the north of Finland at least, two or three buses a day was a handsome number. Points to Serbia, thought Anna. Some things here are still running well.

Anna went to the central bus station in good time to wait for the bus. She also wanted to see the people the locals claimed were making such a mess in the area. The refugees. The melancholy hoots of pigeons rang out in the fresh, early-morning air. Anna passed the Cultural Centre and saw the park in front of which the buses stopped. On the ground there were human-shaped sleeping bags and bundles of blankets, beneath which she could see only black hair and dark faces. A group of men sat around a small bonfire. Litter was strewn around her in every direction. A shocking amount of rubbish. Anna understood the locals' annoyance but she also appreciated that these people probably didn't have the strength to think about something as banal as picking up litter. Anna counted twenty-seven people in total. Most of them were young men, but there were a few women and children too. From somewhere nearby came the sound of a baby crying.

The bus pulled into the stop. The driver waited for the passengers to get off, then hopped out and lit a cigarette. Anna hadn't even greeted him before he was talking to her. In Hungarian. Thank God, thought Anna.

'Don't know what the world's coming to – I can't even smoke in my own bus these days,' said the driver and winced at Anna. She interpreted this as a smile.

'Yes, it's too bad,' she agreed and lit a cigarette herself.

'Every shift is full of that lot,' he said, nodding towards the park. 'Doesn't bother me much, mind. As long as there are paying customers, I've still got a job to go to. I have to say, mind, I've taken a few of them for free. Some of them haven't got two pennies to rub together, though folk round here seem to think otherwise.'

'Have a look at this,' said Anna and showed the driver the bus ticket.

'What about it? It's one of our tickets.'

'Were you working last Friday by any chance? The day this ticket was stamped?'

'Yes, I was.'

Do you remember whether this young man got on in Szabadka?' Anna asked and showed him the photograph she'd printed off the previous night.

The driver looked at her, nervously puffing on his cigarette. 'You with the police?'

'No. Well, yes. But don't worry. I'm only trying to find out who this man is and where he's been.'

'What's happened? Been up to no good, has he?'

'He stole my handbag. And my passport and Visa card. Do you remember him?'

The driver looked again at the photograph, this time more closely. 'I don't usually pay much attention to the passengers. There's too many, you see. Folk come and go, that's about it.'

'He might have been travelling with a child – a girl, maybe ten, twelve years old, in a red skirt.'

'Ah, yes, you get to know the regulars; you recognise them when they get on. I might have seen the boy, I'm pretty sure about it. Not last Friday though, but before.'

Anna felt her heart rate increasing. 'Really? When was that?'

'Quite a few times. He gets on in Szabadka and comes to Kanizsa, and always travels back the same evening.'

'Have you ever talked to him? Do you know his name?'

'He never talks much, just sits on the back seat and stares at his phone. They all do that these days, even the old biddies.'

A phone, thought Anna. The police must surely have it now. How could she gain access to it?

'But you say he wasn't on the bus last Friday?'

'Not on my shift, he wasn't. There's other drivers on this route too. I was on the graveyard shift that night.'

'Who was working that morning?'

'Can't remember. There's quite a gap between shifts, so you don't always see the previous driver. Just pick up the keys and money bag from the station and off you go.'

'Could you find out who it was for me?'

'Sure, no problem.'

'And what about this girl?' Anna showed him another photograph. 'I know it's a bit blurry.'

'I can't make anything out here. But I remember the boy sometimes travelled with a little girl. Not always. Gypsies, both of them.'

'Are you sure?'

'About what? That they travel together?'

'That they're Romanies.'

'Positive. You can tell just by looking at them. I've nothing against them, mind. They pay their way like everybody else.'

Anna gave the man her phone number, thanked him and asked him to get back to her as soon as possible. The driver promised he would.

Three irate-looking women had appeared in the park with rakes and plastic bin liners. Further off, Anna noticed a group of young men. Two of them had shaved their heads, they were wearing camouflage trousers and combat boots. The men were looking at the refugees lying around the park and muttering to one another. Eventually they started walking towards the town hall. One of the skinheads turned and glanced behind him. He looked straight at Anna.

'THE FINGERPRINTS YOU LIFTED from your handbag belonged to you and two unknown people. There was no match in our records,' said Péter. 'Judging by the size of the prints, one set belonged to a child.'

The thief and the girl in the red skirt, thought Anna. She'd invited Péter for a coffee at the Avanti café on the main street through town, saying she couldn't wait until the following evening. She knew this was a risk – people here didn't expect women to be so proactive, so forward. But it was a risk she was willing to take. She didn't have time to think about what was or wasn't considered appropriate behaviour. Péter had agreed, and Anna thought she detected a note of excitement in his voice.

They were sitting on the covered patio outside the café on chairs upholstered with blue cushions. Despite the shade, the air was humid and clammy. Anna leaned as close as she possibly could towards Péter. She was smiling so much her cheek muscles began to ache. They talked about this and that for a while before Anna plucked up the courage to ask about the fingerprints. She suddenly sensed a mild agitation in Péter's body language. Didn't he want to be seen with her? The last time they'd met, he'd taken her all the way to Horgos. And today a couple of passers-by had stopped to say hello to him and shake his hand – an older gentleman in a stylish suit and a younger, scruffier man with stubble. Péter didn't introduce Anna to them, though the older man in particular seemed to expect him to do so.

'What about the security cameras?' asked Anna. 'Are there any in town?'

She realised she sounded too eager, too demanding. Péter remained silent for a moment. He lit a cigarette and ordered a small bottle of mineral water.

'I think you should drop the matter,' he said eventually.

'So do I, but for the time being I'm not going to do that.'

'You're stubborn.'

'Maybe. But I'm nice with it.'

With a teasing smile Anna placed her hand on Péter's. He slowly lifted it away.

'What is it you want from me exactly?' he almost snapped.

'Sorry,' said Anna. She pulled her chair further away from him and sipped her coffee. What on earth had she been thinking? Did she really think she could pull the wool over the eyes of an experienced police officer by playing the ditzy bimbo? Sometimes she felt so stupid.

'Very well,' she said, taking a deep breath. 'I'm going to be completely honest with you. I get the distinct impression your colleagues aren't investigating the death of the bag thief the way they should, and I think there's something untoward going on. I really hope you can help me out.'

'And why would I do that?'

'I don't know. Out of a sheer, altruistic desire to help me?'

Péter laughed. 'Are you still coming to my place tomorrow evening?'

'Are there cameras around the town or not?'

'A few.'

'Where?'

'In front of the town hall and by the school. It's a nasty intersection and we get plenty of fender-benders there.'

'Is there any way I could see those tapes?'

'It won't be easy. But I can try.'

'So I'll see you tomorrow then,' she said, stroked the rough stubble on Péter's cheek and stood up.

Who is using whom here? And why, she wondered.

THE *SZÁRMA* WAS DELICIOUS. The cabbage leaves stuffed with minced meat and poached in a paprika broth really did improve after a few days. Nóra had come home for lunch. Tibor was at work, Gizella at nursery. Anna wondered whether or not to tell Nóra about the fabricated autopsy report but decided to keep it to herself. The fewer people knew she was digging around the case, the better. What's more, she didn't want to put her friends in any kind of danger. And she did suspect that things might get hairy. Why would the police try to hide the thief's real cause of death unless there was something about the case that had to be kept quiet? Anna thought of her mother's words: mafia, politics, big money. What on earth had the young Roma man got himself mixed up with?

'This is so delicious,' Anna said.

Nóra smiled, chuffed at the compliment. 'It's Tibor's favourite. And Gizella likes it too.'

'By the way, do you know the woman that runs the Roma activity centre round here?'

'You mean Judit? I know of her, but I don't know her personally. Why do you ask?'

'Just wondered. I went to her place and had my fortune told yesterday.'

Nóra burst into laughter. 'Really? I've heard she's not all that accurate. Did she predict anything for you?'

'Not really, nothing you couldn't have predicted without supernatural powers.'

'I feel a bit sorry for her, having to make a living like that.'

'I don't think she has many options.'

'Hmm, if only they'd get themselves a proper education, things might be different. I'm not racist or anything, but sometimes I do think they're quite lazy.'

Anna didn't comment; she didn't want to get into an argument with Nóra.

'Are there any skinheads in town? I think I saw a few this morning,' she said, trying to change the subject.

'I'm not sure they're real skinheads. They're just kids. I imagine those refugees have made a few people shave their hair in the last few weeks. Some people are furious about it. You should see the things Újvári Erzsébet writes on Facebook. You wouldn't think such a nice lady could come out with horrible things like that.'

'The far right is raising its head all over the place.'

'I know. It's worrying. Even Tibor has started to change. He's … he's a bit too interested in Hungarian nationalism for my liking. He just sits at the Taverna with his mates every evening talking the same old shit.'

'What shit?'

'Oh, it's nothing.'

'Tell me.'

'Well, they complain about the Jews, the gypsies – and now the refugees, of course. They blame them for everything that's wrong. They're proud of their nationalist opinions. But it's all just talk. In a way I can understand it, though I don't like it one bit. We Hungarians are a minority here, so talk like that gives them a sense of power. Still, it's just bitterness. Powerlessness, bitterness, small-mindedness. Do you want some coffee for dessert?'

'No thanks. You probably have to get back to work.'

'I do, actually. Are you coming to the wine tasting on Saturday?'

'Yes, I think I will. I can ask Tibor more about his interesting opinions.'

'Please don't,' Nóra exclaimed. 'I can't bear listening to it.'

'One more question. Do you know Vajda Péter?'

'No. Who's he?'

'A policeman. I thought I'd ask him to join me on Saturday.'

'You know Béci's going to be there?'

'Exactly,' said Anna.

AS AGREED WITH THE MYSTERY CALLER, Anna sat down on a specific bench at the edge of the park. Children's screams carried across from the nearby playground, but otherwise the park was quiet. Anna was surprised that there were so few people around, though the leafy boughs of the trees formed a green canopy, protecting people from the merciless sun. Despite the shade, Anna felt uncomfortable. She was nervous. The bench was situated between two overgrown bushes, and you couldn't really see into the rest of the park. The perfect spot for a clandestine meeting. Or a crime. Anna looked around but there was nobody in sight. She heard the fluty song of a blackbird in the bushes.

She was just about to send Réka a message, telling her where she was and saying if she hadn't rung in the next thirty minutes to call the police, when she heard someone cough right next to her. The man had appeared out of nowhere and sat down next to her on the bench. Dark skin, short, dark hair, about twenty-five years old, a golden stud in his right earlobe. A Romani. Anna committed the man's appearance to memory as best she could.

'Put the phone away,' said the man, and Anna recognised the voice as the man who had called her in the night. She slipped the phone into her bag.

'Did you bring the cash?' he asked and lit a cigarette.

Anna nodded.

'So what are you waiting for? Let's get this over with.'

She handed over the banknotes, and the man quickly stuffed them in his pocket. Their eyes met for a moment, and Anna noticed the man was every bit as nervous as she was. This had an instant calming effect on her.

'Go to the Kanizsa cemetery tonight. To the chapel,' said the man and stood up, all the while glancing agitatedly around him.

'Why?' asked Anna.

The man took a long drag on his cigarette. 'There's a body you're supposed to see.'

'How did you get this information?'

'I don't know nothing about nothing, I'm just the messenger. Go there at three in the morning. The door will be open.'

'Who told you this? Judit?'

But Anna didn't get an answer. The man was gone as quickly as he had appeared. The smell of cigarette smoke hung in the air. The sounds of the playground had stopped and the blackbird had fallen silent. Anna stood up and ran past the bushes and along the pathway cutting through the park. She scanned the park to find the messenger, to follow him, but he was gone without a trace. Only a solitary old lady, supported by her walking frame, was shuffling through the park towards the spa behind the trees.

IT WAS ALREADY LATE AFTERNOON when Anna and her mother approached Remete Mihály's house near the spa and the park. The house was surrounded by a lawn, its grass mown unnaturally short, with flowerbeds providing splashes of colour. It gave the impression that the garden wasn't a place to spend time but was there simply to provide scenery. The house itself only confirmed this impression. It was so large, it could have accommodated many families. Its brick walls were coated in sherbet-yellow pebbledash, the façade featured a series of grandiose arched windows and a glass door, its metallic frame gleaming in the sunshine. There were many fancy houses in Kanizsa, but this verged on the ridiculous. Why the hell do people feel the need to flaunt their wealth like this? Anna wondered, and thought of Judit's terraced house, whose tiny one-bedroom apartments might house families of five or six and whose garden featured a shared outdoor toilet and shower facilities. Most grotesque of all, however, was the fact that the living conditions of Kanizsa's Romanies were luxury compared to those in which the majority of Roma in this country were forced to live. Anna had seen the cluster of ramshackle huts near the city dump in Újvidék, their inhabitants grubbing around in the steaming piles of rubbish, and the little children with tangled hair begging in the centre of Szabadka.

Her mother pressed the buzzer by the gate. At first nothing but crackling could be heard from the speaker, then came a contrived, saccharine greeting in a shrill female voice. The gate buzzed and opened. Anna shuddered. She couldn't say whether it was to do with all the tasteless self-importance that was on show or because she'd instantly started thinking of those who could barely afford a hot meal.

A path covered in bright-white pebbles led directly to the house, where the mirror-glass door had now opened. A woman stood in the doorway, trussed up in a green trouser suit with a wide smile on her fulsome, Botoxed lips.

'*Jézusom*,' Anna whispered. Her mother gave her a rapid, cautionary shush.

'*Isten hozott!* How nice to see you, Mária. And is this Anna? Goodness me, she's a grown woman. I remember you as a little girl, a shy little thing,' the woman cooed, and held out her heavily made-up face for the compulsory kiss on the cheek.

The woman's cloying perfume tickled Anna's sinuses as she gave the woman formal kisses on both cheeks. She thought she might sneeze. *Kezét csókolom! Sziasztok! Hogy vagytok? Jól vagyunk. Hogy van az Ákos? De jó végre találkozni Anna,* and so on and so forth. Though Anna was more than familiar with all these greetings and pleasantries – she repeated them many times a day with everybody she met – she would never fully get used to them. The words felt every bit as stilted as this house, its garden and this woman – white noise as superficial as a powdered face. She'd tried to talk to her mother about it, but she had simply scoffed disdainfully. The Finns are just like that, sullen and impolite; and it seems you've become just like them, she'd replied.

The woman introduced herself as Anikó and showed them into the living room, her stiletto heels clacking against the stone floor. Anna tried to pull off her trainers in the hallway but Anikó said not to bother. They sat down on bouncy white sofas positioned so that they offered a view through the glass wall and out on to the patio and the swimming pool in the garden.

'What would you like to drink?' asked Anikó and looked pointedly at Anna. Anna flinched; she had the distinct impression the woman had been staring at her for some time without her noticing.

'Beer, wine, *pálinka*?' Anikó continued.

'*Pálinka*, please,' her mother replied. 'Anna?'

'Could I have some coffee, if it's not too much trouble?'

'Not at all, I'll go and make some. Mihály will be back shortly. He always drinks coffee when he gets back from work.'

Anikó clip-clopped into the kitchen. Anna heard the sound of the gas stove lighting and the clink of glasses.

'This is quite a house,' said Anna.

'I know. Anikó is a doctor and Mihály is in politics, so they've no shortage of money.'

'Do they have any children?'

'Two daughters. They both live in Budapest with their families.'

'Did I know them as a child?'

'I doubt it. They're both older than you.'

'Did Ákos know them? Or … Áron?'

Anna's mother was silent for a moment, as though, after the very mention of Áron's name, to speak, to even open her mouth again, required an extra effort. Perhaps it did. Anna realised she had no idea how or if her mother had recovered from the death of her eldest son.

'Csilla, the Remetes' eldest daughter, was in the same class as Áron. They were friends,' her mother said quietly.

Just then there came a loud greeting from the front door, the clack of high heels from the kitchen to the hallway and the mawkish smack of air kisses. The man Anna had met at the wine fair stepped into the living room, his wife just behind him.

'*Kezét csókolom*, Mária. How nice you could make it. We haven't seen you properly in ages. And Anna, *kezét csókolom*.'

Remete Mihály theatrically greeted them and literally kissed their hands.

'What a beautiful daughter you have,' Mihály addressed Anna's mother. 'Why does she visit so rarely?'

'I work in Finland, and I can't take holidays whenever I feel like it,' Anna replied.

'Is that so? And what do you do?'

'I'm a police officer. I work in the Violent Crimes Unit.'

'That's right. I'd heard something to that effect. Did you want to follow in your father's footsteps – is that what made you decide to join the police?'

Anikó appeared carrying a tray laden with coffee cups and plates, a bottle of *pálinka* and small shot glasses. In front of Anna and her husband she placed porcelain cups and silver spoons, then poured some *pálinka* for herself and Anna's mother, and tripped back to the kitchen to fetch the coffee and a selection of cakes. Anna's mother gasped over-the-top compliments about how beautiful the china was.

'I don't really know why I became a police officer,' said Anna. 'I suppose I wanted a job where you have to think and use your body. And every day at work is different.'

'That's nice,' said Mihály, almost to himself.

Anikó brought in the coffee. Her nails were unnaturally long and sharp, and they were decorated with floral patterns.

'You've got lovely curtains, Anikó. Are they new?' Anna's mother gushed.

'Yes. I bought the fabric in Vienna and had them made up here. I think they're delightful, and they go with the sofa perfectly.'

'Anna, just look at these beautiful curtains,' her mother said, and Anna could hear the unmistakeable reproach in her voice telling her that you were supposed to compliment your hosts on their house.

'Yes, pretty,' Anna replied, barely able to hide a yawn. Christ, people had some dull conversations.

Enormous pastries oozing white cream had been laid out on a golden platter. Anna wondered whether it would be impolite not to have one. Anikó and her mother began talking about the dearth of good bakeries in town and about which place sold the best *sampite* cakes. Mihály's telephone rang. He apologised and disappeared into another room to answer it.

Anna sipped her coffee and gazed out at the surface of the swimming pool, sparkling in the sunshine. How nice it would be to go swimming, she thought. It must be nice owning your own pool, you could go swimming every morning in your own garden. She decided to go to the Tisza that evening for a swim.

'Can you use the pool all through the winter?' Anna asked, for want of something to ask. She didn't want to seem so unsociable that her mother would feel the need to chide her later. That had happened plenty of times in the past.

'We don't bother heating it during the winter. Nobody really uses it except the grandchildren when they visit,' Anikó explained. 'Our gardener looks after the pool, keeps it clear of leaves and covers it when necessary. You have to chlorinate the water quite regularly. The little ones like it, but they visit so rarely. Their parents are so busy at work. I do wish they'd visit more often.'

What a waste, thought Anna.

The women's conversation naturally turned to grandchildren, and, at that, Anna knew she would be reprimanded by her mother when they got home. She saw her mother's awkward expression when Anikó told her about how her daughters' children went to piano lessons, played tennis and all had excellent grades at school. Would her mother tell Anikó about Ákos's new girlfriend and her children? Anna doubted it.

'Anna,' came Mihály's voice. He had finished his conversation and was standing in the door to the hallway. 'Come and see what I've got here.'

Anna stood up. Anikó and her mother continued chatting. Anna followed the man into a room decorated in green and set up as an office, with a large desk and two computers. Mihály clicked at one of them and began searching for something.

'This computer has photographs of your father,' said Mihály. 'I thought you might like to see them. Here we are.' He clicked open one of the folders. 'A few years ago I had all my old photographs scanned. It's nicer to look at them on a large screen. Here's our class photograph from fourth grade. Can you find him…?'

The girls and the smaller boys were sitting in the front row, the taller pupils standing in two rows behind them. Their teacher was standing upright at the left-hand side of the group, wearing a white jacket and a pair of thick-rimmed spectacles. The photograph was surprisingly clear, but Anna couldn't identify her father.

'Can't you see him? Look, here,' said Mihály and pointed at the upper-left corner.

True enough, it was her father. He was about ten years old, with short, dark hair, a shirt beneath his woollen jumper. He was looking to one side, away from the camera, and grinning. Someone must have been standing outside the photograph, a pretty little girl in another class, perhaps. The little boy's eyes were exactly the same as those Anna remembered her father had as an adult: laughing eyes, warm and slightly mischievous. Tenderness and longing made Anna shudder.

'That's me next to him. And look at this,' said Mihály and clicked open another photograph.

In this photograph her father was far more readily recognisable. He must have been about seventeen: his long fringe was dangling across his eyes, smoke rose from a cigarette between his fingers. Mihály, who must have been the same age, was leaning against him drinking a beer.

'Those were the days,' Mihály sighed. 'We were good friends. I think about your father a lot. His death was a terrible loss.'

'Yes,' said Anna. She wanted to ask about her father, ask what he had been like as a teenager, whether he'd had girlfriends, what they'd done at the weekends, but the words caught in her throat.

'I heard your handbag was stolen,' Mihály said suddenly.

'Yes. Well, they found the bag, but my passport and credit card had been taken. Do you know anything about it?'

'Of course not. Have you been in touch with the embassy?'

'No,' said Anna. She felt annoyed at herself; she mustn't forget this any longer. 'The thief was a young Romani man. He was found dead by the riverbank. Have you heard anything about it?' she continued.

'Yes, he drowned apparently. Things like that happen next to a large river. Accidents.'

'Did you see the moment when it all happened?'

'No. I was at the other end of the park by that point, but I heard the screams and all the commotion.'

'The thief might have been working with a little girl in a red skirt. Did you see her?'

Mihály thought about this. 'There were so many people at the fair. And I was talking to friends all the time – there are so many of them in town. I don't think I saw your thief. Or rather, I don't think anyone you mentioned caught my attention. A girl in a red skirt … Who could that be?'

'I don't know, but she might know something about what happened after the theft.'

'Really? I'll keep my eyes open. You'll be the first to know if I think of anything.'

'Thank you. That would be helpful.' Anna paused, then decided to take a chance. She lowered her voice. 'Do you happen to know anything about the neo-Nazis in Kanizsa? The young skinheads?'

Mihály's mouth seemed to twitch.

'No,' he said quickly. All too quickly.

'Your party is quite right-leaning, though?'

'You could say that, but we certainly don't support any extremists.'

'Have there been any altercations between the refugees and the local population?'

'No, none whatsoever. It goes without saying we're not particularly happy about people swarming into our town like this and leaving a mess. People are afraid, but there's been no violence.'

'For the time being,' said Anna.

'Shall we go back and join the harridans? Can I ask that you don't mention the refugees in front of them? Anikó can't bear it; she gets very tetchy about the subject.'

Anna consented, but she was curious to know what this man might have to do with the skinheads and the refugees.

EVENING WAS DRAWING IN when Anna finally reached the river. First she'd run round the whole town, then through the Haterem parkland and past the garden centre to the *töltés* path. She was wearing her swimming costume beneath her running clothes. She hadn't brought a towel, but it was only a short journey home and the air was warm.

Anna walked down to the river outside Békavár and took off her running clothes on the jetty in front of the restaurant. Békavár was closed. The shore was deserted. The surface of the water shimmered with hues of black and brown, gleaming like matte silk. The river looked calm, almost sleepy, but Anna knew that the current was powerful.

Without testing the temperature Anna jumped straight in, feet first. The cool, clouded water enveloped her, the cold pushing the air from her lungs and pricking her skin like a thousand small thorns, and the current instantly started pulling her south. She kicked up to the surface and began swimming against the current. She stayed relatively close to the shore, as further out there could be powerful whirlpools, and people had drowned in them. Tired after her long run, she didn't have the energy to swim very far but soon flipped on to her back and allowed the current to carry her back to the jetty. She pulled her running clothes over her wet body and ran home quickly.

What a great feeling, thought Anna as she lowered herself into a hot bath and texted Réka about what she'd done. *Wow!* Réka replied instantly. *I'm coming to Kanizsa tomorrow. See you in the afternoon.*

Anna wondered what to reply. When would she have time to see Réka when she already had far too much to do tomorrow? Réka would be upset if she didn't spend as much time with her as usual. Anna wouldn't be happy about it either.

Can you make it the day after? I've got so much on tomorrow.

Anna stepped out of the cooling water, dried herself and curled up in bed; she needed to try to get a few hours' sleep before her excursion that night. A glorious warmth spread through her tired muscles, and Anna couldn't bring herself to get out of bed again to answer her beeping telephone. It's okay, it'll only be Réka. But when the phone beeped as a second text message arrived, she reluctantly delayed sleep for a while and fetched it. From Réka: *Okay!* From an unknown number: *Kriska Tamás was driving on Friday morning. I don't have his number, but you can get it from the Subotica-Trans office. Best regards. Nagy Vilmos.*

Anna googled the bus company's contact details and saved the number in her phone. After returning to bed she realised that postponing sleep had made it disappear from her grasp altogether. She went down to the patio for a cigarette and sat listening to the chirping of the crickets until it was time to leave for the cemetery.

Anna drove through Kanizsa in the darkness of the early hours. She parked her car by the empty railway station, stepped out, closed the door as quietly as she could and stood for a moment listening to her surroundings. The night was mild, wind rustled through the leaves of the trees and all around was quiet. Deadly quiet. Anna quickly walked towards the cemetery and the tall wall around it, protecting the peace of those laid to rest. The gate was locked. She began walking round the wall heading east towards the overgrown railway tracks that ran close to one corner of the cemetery. She knew there was a crumbling section of the wall along the eastern side, which she could easily climb over. Her heart was beating and she was sweating beneath her black hoodie, and she was ready to pull out her police badge or run away as quickly as possible as she placed her hands and feet in between the bricks, hauled herself on top of the wall and jumped down to the other side. Pain shot up through the cut on the sole of her foot as she hit the ground with a thud. Remaining crouched down, she scanned the graves. If there was someone waiting for her in the darkness of the cemetery, they would have heard that thud and would know she was coming. The thought terrified her. She stayed squatting on the spot for a few minutes. But there was nobody in sight and she heard nothing. There was still time to turn back, she thought. But something told her that this nocturnal visit to the cemetery would prove to be a turning point in her investigation, that after this nothing would be the same again. She made her decision, stood up and set off briskly through the cemetery towards the chapel near the gates, the gravel on the path rasping loudly with each step, as if she was shouting out: *Here I come!*

The chapel door was unlocked. Anna pressed her ear against it, but all she could hear was her own racing heartbeat. If there was anything alive inside this chapel, it knew how to remain perfectly silent.

Anna opened the door, stepped into the cold room and closed the door behind her. She was afraid to switch on her torch, as though bloodthirsty faces would suddenly appear in its beam of light, but when she did she found the room empty. Only a few chairs, a cross on the wall, another door. This too was unlocked.

Anna pushed the inner door open and waited behind the wall for a moment before aiming her torch into the room and peering inside. She pointed the beam into all the corners and along all the walls. There was nobody in the small room. No one except a body covered with a white sheet lying on a gurney. The man who'd stolen her handbag.

She felt a chill running through the soles of her running shoes, up into her legs and spreading out through her body. She would have to work quickly before fear and the chill made her shiver so much she would be unable to examine anything.

Anna placed the torch between her teeth, and for a moment before pulling back the sheet the thought came to her that it might be the murderer lying there instead of the body. He was about to jump up and attack her, kill her, place her on the gurney, pull the white sheet over her head and leave her there. She would be buried in an unnamed grave instead of the Romani thief, and nobody would ever know where or how she had disappeared.

Anna took a deep breath, carefully drew back the sheet, pulled a pair of latex gloves from her pocket and got to work.

As the broken blood vessels in the eyes had indicated, the man had been strangled to death. Beneath the ears there were contusions caused by fingers clasping round his throat. Large bruises had also appeared on the man's neck and his Adam's apple had clearly been crushed. The bruises would have formed only a few days after his death. Someone recently strangled might be mistaken for a drowning victim, particularly if the body was found in or near water. In this case, however, the verdict of death by drowning was completely fabricated. The body hadn't been opened, and Anna doubted whether it had been properly examined. Anna was certain that, if they did open up the body, his lungs would contain no water from the Tisza, no water of any kind. The strangulation marks were now so obvious that even a novice couldn't mistake them. Did the chief of police know that the body was here and not at the pathology department in Újvidék? Had he ordered the forged autopsy report? Or was it someone else? Who had the power to do something like that? Surely, even in this country, not everything was possible?

Anna carefully examined the rest of the man's body and photographed all the marks she found. She paid particular attention to the hands and arms. There were scratches on his fingers and palms, and a number of bruises on his chest. She was convinced they indicated that the man had struggled with the killer before his death, doubtless trying to defend himself. He had been strangled from the front. The bag thief had looked his killer in the eye at the moment he'd died.

***

On her way back home Anna took a detour down the street where Péter had told her he lived, though she wasn't sure why. Was she hoping to see the lights on in his kitchen, to see him standing in the window, inviting her in, where he would take her in his arms and let her talk away the fear and horror that gripped her? But, like every building in town at this time of night, Péter's house was dark.

Once she was home and safely behind the locked bathroom door, she took off her hoodie and noticed she was still wearing her latex gloves. She pulled them off, wrapped them in a ball of paper and flushed them down the toilet. Then she went outside for a cigarette, set her alarm clock to wake her up in five hours' time and took one of the sleeping pills she'd bought that day without a prescription.

JUNE 9th

'YES, I REMEMBER THEM. They got the 12.30 bus to Kanizsa. I've seen the man on the bus before.'

Kriska Tamás was a tall, rakish man in his forties who wore his thinning grey hair tied in a ponytail. Ever the young rocker, thought Anna.

'Has something happened to them?' he asked, suddenly concerned.

'The young man stole my handbag, and a while later he was found dead by the river. I don't know where the girl is, but I have to find her.'

'She travelled back to Szabadka on Saturday morning.'

'What?'

'Yes, I remember it well. It was the first bus of the day. I don't think there were any other passengers. She looked as though she'd seen a ghost. She went straight to the back seat and curled up so small I couldn't see her in the mirror. Poor girl.'

'Where did she get off?'

'At the bus station in Szabadka.'

'Was there anyone to meet her?'

'I don't remember.'

'What language did she speak?'

'I don't think she said anything at all.'

'She must have said where she was going when she bought the ticket.'

'I don't think she did.' He frowned as he thought.

'Did she say Szabadka or Subotica?' Anna asked impatiently.

'They're the same thing. I never pay that any attention.'

'Try to remember.'

'I'm trying,' said the driver, now as impatient as Anna. 'Yes, I remember. She didn't say anything, so I asked whether she wanted to go to Szabadka and she nodded. She looked very frightened.'

'In what way?'

'She kept looking over her shoulder, wouldn't look me in the eye. I remember wondering what she might be afraid of.'

'Did you see which way she came from when she arrived at the bus stop in Kanizsa?'

'No. She just appeared out of nowhere. Maybe she'd been waiting at the stop for a while.'

'Thank you for this. Thank you very much.'

'No problem. Sorry I can't help you any more than that.'

You've already helped me a great deal, she thought. The girl is no longer in Kanizsa. She probably lives in Szabadka; I'll have to go there and find her. Anna looked at her watch. It would soon be time to go to Judit's club. After that she would have a few hours to start the search for the girl.

She pulled her phone out and called Réka. She was still in Szabadka and promised to help. She said she knew of a few neighbourhoods where there were lots of Roma. They could start there. They agreed to meet at the bus station in the centre of Szabadka.

THE KANIZSA WARD of the Vojvodina Roma community met at the municipal library at the intersection of Dajmaniceva and Nikole Tesle. The building was relatively new, complete with beautiful turrets and patterned roof tiles, but Anna didn't know of anyone here who used the library. Anna had never visited the building herself. She thought she might first look at the selection of books and perhaps borrow some holiday reading, but to her disappointment the loan desk was closed. It was siesta time. From the courtyard, however, there were doors leading into rooms where there seemed to be some kind of activity. A large room belonging to the local folk-dance society echoed with violin music and the stomping of feet, and was full of girls in traditional dresses and boys in white shirts. The door to the pensioners' clubroom was locked. When Anna finally found the right room, the Romani homework club was already under way.

Judit noticed Anna as soon as she entered.

'So, you decided to brave the club after all? Welcome!' said Judit and hugged Anna. She smelled of fresh soap. Her long, black hair flowed across her shoulders and large golden rings dangled from her ears. She was wearing a pair of tight jeans and a white blouse; she looked very slim and beautiful.

'It's nice to be here. Thank you for inviting me,' said Anna. 'So, what goes on here?'

'Schoolchildren come to the club and we help them with their homework. The little ones are already here and the older children will start to arrive in about an hour, when their lessons end. As I said, many of these children's parents can barely read, so we started up the homework club to help them get the most out of school. Parents are welcome too. We try to teach them about what school can give them; we tell them how important it is to have a routine – to go to school every day, to arrive at classes on time, that kind of thing. We can't expect children to be motivated about their own education if their parents don't understand that they have to go to school every day.'

Judit chuckled blithely, though Anna found the subject very serious.

Some of the children were sitting round a large table, tucking in to a snack, and some were already sitting at small desks, quietly getting on with their homework. A few adults had arrived too. Judit introduced Anna to everyone, and before long she found herself sitting down next to a little girl called Blanka and helping her with a maths problem. The girl was in the second class at school and she was smart. She was quite good at maths, but she seemed to enjoy Anna's company and attention. Seeming a little proud that this new lady from abroad was suddenly her friend, she began to dally over her homework.

'What do you want to be when you grow up?' Anna asked the girl once she'd finished her maths questions and her textbook was carefully packed in her large, pink bag.

'A hairdresser, that would be nice,' said Blanka.

'You're very good at maths. You could become an engineer!'

The girl looked at Anna in bewilderment. 'What's that?'

'There are all kinds of engineers. Some invent machines, others design buildings or roads. You have to be good at maths if you're an engineer.'

'Boring. I want to comb long hair and plait it.'

'I'm sure that will be nice. What does your mum do?'

'Nothing. Well, I don't know really.'

'And your dad?'

'My dad goes into town every morning. Sometimes he helps out at a restaurant.'

'Well, what's most important is to study hard,' said Anna and immediately felt too teacherly. 'Then, when you're grown up, you can do what you want.'

'We can't afford to go to school,' said Blanka with a smile. 'Can I plait your hair?'

Anna nodded, and the girl gripped her hair, gently but firmly, and began plaiting it. Anna could hear the girl's concentrated breathing and felt the warm flow of air against her ear, as light as a butterfly. Emotion welled within her. Was this what it would have been like to have a child, a little girl of her own?

When the plait was ready Anna thanked the girl, whose eyes sparkled with pride. Judit stood up from beside another girl and asked Anna outside for a cigarette.

Out in the yard Anna took one of the slim cigarettes Judit offered. They smoked in silence for a moment.

'Well, what do you think?' Judit asked eventually.

'What you do here is so important,' said Anna and truly meant it.

'Thank you. It's not easy, but someone's got to at least try and do something. We have a festival of Roma culture here too – music, that sort of thing. We held the first festival a few years ago now.'

'That sounds great,' said Anna. Putting her cigarette out, she pulled the printed pictures out of her bag. By now they were slightly crumpled. 'I've managed to get some photographs of the man and the girl who stole my bag. Would you look at them and see if you recognise either of them?'

'Of course.'

Judit scrutinised the dark photographs, enlarged and printed on sheets of paper, then shook her head.

'I'm afraid I don't think I've seen them.'

'Are you absolutely sure?'

'These photographs aren't very clear, but, yes, I'm sure. I don't know them. They're definitely not from round here.'

Something told Anna that the woman was lying. She couldn't say why she thought this, because Judit looked and sounded utterly convincing. Perhaps that was precisely the reason. She was every bit as convincing as when she'd read Anna's cards.

Judit handed the photographs back. 'I have an offer to make you,' she said.

'What's that?'

'I could sort out a parcel for you. You can use it to … to banish the evil things around you. I'll prepare it myself. It won't cost much.'

A fene egye meg, Anna cursed to herself. Is this what all the premonitions about death and danger were about? Selling her something to trap her demons? No. Enough was enough, not even if Judit was dying of hunger.

'No, thank you. If you need money, I can give you some without the parcel.'

'It's not about the money,' said Judit, clearly hurt. 'It's just I happen to see more than—'

'No, thank you. Believe me. You do excellent work with these children and for that you have my utmost respect, but I simply don't believe in any supernatural nonsense.'

'Very well,' said Judit and flicked her cigarette to the ground, where it lay smoking at her feet. 'I have to be getting back. The children are waiting for me.'

'I hope I haven't offended you.'

'Of course not. My cousin is getting married tomorrow here in Kanizsa. Come along, if you fancy.'

'Even if I don't buy your parcel?'

Judit laughed lightly. 'Everyone does as they see fit. Come along, by all means. It's going to be quite a day.'

ARRIVING IN SZABADKA, Anna drove around the centre of the town for a short time, searching for a parking space. She found one on a side street some distance from the bus station and walked the rest of the way.

As she approached the station she saw Réka waiting out front in a white summer dress, beauty and happiness shining from her like an angel. Anna stopped for a moment and looked at her friend. I don't think I could ever radiate that much harmony, she thought. I'll never achieve anything like that. But perhaps I'll achieve something else. Something for the greater good, something selfless. Ultimately that's what my work is all about. Every time I catch a criminal I make the world a slightly safer place for the people around me. Surely that's a far greater achievement than starting a family? Then she shook her head. Why am I always comparing things? Comparing myself to other people, Finland to Serbia? Stop it, now, Anna instructed herself.

Réka noticed Anna and rushed towards her with a smile and a hug.

'I've done a bit of background work,' Réka said eagerly. 'I wrote an article about a Roma family a few years ago. I called them and they've agreed to meet us.'

'That's great, Réka. Thanks.'

They walked back to the car, the sun beating down from the cloudless sky, and Anna wished she'd put on a dress instead of her sweaty jeans. As they approached the outskirts of town, the houses became smaller and more run-down. The centre of Szabadka was full of buildings in the art nouveau style, but the further out they drove, the more the houses revealed the extent of modern poverty. Nobody could afford to take care of the façades of the buildings, and they had been left to crumble.

'This is the one,' said Réka when they arrived at a grey, three-storey concrete block.

They stepped into a stairwell that smelled of urine and where the lights were broken. They walked up to the second floor in the dark and Réka rang a doorbell. A little girl opened the door, and stared, petrified, at Anna and Réka for a moment before disappearing back into the apartment.

'Come on in,' someone called out. 'Don't worry about Amanda, she's terribly shy.'

Anna and Réka stepped into the tobacco-smelling apartment. A plump lady appeared in the hallway, wiping her hands on her apron.

'Réka, *Isten hozott*! How nice to see you after all this time.'

Reka performed the usual polite greetings and introduced Anna.

'She's a police officer from Finland. But her family lives in Kanizsa. We were wondering if you could help us.'

The woman gave Anna a suspicious look but showed them into the kitchen, where a large pot was bubbling on the stove.

Sitting down, Anna let Réka explain.

'My friend is looking for a little girl and a young man.'

Anna pulled out the photographs and placed them on the table. She instantly saw that that the woman recognised the faces but seemed reluctant to admit it.

'Why are you looking for them?'

'The young man was found dead in Kanizsa on Saturday morning,' said Anna. 'On the banks of the Tisza. I want to know who he is. And there was a little girl with him that night, at least for part of the time. She's about ten years old. I'd like to find her.'

The woman looked at Réka and Anna in turn, then back at the photographs. Eventually she came to a decision.

'Let me make a few calls,' she said.

The woman went into the living room, if indeed it could be called that – it clearly also served as a bedroom to many people. She made a total of three phone calls. But her low, melodious voice was so quiet that Anna couldn't quite make out what she was saying.

'She'll come up with something soon,' Réka whispered.

'I doubt it. They're going to keep quiet. Mark my words.'

'No, she'll tell us something. I've got a feeling about it. Call it journalist's intuition.'

The woman finally returned to the kitchen. Little Amanda peered, smiling, from behind her legs.

'Would you like some coffee?' the woman asked.

'No, thank you.'

The woman looked at Anna, sizing her up, as if she were still wondering whether or not she could trust this strange woman, a police officer at that. Réka gave her a reassuring smile. Eventually she spoke.

'Lakatos Sándor hasn't been seen for a few days. He goes to Kanizsa quite often.'

'Who is Lakatos Sándor?'

'I don't know him very well. I knew his parents, but they've been dead for years. Poor child.'

'Where does he live?'

'Here and there. Last I heard he was staying with a friend. But they haven't seen him there for a while, though apparently there's nothing out of the ordinary about that. The boy does as he pleases and doesn't tell them where he's going or when he'll be back.'

'What about the girl?'

'Dzsenifer is his little sister. Sándor looks after her.'

Anna and Réka looked at one another. The case had finally taken a step forward, thought Anna. At last something concrete to investigate, to follow up on. Yet still she had a suspicion she was heading into a dead end.

The woman wrote Sándor's friend's address on a piece of paper and handed it to Réka. Réka thanked her profusely and gave her a thousand-dinar note. The woman looked content.

'Don't hesitate to get in touch if you need any help. You're good people. I'd be happy to help.'

Out in the yard Anna and Réka waved to the shy little Amanda, who was peeking at them from the living-room window. The figure of Amanda's mother could be seen further back inside the room. She was speaking on the phone. Anna and Réka got into the car, which, having been parked in the direct sunlight, was now as hot as a sauna.

LAKATOS SÁNDOR'S FRIEND LIVED in a ramshackle hut outside Szabadka, in a small village consisting of a few similar shacks. A group of scruffy children were playing football in the yard and two small dogs yapped at their heels. The sight was like something from a favela in Rio. The children stopped playing momentarily and stared in awe at the Punto, covered in a coating of grey dust, carefully driving along the uneven path between the shacks. Anna and Réka stepped out of the car and greeted the children, who soon continued their game.

The structure patched together from boards and sheets of corrugated iron was dark and dirty. There was only one room, its floor covered in a collection of mattresses, with a black stove in the corner. Does that small stove keep this place warm through the winter? Anna wondered.

Anna and Réka introduced themselves to a young man with bad teeth sitting on a threadbare sofa. There was a suspicious, almost hostile expression in the man's eyes, and he wouldn't tell them his name. A small boy's head appeared in the shack's only window. The man jumped to his feet and bellowed a litany of swear words, and the head quickly disappeared.

'You know Sándor, is that right?' Anna began cautiously. The man nodded. 'When did you last see him?'

'Last Friday. Why are you asking? Has something happened?'

'Where were you on the night between Friday and Saturday?' asked Anna.

'None of your fucking business, lady.'

'It is my business,' said Anna carefully. 'Sándor stole my handbag that night. But the next morning he was found dead by the river.'

At that, something else flashed in the man's eyes, something other than hatred and mistrust. It was fear. Worry.

'Why should I believe you? What are you, some kind of cops?'

'I happen to be an officer, yes, but I work in Finland. Here I'm just on holiday, visiting family in Kanizsa. It's my belief that the local police don't want to investigate Sándor's death properly, and that's why I've decided to look into things myself.'

The man listened to her reflectively. He was clearly weighing up whether or not he could trust these two white women.

'How did he die?'

Anna showed him a photograph she'd taken at the chapel in the cemetery.

'Fuck it!' he shouted. 'The motherfuckers have killed him!' He fell silent, tears rolling down his cheeks. 'I was out drinking in Palics on Friday night. We came back here for a party. Plenty of people can tell you.'

'Who are these people you're saying killed him? And why? We want to get to the bottom of this.'

The man scoffed derisively and wiped the snot and tears from his grimy face.

'You'll never find out who did it.'

'Why not?'

The man looked at Anna as though she was a halfwit. '*A kurva életbe*, because our lives are worth nothing. We get accused and convicted of crimes we haven't committed, but if someone does something to us, nobody gives a shit. Nobody's interested.'

'I'm interested,' said Anna. 'I want to know what happened. And I'm sure his little sister wants to know too. Do you know where she is?'

The man glanced almost involuntarily out at the yard, where the distant sound of children playing could still be heard.

'Is she here?' asked Anna.

The man said nothing.

'She's here, isn't she?'

Still the man didn't answer. He scratched his skinny arm, and it looked as though he wanted to make a run for it. Anna pushed the door open and shouted into the yard.

'Dzsenifer! Dzsenifer! In here, right now!'

The children's game stopped. The small, dark heads turned and stared at Anna in confusion. One of the children glanced behind the shacks, and Anna glimpsed a head of black hair disappearing round the corner.

Anna ran after the girl, but she was nowhere in sight; it was as though the earth had swallowed her up. Anna made a quick tour of the area surrounding the shacks, checked in the bushes and ditches, but she found nothing but discarded plastic bottles. Further off was a cluster of detached houses. If the girl has run inside one of them, thought Anna, I've no chance of finding her.

'Listen, you,' said Anna as she returned to the shack. 'When she comes home, you call me immediately. She might have seen Sándor's killer.'

The man hesitated, rubbed his scabbed arm. He lit a cigarette.

'Don't you get it? Her life might be in danger,' Anna shouted.

'Fine, I'll call you,' he promised and Anna gave him her phone number.

As Anna and Réka walked back to the car, the children in the yard stared at them, terrified.

'Wait,' the man hollered from the door just as Anna turned the key in the ignition. She rolled down the window.

'You might want to ask round the camp about Sándor,' he said.

'What camp?'

'The refugee camp, where else?'

'Why should I ask round there?' Anna asked.

'Sándor went there a lot.'

'Why?'

'How should I know? Probably selling something.'

Anna closed the window and turned the air conditioning on full. The cool flow of air felt wonderfully refreshing.

'Will you take me back to József's?' asked Réka.

'Sure. But do you know where the refugee camp is?'

'Sort of. I've never been there, though.'

'I think I need to pay the place a visit.'

'I'm not coming with you. God knows what kind of diseases I might pick up,' said Réka and tapped her stomach.

Do you really believe all that propaganda too? Anna thought, but didn't say it out loud. Still, she understood the pregnancy had made Réka wary.

'Do you want to have dinner at our place?' asked Réka.

'Thanks, but I really don't have time. Say hi to József for me.'

They promised to call one another if something new came to light. Then Anna drove off back to Kanizsa, wondering what strange kind of web she was getting herself mixed up in.

RONALDO IS SILLY, thought Dzsenifer. He always passes the ball to the other boys and never to me. She sat down behind the shack in a huff, picked up a ladybird waddling in the soil and watched as it scuttled along her arm and up towards her armpit before spreading its wings and clumsily flying off. The others carried on playing in the yard as though Dzsenifer didn't exist at all. Stupid boys. Idiots. She heard their cries, their laughter, and thought that if her brother was here, he'd give them what for. *Let Dzsenifer play too*, he'd say.

But her brother hadn't come back. Even though Dzsenifer had clasped her hands together every night and prayed to God and Baby Jesus to bring him back. Rambo let her sleep in the shack and sometimes even brought her a bite to eat. But it wasn't the same. Her brother had taken proper care of her.

She wondered what it would be like to be the blonde-haired girl who lived in the big house near the shacks. They'd been in the same class at school in first year. The girl had a mother and a father and a happy, little black dog that Dzsenifer had once been allowed to stroke. The girl had told her the dog's name; she'd seemed nice, smiled and even walked a short distance with Dzsenifer. But at school the next day she pretended not to notice Dzsenifer at all, and never spoke to her again. Dzsenifer might as well have been invisible to all the girls who lived in big houses and had their own rooms and who progressed through school as they were expected to.

Dzsenifer heard a car pull up in the yard. The boys' hullabaloo stopped for a second but continued almost instantly. The sound of two car doors slamming shut, two women's voices, then Rambo's voice. Dzsenifer stood up and warily peered through the soot-covered window and into the shack. Dzsenifer froze to the spot. The woman from the passport was standing there. Panic gripped Dzsenifer's stomach so hard that she thought she might be sick. That woman was looking for her. She'd stolen the woman's passport, and now she'd been caught. Would she be sent to prison? Or killed? Would that woman attack her, just as her brother had been attacked? Dzsenifer felt her throat tightening. She heard the shack door creaking open. Then someone called out her name.

Dzsenifer darted away, running as fast as her little legs could carry her, slipped into a side street full of potholes, with a line of run-down houses leaning next to one another, as if holding each other upright. She took a shortcut across an empty plot of land towards an overgrown path and headed towards the neighbourhood with the bigger, better houses. She knew that near where the blonde-haired girl lived there was a huge house that had stood unfinished for years. Dzsenifer often played there, in and around the bare concrete blocks. She dashed into the building, ran up to the third floor and curled up in a corner among the cobwebs. She didn't dare lift her head from her knees until it started to get dark.

When dusk had fallen, she creeped into a nearby yard and stole a sheet hanging out to dry.

She wrapped herself in the sheet like a caterpillar in a cocoon and lay down to sleep in her very own hideout, high up in the windowless building.

THE BED WAS LARGE AND SOFT. The sheets had clearly just been changed. They smelled fresh, as though they'd been dried outdoors, and felt crisp against the skin. Two candles burned in the room, and the quiet baroque music playing in the background had stopped.

'Would you like some coffee?' Péter asked Anna, holding her tightly in his arms.

Anna lay there, relaxed. It felt good that he hadn't started talking immediately, got out of bed or turned his back to her, but lay next to Anna for a long time, gently stroking her back.

'Not this late at night. But a cup of tea would be nice. And a cigarette.'

Péter slowly slipped his arms from around her, climbed out of bed and pulled on a dark-grey dressing down. Anna heard him go into the bathroom, listened to the sound of the tap running. Then she made out the sound of bare feet walking across the wooden floor towards the kitchen. Anna noticed a soft, green toy frog on the rug next to the bed, then heard the sounds of cups knocking against one another, the tap again.

Péter returned to the bedroom door, a lit cigarette in his mouth, an ashtray in his hand.

'Here,' he said and handed Anna the cigarette.

'Thanks.' And then, as if in passing, 'You haven't seen the bag thief's body, have you?'

Péter hesitated for a second. He looked at her curiously, then pulled a cigarette for himself from his dressing-gown pocket and lit it.

'The official verdict was accidental death. Drowning. The case has been closed.'

'I know that. But did you see the body?'

'Yes. I was at the scene.'

'What were your impressions? Did it look as though there had been a struggle?'

Péter drew sharply on his cigarette. He was clearly in two minds as to whether or not to talk to Anna about the case. Anna waited patiently. Something told her it was best not to pressurise him.

'Tea's ready. Take a dressing gown from the wardrobe so you don't get cold,' said Péter and went into the kitchen.

Anna followed him. 'What will your wife think about me using her dressing gown?' she asked, and took a sip of tea, which tasted of stale, artificial fruit flavouring.

'Nothing much.'

'Where is she now?'

'At her parent's. We've just started a trial separation. She moved out last week.'

Péter sighed. Anna saw a flash of sadness in his eyes.

'I see you have children too. I saw the soft toys in the bedroom.'

'Just one. Sámuel is five.'

Anna didn't enquire further, as she could tell Péter didn't want to talk about it. That was fine by Anna too. To her mind there was nothing more unattractive than a recently separated man continually talking about how ruthless his ex had been, how unfair their divorce was, while all he wanted was to get into another woman's panties.

'Listen, Anna. I think you should forget about the bag thief.'

'How many times have I heard that these last few days?'

'You should try and accept that it was a simple accident.'

'I could do that if I didn't know for a fact that he'd been strangled.'

Péter's eyes narrowed. For a fleeting moment Anna wondered whether he was angry. Or startled. This game might be more dangerous than I could ever imagine, she thought, and felt a knot of fear at the bottom of her stomach.

'How on earth have you got that into your head?'

'I've got photographs.'

'What photographs?'

'Photographs of the body. I know he didn't drown.'

Péter looked at her for a long, silent moment.

'All right,' he said eventually. 'It did look as though there was a struggle by the riverbank. But I'm not a crime-scene investigator and I don't know what was found there, because the investigation was wrapped up before it had even properly started. I'll admit I thought it was a bit strange, but when I heard the victim had drowned, I didn't think any more of it. And if you ask me, you shouldn't think about it either.'

'Is that how you work?' asked Anna. 'You just obey orders even when you know they're wrong? You let a manslaughter – which might be a murder – go uninvestigated for the sake of an easy life?'

Péter lit another cigarette. Anna saw that he could barely contain his agitation. Had she gone too far? Péter was a nice man – funny and gentle – but Anna knew only too well that first impressions weren't always what they seemed.

'Would you like a glass of *fröccs*?' Péter asked and took out a bottle of white wine and some sparkling water.

'Yes, I would. *A fene egye meg*, right now there's nothing I want more than wine and beer and Koskenkorva and *pálinka*. Anything at all, as long as it's got alcohol in it, even aftershave will do. Christ, who have I been kidding, trying to have some kind of dry spell?'

'What's that?' asked Péter, genuinely bemused.

'Oh, it's a Finnish thing. Lots of people go without alcohol for the whole of January to curb their alcohol intake for a while. I've been trying to have a dryish summer because I wanted to work out more than usual. Back home it would have been easy, but here I've been a bit lax.'

Anna didn't mention that in recent months she'd begun to think about her alcohol consumption more seriously. She'd noticed she often drank more than one glass of wine of an evening, at home by herself, and that she'd even started to enjoy the feeling of fuzziness that helped lull her to sleep after a few beers.

'Sounds boring. And harsh. Come on, you're on holiday.'

Anna thought about the man's words. In those two adjectives he'd summed up the essence of her life: boring and harsh. Anna felt something growing in her mind, a tiny seed with a sprout pushing through its casing. I don't want to be boring and harsh to myself. I'm tired of that. I've had enough of the Anna that clings to the remnants of her past with the last of her strength, the Anna that doesn't belong anywhere or to anyone, the Anna that barely belongs to herself.

'Why are you so quiet suddenly?' asked Péter, gently taking Anna's chin and turning her head towards him.

Anna looked at his face. She noticed a small scar on his cheek and touched it lightly.

'There's a wine tasting at Sagmeister's on Saturday. I was thinking of drinking a barrel or two.'

'You realise you're a budding comedienne, don't you?' Péter teased her.

'Oh yes, people find me as entertaining as a slice of stale bread.'

'I think you're funny. If only you'd chill out and just be yourself.'

Whoever that is, thought Anna.

'Don't worry, I'm a laugh a minute,' she said. 'I do more work than is legally possible and the rest of the time I spend running my knees and ankles to bits. That's the kind of comedienne I am.'

'Maybe it only comes out here, where you can speak your own language,' said Péter. He wasn't to know that his words were like a punch in the gut. A short, sharp slap that left Anna almost having to catch her breath.

'Pour me a glass,' said Anna.

'I go running too, you know. Would you like to go for a run together some day?'

Anna was thrilled, more thrilled than she wanted to admit to herself.

'If you help me look into a few matters, I might consider it.'

'What do I have to do?'

'If at all possible, could you look into your files and records and see if there's any mention of a Lakatos Sándor.'

'Is that the name of the bag thief?'

'Yes.'

'How on earth have you found that out?'

'Let's just say, it wasn't exactly difficult.'

'What about the photographs?'

'It's a secret.'

'Are you absolutely sure he was strangled?'

'Yes.'

Péter thought for a moment.

'All right then. I'll see what I can find out about this Lakatos, if it'll help you. You won't leave the case alone even if I ask you to, will you?'

'Thank you. So, shall we go running tomorrow?'

'Why not?'

'I'll whip your arse, you should know that. I'm in pretty damn good shape.'

Péter laughed and grabbed Anna in his arms. 'We'll see about that. I hope you're not a sore loser.'

ANNA TRIED TO CREEP into her room as quietly as possible, but her mother was sitting in the living room waiting for her, just as she had done in Koivuharju when Anna had been out too late.

'Where have you been?' her mother asked and switched off the television. Anna caught a glimpse on the news of Keleti railway station in Budapest, where hundreds of people were sitting or lying on the floor in the waiting hall and around the building. *A record number of immigrants has arrived in Hungary today*, said the newsreader just before the screen went blank.

'I wanted to see that,' said Anna.

'It's on the news from dawn till dusk, you can't miss it if you switch on the television. You can catch it tomorrow if you want.'

'Did you notice they used the word *immigrant*? Why don't they call them refugees?' Anna asked, though she knew the answer. The word 'immigrant' implied that these people were moving voluntarily, and that was precisely the message the Hungarian media wished to give their audience.

'Yes, I noticed,' said her mother. 'Where have you been?'

'At a friend's place. Why? Do I have to account for my whereabouts at all times?' Anna snapped indignantly.

'Tibor and the others were asking after you. They came knocking on the door. And yes, while you're under my roof you are accountable. You know how worried I get.'

'Fine, I'll try and remember.'

'Réka's having a baby,' said her mother.

'I know. Isn't that great?'

'Yes. It just made me wonder when you're going to settle down.'

Anna closed her eyes, took a deep breath and counted to ten before continuing with exaggerated calm. 'Mum, please. I don't want to talk about this.'

'Well, I do. I'm concerned about you.'

'There's no need. Can't you just accept I don't want to start a family?'

'But is that really so, Anna? If that's the truth, I'll accept it, even though it makes me very sad.'

Anna said nothing. She sensed the smell of Péter's sheets in her hair, his sinewy body around her, and thought that she'd never met a man with whom she'd felt so at ease.

'I think deep down you would like a husband and children, and I don't want you to be unhappy,' said her mother.

'I'm not unhappy.'

'Maybe not yet, but what happens when you get to my age and you're still by yourself?'

'I'll cross that bridge when I come to it,' Anna retorted. 'Besides, you're by yourself here, too. Why didn't you get married again? You could find yourself a widower or a divorced man with a few children of his own to give you grandchildren.'

Anna regretted the words as soon as they'd left her lips; she could see she'd struck a nerve. A hidden nerve. Her resilient mother's Achilles heel. But she refused to remain silent any longer. She had to speak up if she ever wanted her mother to stop pressuring her, if her mother was ever to understand her, even remotely.

'It isn't…' her mother said quietly. 'It wasn't that simple.'

'You see? Why should it be so simple for me then?'

'Anna, I was wracked with grief. I'd lost my son. And my husband. Can you imagine the scars something like that leaves on you?'

'If you'd ever talked to me about it perhaps I might be able to imagine. But we've never talked properly about Dad or Áron. It's as if you've swallowed your tongue every time anyone even mentions them.' Anna noticed she had raised her voice.

Her mother slumped back on the sofa. Anna saw a tear run down her cheek.

'I'm sorry,' Anna said, trying to make amends. 'Forgive me. I didn't mean to hurt you. It just frustrates me that my life doesn't seem good enough for you the way it is.'

'You're right,' said her mother and wiped her face on a tissue. 'I haven't talked about things that needed to be talked about. I couldn't. They're too big, too … terribly painful.'

Anna sat down beside her mother and hugged her. Her slender shoulders trembled in Anna's arms, then her whole, fragile body began to shake.

'I know that,' said Anna. 'I loved them too.'

'Oh, poor girl. All the things you've had to deal with,' her mother said through her tears.

JUNE 10th

'I'M GOING TO FIND OUT what happened to that Roma boy if it's the last thing I do.'

Anna and Réka were sitting on the jetty outside the Békavár restaurant with cups of coffee and fresh bread rolls filled with ham they'd bought at the bakery. The Tisza calmly glided south right beneath them, the surface of its dark waters glinting in the sunshine. It was a hot day again. Anna lay down on the jetty.

'I'm worried. You might be putting yourself in danger,' said Réka.

'I'm going back to Finland in a few weeks. Besides, I am a police officer, you know. I'll be fine.'

'And what happens when you work out who killed him? If people are trying to hush the whole thing up, it means there's a reason they don't want the truth to see the light of day.'

'Once I get back to Finland I'll contact Interpol. I'm not leaving it at this. And the press should be interested too. Fancy a great scoop?'

'For *Magyar Szó*?' Réka laughed. 'Yeah, right. It's never going to happen.'

'For an international paper then.'

'This really isn't such a big deal.'

'I've got an itching feeling that it might be.'

'Come on, think about it. What would be my headline? "Corrupt Serbian law enforcement won't investigate possible murder of itinerant gypsy"? Who's going to be interested in that? It's not really news to anyone.'

'Yes, but *why* won't they investigate it? That's the interesting bit.'

'Someone has paid them not to pursue it any further.'

'Who? And why?'

'Somebody important killed the boy and doesn't want to go to prison.'

'Why would somebody important murder a pickpocket from Szabadka? And in the bushes by the riverbank? If it was two drunken guys who'd got into a fight, I could understand it. But that's not what happened. Somebody followed him, or took him into those bushes and killed him there.'

'I can't believe you actually went into that chapel in the middle of the night. It could have been a trap. You're crazy.'

'I had to. I sent the photos to Linnea straight away – she's a pathologist colleague in Finland. Hopefully she'll take a moment to look at them before going on holiday.'

'It was probably another gypsy who wanted his share of the loot. They got into a fight and it ended up with one of them dead.'

'Then why won't the police investigate it, if that's all that happened? There would be nothing to hide if that was the case. In fact, it would be yet another piece of evidence that all gypsies are petty criminals.'

'True,' said Réka pensively.

They drank their now-lukewarm coffees and gazed out at the Tisza in silence.

'The little girl, Dzsenifer. She was there,' said Anna. 'She saw what happened.'

'What if the case is somehow linked to you?' Réka said.

'What? How could it be linked to me?'

'It's just a thought. Because it was your bag that got stolen, your passport.'

This hadn't occurred to Anna at all. She pondered Réka's suggestion a little, but she still couldn't imagine the theft of her handbag was anything other than an unfortunate coincidence. The thief might have snatched any number of handbags that evening. But what if she was wrong? What if she and her bag had played a direct part in the man's death? The thought chilled her.

'I must talk to Dzsenifer.'

'Please be careful, Anna. This is starting to look pretty frightening. If I were you I wouldn't even trust Péter, no matter how good he is in bed.'

'I know. But I don't have many options, if I'm ever going to get to the bottom of this.'

'I can help you out. I'm a professional when it comes to digging up the truth.'

'I don't want to put you in danger. Particularly not now, not with…' Anna pointed at Réka's stomach.

'Having a quick look in the paper's archives can't be all that dangerous.'

'All right then. Why do you think that guy suggested we ask around the refugee camp?'

'He said Sándor might have had business going on there.'

'What business did he mean? Could Sándor have been involved in people smuggling?'

'I get the feeling half the town is involved in it one way or another. They smell easy money and they don't hang around. There was a terrible accident here a few years ago. A group of refugees drowned in the Tisza.'

'That's awful. Just like in the Mediterranean.'

'Exactly. I remember there was talk about a Kanizsa local being somehow embroiled in it. Something like that. I'll look into that first.'

'Great. Réka, you're a treasure. And I need to get to the refugee camp as soon as I can find time. There's so much I need to look into. It's annoying this is taking up my entire holiday and we won't get to spend much time together.'

'We're together now, aren't we?'

'You know what I mean. But this case won't leave me in peace. I feel I've just got to work out what's going on here.'

'Don't worry, I understand. I'll help you as best I can, and next time you're here we can relax properly.'

'Thanks,' said Anna. Only next time it won't just be the two of us, she thought. 'I really have to get going. My mother and I, and Ákos and his new girlfriend are all going to Nagy Béla's place for lunch. It's weird how all my father's old friends are suddenly so keen to see me.'

'What?' Réka nearly screamed. 'Does Ákos have a girlfriend?'

'Yes,' said Anna, curt and almost sour.

'Who is it? Why didn't you tell me?'

'I haven't had time to think about anything except this damn handbag thief. She's called Kata, apparently she and Ákos were in the same class at school, or something like that. A divorced mother of two.'

'Oh, Kata! I remember her. She's really nice. I just hope Ákos can grab himself by the scruff of the neck and get his life back together.'

'Me too. Listen, we'll talk on the phone soon. Be careful.'

'You too.'

THE FISHERMAN'S HOUSE was typical of many of the old houses in Kanizsa. It was long, painted in pastel pink, and its beautiful old windows had been replaced during the 1970s, making them larger and uglier. As was the case at many other houses, a cherry tree stood in the strip of garden at the front. The red of the fruit was already beginning to deepen. In the courtyard there were plum, peach and walnut trees, and at the back of the garden was a small greenhouse containing tomatoes, cabbages and aubergines.

The fisherman's wife, Emese, was standing at the gate to welcome the Fekete family. She paid particular attention to Kata, and so had Anna. Kata had joined them at the fisherman's house, so Anna was also seeing her now for the first time. Short, peroxide-blonde hair and some delicate make-up. A tall, slim body, average clothes. Not a stunning beauty, but certainly not ugly. She was perfectly normal, thought Anna, and couldn't decide whether this was a good thing or not. She'd been expecting something different, someone perhaps more Bohemian.

Nagy Béla was sitting on the covered patio in the courtyard, surrounded by trestles with thick vines winding their way upwards. He gestured to his guests to join him. It was a nice, warm day, 27°C in the shade, with a gentle breeze rustling through the vine leaves. The grapes were still tiny and bright green and would mature much later in the autumn. Anna recalled the taste of grapes plucked straight from the vine, their juicy freshness and sweetness, their sugary liquid running down her fingers. Imported grapes in the supermarket never tasted anything like this – that's probably why she never bought them. Wouldn't it be nice to spend an entire year here? thought Anna. To experience the smells and tastes of the changing seasons. In particular she noticed how she yearned for fresh fruit. Not even organic produce could compare to ripe fruit plucked straight from the tree.

'Would you like something to drink?' asked Emese. 'Coffee? *Pálinka*? Beer?'

'I think I'll have some *pálinka*, please,' said Anna's mother as she sat down in one of the plastic chairs.

'Coffee for me, please,' said Anna.

'I'll be fine with water, thanks,' said Ákos.

'Sure you don't want to taste our *pálinka*?' Emese tried once more. Anna noticed the furrows in her mother's brow deepen.

'Thank but no thanks,' said Ákos. He seemed relaxed.

'Ákos has had a few problems with alcohol so now he doesn't drink at all. But I'd love some,' said Kata, upbeat and matter-of-fact; and at that moment Anna knew she liked her.

'Yes, best not to touch the stuff at all,' Ákos agreed.

Anna wondered when her brother's once shameful addiction had suddenly become the subject of breezy afternoon conversation. Her mother continued to frown, though, and Emese also seemed embarrassed, and at a loss for words she disappeared inside the house to fetch the drinks. Anna glanced at Kata and they smiled at each other like secret allies.

'So, how are you keeping, Ákos?' asked Béla with a hearty smile.

'Very well, thank you, as you can probably see,' her brother said and looked at Kata, clearly besotted.

'So, does this mean you're going to move back here permanently?' asked the fisherman. Anna's heart missed a beat.

'I'm going to stay at least all summer. I'm planning to look for work. Kata and I will think about what to do in the autumn, whether to move to Szeged where Kata works or stay here on the Serbian side. Or whether we all go back to Finland.'

Anna listened nervously. She'd wanted to ask her brother the same question when they were alone, to talk calmly about his plans, because more than anything else she was afraid that he would stay here – and she'd decided to tell him that. But not now, not here. Not in front of all these people, because saying it out loud would have brought her to tears and she didn't want that to happen in the company of strangers.

'The wages are good in Finland,' said Béla.

'Yes, but it's extremely difficult to find work there unless you speak the language perfectly, like our Anna here. I don't speak it all that well, and Kata speaks even less. Besides, I haven't really got any qualifications. My studies came to an end when the war broke out.'

'It's the same everywhere. But Anna is quite a special case,' said Béla. 'She's just like her father, don't you think, Mária?'

'In her choice of career, at least,' her mother replied grimly.

'What's wrong with that? It's a fine career.'

'And a dangerous one,' she replied.

To Anna's relief, Emese returned to the patio with a tray and began busying herself with setting out glasses and pouring drinks, and the conversation turned to last year's *pálinka* and the autumn's fruit harvest. The awkward topics of conversation were soon forgotten about and Anna eventually relaxed. Kata was talkative and sociable – she seemed to be able to chat with Béla and his wife about anything at all – and Anna began to appreciate why Ákos and her mother were so taken with her. She might not be a beauty but she was witty and amusing.

'Speaking of your father, Anna, come and look at this,' said Béla, standing up and walking inside the house.

The interior of the house felt pleasantly cool, and it took a moment before Anna's eyes became accustomed to the dimness after the bright glare of the sun. The fisherman led Anna into the living room, opened one of the drawers in the bookshelf and pulled out a pile of old photographs.

'Look. That's me and your father, as young boys,' he said. 'We often went fishing together. Did you know your father was a keen fisherman?'

'No,' Anna replied and looked at the small, faded, sepia photographs showing her father in old-fashioned clothes, sitting in a boat on the Tisza and proudly holding a large carp up to the camera.

'He certainly was,' said Béla 'I knew him since he was a boy.'

Anna stared at her father's laughing eyes long and hard, tried to grab hold of her own blurry memories, to focus them in her mind.

Could she remember anything about him at all? His voice, his smell, his arms around her little body? His embrace. That had stayed with her. She must never let go of it.

'Mum never talks about him,' Anna said quietly.

'It's not surprising. It was a blow to us all when he died – for your mother especially.'

Anna went through the photos once more. Dad's thick moustache. Dad in his uniform. Dad's kind eyes. Dad in his class photograph, the same photograph as Remete Mihály had shown her.

'Were you all in the same class?' asked Anna and began examining the old, faded photograph more closely.

'Who do you mean?'

'You and my father, Remete Mihály and Molnár László?'

'László is a year younger than the rest of us, but he was part of our gang. Those were the days.'

'Who else was in the gang?'

'Let me see, there was Fejős Lajos, Almási Ottó, loads of people. In those days groups of friends were big, we wandered around in a huge herd, and there were kids of all ages too. The smallest ones ran behind us and the oldest among us were almost adults. At least that's what they looked like to us. We played football, ran around the park and swam in the Tisza. Then, when we were a bit older, we drank a lot and teased the girls. Many of them are dead and buried. That's what happens when you start to get old – you suddenly notice your friends disappearing one by one.'

Béla looked into the distance, his eyes clouded a little. Anna could hear the murmur of voices drifting in from outside. Now was a perfect time to find out what Béla was holding back.

'Why didn't you tell me you were at the wine fair too?' she asked quietly.

Béla looked perturbed. 'What?'

'You didn't mention that you were at the wine fair, but I saw you in one of the photographs a friend of mine took that night. Why didn't you tell me?'

'Well, I … it didn't occur to me. I went down to the fair briefly. I think I was there less than half an hour.'

'In the photograph you were standing right behind me just moments before my handbag was stolen. You might have been standing very close to the thief, right next to him even.'

'Really? Goodness me.'

'Did you see the theft?'

'No. As I said, I only popped into the fair. I must have just left when your bag was stolen.'

'Who did you speak with at the fair?'

'Lots of people. László invited me down there. But I couldn't find him anywhere so I decided to go home.'

'Do you recall seeing a little Romani girl in a red skirt? She must have been about ten years old.'

'Not that I remember.'

'You said you saw a flash of something red down by the riverbank when you found the body, though?'

'That's right, there was a flash of something. You're telling me it was a little girl?'

'Yes. This is her photo. She's the thief's younger sister.'

Anna showed him the photos from the wine fair. Béla looked at them, his brow furrowed. Anna noticed that his hands were trembling ever so slightly. Was this because of old age, or something else?

'I don't know anything about these people. And I don't want to know anything about them either. All I want is to do my job in peace and quiet.'

'So why did you take me to the place where you found the body?'

'Because I thought there was something suspicious going on. But I don't think so any longer. I don't want to talk about this anymore and I'd advise you to forget all about it.'

You can be sure I won't forget about it, thought Anna. If only you knew how suspicious things looked right now. But perhaps you know only too well.

WHEN ANNA ARRIVED at Judit's cousin's house, the celebrations were already in full swing. People were playing violins and guitars, and dancing in the yard, and straightaway someone pressed a glass of *pálinka* into Anna's hand. She took a cautious sip. It was peach *pálinka*, stronger than usual. The bride and groom were both dressed in white. They looked like cake decorations as they sat behind a table reserved only for them. Anna saw Benedek and waved. The boy smiled and waved back at her.

A sweaty Judit made her way through the crowds of guests and hugged her. 'Come and dance,' she said and began pulling Anna past the orchestra towards the crowd of revellers.

Anna was reluctant. 'I don't really know how.'

'Nonsense. At weddings everybody knows how to dance. Come on!'

And so Anna followed Judit, joined the energetic throng of dancers and let her hair down. It was easy to catch the infectious rhythm of the music, the trumpets blared and the violins squealed so much, she didn't have to think about dancing at all, her legs and body moved of their own accord. Anna had never experienced anything like it before. Given that she normally only danced when she was drunk, now she allowed her body to be carried away by the music and forgot about herself. There was nothing but the psychedelic rhythm of the accordions and the beat of the dance; the collective movement of bodies blended with the music, forming something extraordinary, a figure with no defined edge. Dust flew up from the ground as they stamped their feet. The evening had darkened, but the air felt as warm as if a lightless sun were still burning down upon the partygoers. Laughter, noise, the rhythmical thud of feet. The brassy chaos of the trumpets. The dance continued, on and on, at least that's what it felt like. Until Judit tugged at her sleeve and invited her to have something to eat. It was as if Anna woke from a trance, and for a moment she stared at Judit's laughing face without fully understanding where she was.

As they edged away, the amorphous throng continued dancing and playing, new people joining in as others pulled themselves from its centre of gravity.

'Let's have a cigarette first,' said Anna. I need to come back to earth before I can eat anything.'

Sweat trickled in rivulets down her cheeks. She surreptitiously tried to sniff her armpits; her deodorant was holding out.

Anna and Judit lit their cigarettes and watched the crowd of dancers.

'I've never danced like that before,' Anna said eventually.

Judit laughed. 'I don't think anyone can resist music like that. I certainly can't.'

'Thank you for inviting me. This is quite an experience.'

'I thought you'd like it. Come on, let's go and eat.'

Anna threw her cigarette to the ground and followed Judit as she darted through the crush of revellers towards a long table laden with all manner of delicacies. Further away there was a small bonfire with a whole pig roasting on a spit propped above the flames. A group of children had gathered and stood throwing twigs into the fire.

For the sake of politeness Anna took a slice of cake, though she wasn't very hungry. To her great astonishment she wanted to go back and dance some more. And that is what she did.

When a combination of sweat and thirst eventually forced Anna to leave the group of dancers, Judit had disappeared and she couldn't see Benedek anywhere either. Anna looked at her watch and noticed she'd been dancing for at least an hour. She'd completely lost her sense of time. She went to the dining table to fetch some water, gulped it down and looked out across the assembled guests. People had stuffed banknotes into the bride's hairpiece and the front of her dress. The notes were dangling here and there, making her look almost like a scarecrow.

'Are you the Fekete girl?' Anna heard a gruff voice say behind her.

She turned and saw a wrinkly old man, his bright eyes looking her up and down.

'I'm Fekete Anna,' she replied, wiped her sweaty hand on the hem of her skirt and held it out to greet the man.

He gripped it in his own rough, sturdy hand. 'Kolompár Lukács. It's my son's girl that is getting married.'

'Oh, congratulations. What a great wedding. I'm privileged to be here.'

'Judit brought you, did she?'

'Yes. Didn't she …? Is this…?'

'Don't worry. You're perfectly welcome. Everyone's welcome at our weddings. Except Bangót.' The man muttered the last words so quietly that Anna wasn't sure whether she'd heard him right.

'Great music here too,' she said. Having felt so welcome and joyful, she now felt awkward and out of place. The man was still looking at her with his bright, unblinking eyes. Staring at her. He took a sip from his bottle of beer, and some of it trickled down his chin.

'I hear you've been asking round about the boy that died on the riverbank,' said Kolompár Lukács without taking his eyes off her. 'He was one of ours.'

Anna was suddenly alert.

'Yes, I've been asking this and that. There's something suspicious about the case.'

'Everything's a little suspicious. Nothing's ever out in the open in this country. Nothing.'

'For some reason the police don't want to investigate the case properly,' Anna ventured. She had the impression the old man wanted to tell her something important.

He swilled down what was left in his bottle and burped. 'Listen, girl. That's the way of the world. When it's one of us, they never investigate anything. Why should they? All gypsies are thieves and crooks. You don't need an investigation to prove that.'

'Surely it can't be like that,' said Anna, in a coaxing voice.

The man scoffed.

'Even here in Serbia everyone is equal in the eyes of the law…' she continued.

The old man burst into a cackle. He laughed so much that tears rolled from his eyes. 'That's right, that's just how it is. The law is one thing, and the way of the world is another. Just like in your father's case.'

'What case?' said Anna and felt a cold hand squeeze her gut.

'Your father was that policeman, right?'

'What policeman?' asked Anna.

'Fekete, the one that got himself killed.'

'That's right. But that was a long time ago.'

'You must have been a little lass back then.'

'I was.'

'It was bad luck. For your father, I mean. And you too, mind. It's not easy growing up without a father – though who am I to judge? My own father played no part in my life after getting my mother knocked up. We didn't see him much after that. They say he was handsome. I've got my father's genes,' said Lukács and smiled to reveal his toothless gums.

'Do you know what happened to your father?' he asked eventually.

'Of course I do. Well, I know something.'

'So tell me,' the old man commanded her. From his voice Anna could tell the man was certain Anna knew nothing at all.

'He was shot. It was to do with the mafia. The shooter was caught and executed.'

'That's the official story. They still had the death penalty back then,' said Lukács. 'Did you know the accused was a gypsy?'

'No. I mean, there was some mention of it,' said Anna, now unsure of herself.

'That's right. He was one of us. And he didn't do it.'

'What?' The knot in her stomach tightened. It was as though she could barely breathe.

'He didn't shoot your father. He was framed for it.'

'What are you talking about?' Anna was becoming agitated. The cold fist gripping her stomach rose higher and higher. It was now constricting her throat.

'It's true. It happens round here all the time.'

'Who was it then? The shooter, that is?'

'I don't know who the real killer was, but the gypsy boy didn't shoot your father, that's for sure.'

'How can you be so sure?'

'He had an alibi, but the people giving him that alibi were our lot too, so the police didn't believe them. It really is a while ago now. So long ago, there's no point dwelling on it. I just wanted to tell you, seeing as you popped up at the wedding. I don't think anything happens by accident, especially not if Judit invited you here.'

'Does Judit know something about my father's death, then?'

'Judit is still young, but she knows a lot of things. People still talk about your father's case, though not all that much these days.'

'Did you know him?'

Again Lukács guffawed. 'He took me to the cells, more than once, Fekete István. He had a good reputation. He was a decent man, your father.'

'I work for the police too, now,' said Anna.

The old Romani looked her up and down. 'I'll say this much, I'd rather be taken to the cells by you than your old man.' He chuckled. 'Come on, girl, let's dance. Now's no time to worry about the past. Tonight we celebrate!'

But Anna didn't want to dance any longer. The trumpets and violins hurt her ears, made her wince, and the noise of the crowd was beginning to irritate her. She left without looking for Judit, without congratulating the bride and groom, without saying a word to anyone. The party atmosphere had vanished.

Anna slowly walked towards the town square. The lights in the bakery were still on, but she couldn't see anyone inside. The sound of men talking carried through the open door of the Gondűző bar. Thick, grey smoke puffed out into the street. Young people were walking up and down. She couldn't think of anything, didn't know where to go, what to do. Her head felt as empty as a dried-up well. She wandered through the dark town smoking a cigarette and pondered how quiet it was, pondered herself, her life.

Who am I? What makes us who we are? Our language: I have two of them. Our home: I have two of them as well. Work, friends, hobbies – all far too superficial. Our family, our roots. What do I have left of those? The memory of my father. A memory now suddenly prodded with a burning iron, branding me so that the smell of burning skin rises into the air. She wanted to talk about her father, about Áron. But she didn't know how she could ever bring up with her mother what she'd heard at the wedding.

The weight in Anna's chest felt heavy and her legs were like lead. They carried her somewhere, one step at a time. Towards Péter's house. Anna didn't even attempt to withstand the will of her feet.

JUNE 10th

Many times during the course of his life he had wondered what was ultimately true and what was false, what was reality and what merely illusion, and how much of it was nothing but a web of words and thoughts in our brains, a tapestry of our own making.

He felt almost dizzy every time he thought about it and began to wonder whether reality truly existed as we understand it in everyday observations. What if his private hell was simply a product of his own thoughts, and nothing else? What if no one but he carried this thought inside them, like a slowly spreading cancer, a tumour that could not be operated away. Did it exist only to him? Did the world around him exist in another reality, another time dimension, a place where the world inside his head was utterly insignificant?

The worst of it was the guilt. Sometimes he thought the worst thing was constantly keeping up the façade, wearing a mask that he could never remove but that made his true face clammy and, like the severest form of asthma, made it hard to breathe. He hadn't had to lie for years, and in his own head the lies had begun to resemble the truth so vividly that the mask had merged with his own features. Nowadays what plagued him the most was the fact that the mask essentially hid him, hid the truth that only he knew, hid the inescapable fact of his guilt.

Over the years he had learned to live with it. Days could go past, sometimes weeks at a time, when he wouldn't recall the matter. Rather, he remembered but he didn't think about it. Everything had been just fine; at times they were even splendid. He had lived a respectable life. He had worked hard, looked after his family, even looked after local stray cats. Nobody had any reason to think ill of him. He had done a lot of good.

If that woman, Fekete Anna, weren't doggedly digging around in his business, in his private hell, it might all remain hidden behind the mask forever. And that would be a good thing, best for all concerned. For if only one person knows the truth, lies can be almost true.

But now it had happened. Anna's suspicions had been awoken.

Drops of sweat appeared on the man's brow and armpits. His heart was thumping. He paced back and forth across his office and thought hard about what to do. What the hell should he do next?

He sat down in an armchair and looked out of the window, took long, concentrated breaths and counted to twenty. He lit a cigarette. He sucked the smoke deep into his lungs and exhaled it slowly through his nostrils.

He thought about the possibility of a bribe. But Anna was from Finland. There weren't the same levels of corruption over there. On the other hand, if the sums involved were large enough, people's morals had a habit of loosening. He'd seen this first hand more than anyone would believe. But he had to remember this was about Anna's father. An emotional attachment always made things more difficult. And it meant that such things didn't necessarily have a price.

Just stick to the old story and you'll be fine, he told himself. My story didn't arouse any suspicions at the time, so why should it arouse them now? This is no time for panic or rash decisions. A cool head will see me through. It had worked in the past and it would work now.

But somehow he had to watch his back. That much he understood. After smoking three cigarettes and giving the matter careful consideration he knew he had to find and kill the Lakatos girl. He didn't like the idea. Killing a child was in a different league from killing an adult. On the other hand, the tinkers breed like mosquitoes. And the girl's an orphan. Her life will probably be nothing but a cycle of endless poverty and suffering – he'd be doing her a favour by putting her out of her misery. Besides, the most important thing now was keeping his life and the life of his family from falling apart. You always had to put your own family first, he mused. That's right. I'm doing this to protect my children, my good name, my honour. And if Fekete Anna doesn't take a hint and back off from her little investigation, I'll have no choice but to take action against her too.

JUNE 11th

From: Linnea Markkula <linnea.markkula @poliisi.fi>
To: Anna Fekete <anna.fekete@poliisi.fi>

Hi Anna,
I asked Kirsti from forensics to look more closely at a few of those photos. She and I are going out to celebrate the beginning of the summer holiday tonight and I promised her a bottle of champagne if she helped me out. As usual, she came up with the goods. I would too if I knew it was going to land me a bottle of Charles Heidsieck (hint hint).

Judging by the photos, I can confirm the guy was strangled, just like you said. The elongated bruises on the neck left by the killer's fingers and the chafing marks on his skin are perfectly obvious. Just by looking at it I'd say his thyroid cartilage was crushed. On top of that there are signs of a struggle dotted all over the body – he probably tried to defend himself against his attacker. These marks aren't old; they look as though they occurred at the same time as the strangulation marks. I'd need to get my hands on the body to give you a more precise time of death, but under these circumstances that's out of the question. Still, I'm planning on getting my hands on some live meat pretty soon, preferably this evening. The kids are off to their Dad's place for two weeks :)

You asked whether the man would have been able to run around and steal your handbag if he'd been beaten up *before* bumping into you. In my opinion, no. I'm fairly sure he's got a broken rib on the right-hand side, and the other injuries are such that he wouldn't have been able to run away from you for several kilometres. If he'd been in a fight earlier in the day and broken his rib then, you'd have caught up with him easily, but in that case I don't think he would have been out pickpocketing but in hospital or at least in bed in terrible pain.

I hope this is helpful. Now I'm going to switch off my work phone, my work computer, my work persona, enjoy my freedom and find myself a summer fling. Or two! It would do you a world of good too.

Linnea

Anna locked her bedroom door and examined the photographs again, paying particular attention to the marks Linnea had mentioned. She couldn't see a broken rib in the photos but trusted that Linnea knew what she was doing.

Someone had attacked her handbag thief – by now Anna thought of him as her own thief – he had tried to defend himself and eventually succumbed to the assault. Anna thought back to the evening of the wine fair. Had someone first witnessed the theft, then followed the thief? If that were the case, the killer must have been at the fair too. Was it someone who wanted their share of the contents of Anna's bag? Once again Anna went through the list of people she'd met that evening, thinking back to all the kisses on the cheeks, and looking through Nóra's photographs, which she'd uploaded to her tablet. She searched for any observations she'd made around these moments captured in still life. Faces. Clothes. Bodies. Something, anything she could latch on to.

But her memories were nothing but a blur of pixels. She hadn't paid attention to anything out of the ordinary. Except Remete Mihály, but it was hard to imagine this slimy, self-assured, successful figure of a man wading through the undergrowth by the Tisza in the dark of night, let alone beating anyone to death. Men like that never get their own hands dirty, thought Anna. Men like that get other people to do their bad deeds. The gang of skinheads fitted the bill perfectly. The local far-right extremists would hardly look favourably on a Romani pickpocket from out of town turning up and stealing an innocent woman's handbag.

I must find those young skinheads, thought Anna. Talk to them face to face. She tried to work out how she could do this, but her thoughts kept wandering back to her father. Was the old Romani man telling the truth? Anna knew from experience that minorities often pulled out the racism card all too easily. Failure, setbacks and all manner of imagined wrongs were routinely blamed on the prejudice and hegemony of the dominant culture. Any wrongs they committed themselves were turned into a reflection of the wickedness of the ruling classes. Anna had often pondered that the racist and xenophobic attitudes of the dominant culture offered minorities a cruel, twisted sacrament – absolution, a pardon of sorts – that didn't help anybody but which widened the gap between cultures and whipped up resentment on both sides. She felt a growing desire to find out exactly what happened on the day that had been her father's last, but at the same time she felt a deep sense of powerlessness: her lack of resources and the time she had left here were barely enough to investigate the bag theft.

Anna gave a start as the phone rang. The Romani man from the shantytown in Szabadka, the one who wouldn't give his name, was calling to tell her that Dzsenifer had returned home.

THIS TIME THERE WERE NO CHILDREN or dogs in the yard outside the cluster of shacks. The sun had dried the clay earth amber-brown, leaving it full of cracks. A gust of wind caught a green plastic bag and blew it against the car windscreen. Lakatos Sándor's scrawny friend was waiting for her at the door. This time he introduced himself. His name was Rambo.

Anna had set off immediately after his call, taking the most direct route to Szabadka, and paying little attention to the speed limits. Though she knew the Serbian police were vigilant and that there were plenty of them, she was determined not to let the girl slip through her fingers again. She must find out what the girl had seen.

She was sitting at a cluttered table eating a sandwich.

'Hi, my name's Anna,' she said, trying to sound as friendly as possible.

'Hi,' the girl replied quietly, munching her sandwich and gazing at the crumbs falling on the table.

'Are you Dzsenifer?'

The girl nodded warily.

'I'd like to ask you a few things. Is that all right?'

The girl looked up at Rambo – these Roma names are quite something, Anna had thought as she shook his hand out in the yard – and he nodded back at her.

'How old are you?'

'Ten.'

'Were you in Kanizsa last Friday?' asked Anna.

'Yes,' the girl replied and continued gobbling her sandwich.

'Were you there with Sándor?'

'Yes,' she replied and immediately started to cry. Rambo poured water into a stained kettle but didn't ask whether Anna would like anything to drink.

'Cut out the bawling and tell her what happened,' he snapped.

Anna wanted to order him out of the room but decided against it, thinking he was unlikely to listen to her. Dzsenifer lowered her sandwich to the table and wiped away her tears.

'Sándor was just lying there. I tried to wake him, but he wouldn't get up. I knew he was dead. I knew that horrible man killed him.'

'What horrible man?' asked Anna carefully.

'I don't know who he was. I'm scared.'

'It's all right, there's no need to be frightened,' said Anna. 'You're safe now. Why did you go down to the river?'

'Sándor has a hideout there. He knew the place. He took people there sometimes.'

'What people?'

'I don't really know. But he earned money from it.'

'Was he taking people there that night?'

'No. But sometimes he took people to a boat. He said it was a good place because nobody knew the way. We were going to sleep there and leave on the first bus in the morning.'

'Tell me everything that happened that night, Dzsenifer.'

'We agreed to meet at the river, and when I got there Sándor was there with that man.'

The girl began to cry again. Anna waited patiently, but Rambo was pacing up and down the room and cursing to himself.

'Sit down,' Anna told him.

Rambo pretended not to hear, instead glowering at Anna, his expression furious. Anna could see that his agitation frightened Dzsenifer.

'Sit down or go outside,' Anna ordered in her firm police voice. 'Right now! You're making Dzsenifer nervous.'

Rambo slumped on to a stool. Anna waited for the charged atmosphere to pass, then turned back to Dzsenifer.

'Take your time and tell me what you saw at the river.'

'Start talking, Dzseni!' Rambo hissed at her.

'I heard them shouting at each other and I hid behind a bush. Sándor tried to punch the man, but the man hit him back and

Sándor fell down. Then the man jumped on top of him and started squeezing … I was too scared to watch any more. I crawled further away and hid under a thick bush. I was very, very frightened. But the man didn't see me.'

Thankfully, thought Anna. Did the strangler even know there was a witness to the murder?

'I was scared when I saw you here last time. I thought someone had come to kill me,' the girl sobbed.

'I'm not surprised,' said Anna and cautiously held out a hand towards the girl. Dzsenifer didn't pull away but let Anna stroke her head of black, tangled hair. 'It's all right. You're not in any danger. I'm going to find out what happened to your brother. I want to help you.'

'My brother told me never to trust white people.'

'You can trust some white people. You can trust me.'

The girl hunched her shoulders, making her appear even smaller in her chair, and leaned her head towards Anna. Anna caught the girl's smell, a mixture of dirt and children's sweat, and she was consumed by a desire to take the girl home, put her in the bath, wash her clothes, brush her thick hair until it was smooth.

'*A fene egye meg*, who the hell killed Sándor? I swear he'll pay for this,' Rambo shouted.

'Stop it,' said Anna. 'We don't want to frighten Dzsenifer any more.'

The water began to boil and Rambo jumped up, fetched a cup and dangled a used teabag in the water. He offered Anna some. She politely declined.

'The man was quite old,' said Dzsenifer.

'How old?'

'At least thirty or forty. His hair was all grey.'

'Dzsenifer. I'm just over thirty. Was the man the same age as me?'

The girl looked at Anna with teary eyes and shook her head. 'You're much younger.'

'Would you recognise the man if you saw him again?' asked Anna.

Dzsenifer began to cry once more. 'I never want to see him again. He squeezed Sándor's throat.'

'What kind of clothes was he wearing? Was he a big man?'

'I don't know.'

'Was he bigger than Rambo or smaller?'

The girl glanced over at Rambo. 'He was fatter. I'm really, really scared.'

'I'm not surprised. I would have been scared too. You were very brave.' Anna paused, and stroked the girl's hair again. 'Do you know what happened to my passport?'

Dzsenifer looked up, terrified, and quickly shook her head.

'No, I don't know. I don't know anything,' she spluttered. 'I'm sorry.'

'It's all right, I can get a new one,' said Anna. She was certain that either the girl or the crafty-looking Rambo had already sold the passport, but she didn't want to cause Dzsenifer any more distress. She would get a new passport – as long as she remembered to contact the embassy in Belgrade, that was.

'Could I have saved Sándor?' Dzsenifer suddenly asked in a fragile, little voice.

'No, Dzsenifer, you couldn't. You did the right thing by not getting involved. That man could have done something bad to you too.'

'Who's going to look after me now?'

That was a question Anna didn't know how to answer. She nodded to Rambo to step outside with her, then asked him why the girl wasn't at school. Rambo stared at his shoes and said Sándor had taken care of Dzsenifer's schooling and claimed he knew nothing about it. Anna asked about any other relatives and social workers, but he said that Dzsenifer didn't have any other relatives and the authorities would only take her to an orphanage. We'll take care of her here, the man assured her and even promised to find out at which school Dzsenifer was enrolled.

Anna looked at the dismal surroundings, the run-down shacks, the piles of rubbish strewn across the yard, the gaunt, grimy man in front of her. She decided to ask Réka for advice. There must be a child protection agency here too, she surmised. The girl must be taken to safety. Fast.

'Very well,' said Anna. 'But don't let her roam around by herself. If Sándor's killer knows there was a witness, Dzsenifer could be in real danger.'

'Okay.'

'And tell her to have a wash. Are there facilities round here where you can do the laundry?'

'Listen, lady, don't start telling me what to do. We'll look after Dzseni here.'

'Okay. Now, tell me everything you know about Sándor's little business scams.'

'He was up to all sorts.'

'Dzsenifer said she saw him taking people down to the river.'

'All right, I'll tell you. But only because it might help catch the bastard that did this. Sándor had some business going on with these refugees. He organised transportation for them. That's why he was in Kanizsa.'

'People smuggling?'

'If you like. I mean, he didn't drive them himself, he was just a go-between. A link between the refugees and the drivers.'

'Do you know who he visited when he went to Kanizsa?'

'No. I doubt even he knew their names. Everything was hush-hush. He just looked for the right kind of people at the camp and took them to the drivers. He didn't talk about it much, and I didn't ask him. But he bought us food whenever he got paid. He was a good guy. God, I miss him. If I had enough money I'd get the fuck out of here. I'd take Dzsenifer with me and sort us out a decent life in the West, a life with some dignity.' Rambo's face contorted with suppressed grief and anger.

Anna told him to call her if he learned anything at all about what Sándor had been up to or if Dzsenifer told him something new.

She got back into her car and drove a little distance back towards the town centre, then stopped by the side of the road and called Réka.

Réka promised to find out which department at the Szabadka social services was responsible for Dzsenifer and would take care of the girl's welfare.

THE GROUNDS OF THE NAGY-SAGMEISTER vineyard were not situated in Kanizsa but further away on the slopes of Fruška Gora where people had made wine since time immemorial. The wine itself was bottled in the town. The owners had renovated an old industrial warehouse in the town centre, fitting it with steel vats and oak caskets. The space also housed a tasting hall where long tables had been set with candles. A lively group of people had gathered round the tables, mostly Anna's old friends from school. The bottles of wine were lined up on a platform built along one of the walls. Anna suspected there would be very little swilling and spitting at this particular wine tasting.

Béci spotted Anna straight away and came to say hello. The gentle hug and kisses on the cheek passed as though there had never been anything between them. I'm getting good at this, thought Anna. Meeting my one-night-stands then brushing them off again – I'm especially good at the brushing off bit. Béci held out a glass of wine. Anna gripped it, turned away before she could register the note of disappointment flash across his face, and quickly emptied the glass. I hope Péter turns up soon, she thought.

'How are you? Where have you been? We've been trying to get hold of you,' Nóra babbled as she arrived with Tibor, Ernő and Véra in tow.

'Have you got any new information?' asked Anna excitedly.

'About what? Your handbag? No, of course not. We wanted to invite you down to the Tisza. We were all there yesterday.'

'I was at a gypsy wedding. Judit took me.'

'Wow. That's quite an honour. Their weddings are apparently a lot of fun. Look at Béci; he's staring at you all the time.'

Anna didn't turn round. Instead she poured herself some more wine. The voices around her seemed to grow louder. Someone had put music on.

'Have any of you ever heard of a guy called Rambo?'

'He's the actor, isn't he? No, the film,' said Ernő.

'Don't be silly. He's a Roma man in Szabadka.'

'How would we know anyone like that?'

'What about Lakatos Sándor?'

'Never heard of him.'

'Since when have you become best buddies with the tinkers?' said Tibor. 'Didn't one of them just take your passport? Are you sure you should be hanging about with them?'

'I'll hang around with whoever I want. So far the people I've met have been very nice,' said Anna.

'Most of them are work-shy scroungers. They're only interested in hand-outs, then they go to Germany and whereever and beg in the streets. They should get proper jobs.'

'Perhaps nobody will give them a proper job,' Anna suggested.

'They wouldn't take one if you offered it. They don't want to work.' Tibor had raised his voice. 'And that fortune-teller you're suddenly best friends with, you know she's married to a convicted criminal?' he shouted. Anna could hear the agitation in his voice.

'You mean Judit?'

'That's right.'

'She told me her husband was working abroad.'

'Working abroad!' Tibor laughed. 'He's banged up in the Szabadka prison. Though he's probably been begging in the West with the rest of them. I suppose you could call that work. He can put it on his CV.'

'It's harder work that you've ever had to do,' said Anna, feeling herself becoming irritated. 'Nobody would sit out in the streets all day, in all weathers, to be humiliated by passers-by, unless they really had to.'

'I can tell you don't live round here anymore,' said Tibor. 'You wouldn't think that if you did.'

Nóra rolled her eyes and Anna decided not to push the matter. She was upset that Judit had lied to her. And Tibor's words had hurt her so much, it was all she could do not to show it.

'Go and talk to poor Béci,' said Véra.

'I don't want to.'

'Why not?'

'I'm not in the mood.'

'Anna, now you're just being impolite. You can still talk to him, can't you, even if you're not interested in jumping into bed with him?'

'I suppose so,' Anna admitted and emptied her glass. The alcohol swirled pleasantly in her head and her limbs tingled. She could feel herself relaxing; a few words with Béci might not be all that awkward after all. They might even help her forget about her conversation with Tibor.

Béci broke into a broad smile when he saw Anna coming towards him.

'Hi, how are you doing?' asked Anna, raising her glass.

Béci clinked his glass against Anna's. They each took a sip and looked each other in the eye.

'I'm fine, thanks,' Béci said. 'I decided to come home for the weekend. I hear you're staying all month.'

'Is that why you came?' Anna teased him, emboldened by the wine, and regretted it at once. Do not flirt with him, she commanded herself.

'There were other reasons too. But yes, that was one of them.'

'How are your parents?' The question was a diversion tactic, trying to steer the conversation back to banal pleasantries.

Béci noticed and made his own effort to get back to more personal topics. 'They're very well, thanks. Listen, do you want to meet for coffee? Tomorrow, maybe? I'd like to talk things over with you.'

'What things?'

'You and me.'

'There is no "you and me".'

'Okay, you know what, fuck you, Anna,' said Béci. An angry furrow appeared at the corner of his mouth.

'What?'

'I said, fuck you. You're the most selfish woman I've ever met. You don't answer my emails or text messages, even though … even though we had such a good time together.'

Béci was drunker than Anna had thought. Talking to him had been a mistake. Sleeping with him had been an even bigger one. And if there was one thing Anna disliked, it was men that didn't take a hint when they were being dumped.

'In that case you should think yourself lucky that nothing ever came of "you and me". Think how awful it would have been if you'd ended up having to deal with such a selfish woman,' said Anna and polished off yet another glass of wine.

'Looks like you're an old drunk too,' said Béci, his voice dripping with resentment.

'That's right, I'm an AA regular. Fat lot of use it's done me. Give my best wishes to your mother. And take down those teenage posters in your room. They're ridiculous.'

Anna spun round, turning her back to him with such force, she staggered. The alcohol had gone straight to her head, and it felt good. Damn good. She texted Péter and asked him not to come inside but to wait for her at the gate. He replied to say he'd just arrived.

'What's the matter now?' asked Péter, at a loss, as Anna stepped through the gate and into the street.

'Let's go somewhere else.'

'But I wanted to taste the famous wine,' he said, disappointed.

Anna pulled an unopened bottle of Pinot Noir from her bag and handed it to Péter.

'There. Let's go. It's going to start raining soon.'

'How much does the wine cost at this place? And where are we going?'

'It didn't cost anything. Let's go to yours.'

'You didn't pinch it, did you? Anna!'

'Don't tell the police.'

THE NIGHT WAS DARK AND WARM. Dzsenifer couldn't sleep in the cramped shack. Rambo had gone off somewhere with his friends and made Dzsenifer promise to stay put. *You mustn't go anywhere without me*, he'd shouted at her, and she had promised she wouldn't.

She was afraid. The rumble of thunder could be heard in the distance. She was afraid of storms, though she'd never admitted it to anyone – not even her brother, who she missed so much that her stomach hurt. She fetched one of Sándor's dirty T-shirts from the pile in the corner of the room that served as a wardrobe, clenched it tightly in her arms and curled up in bed.

The black night behind the window flashed brightly, as if it were lit up by the strobe lights at the Turbofolk concert she'd seen on television. The boom followed shortly afterwards. The storm was coming closer. Dzsenifer was close to tears. She pulled the T-shirt over her head and felt the sharp smell of sweat in her nose. She'd never been this close to her brother. And never this far away. Water started pattering against the shack window.

Even if she hadn't been wrapped up in bed, her eyes covered with the T-shirt, there was no way she could have prevented what happened next.

She heard someone step into the shack. Had Rambo come back early? But, before she knew it a sock or some other stinking rag was stuffed into her mouth, a sack was pulled over her head and her little hands and feet were tied with a rough length of rope so tightly that any attempt to kick felt like she was cutting herself with a knife. Dzsenifer didn't even have time to cry out. If she'd just been able to shout, someone in the neighbouring shacks might have heard her.

The attacker snatched her into his arms and carried her out. Dzsenifer felt the cool, stormy air and the rain against her bare shins. She sensed a bolt of lightning flash somewhere nearby and heard the boom that almost burst her ears immediately afterwards. At that point she fainted.

She was unconscious as the attacker bundled her into a car and drove away.

ANNA AND PÉTER WALKED through the town to Péter's house. Storm clouds were gathering across the western sky, making it darker still. The metal gates opened with a screech, and they stepped into the pleasant garden at the front. Péter fetched a corkscrew and some glasses from inside and they sat down on the patio. Lightning flashed far across the sky. Anna noticed a child's shovel and sand bucket tumbled to one side of the paving.

'When was the last time you saw your son?' she asked.

'Today. He and my ex came over to collect some clothes.'

Anna tasted the wine. Through her drunkenness she could hear the note of wistful sadness in Péter's voice.

'Have you found any new leads?' she asked, changing the subject.

'Bits and pieces ... This wine's pretty good. I'll have to start buying from them directly. The selection in the supermarkets is pretty lame.'

'Was Lakatos known to the police?' Anna went on, refusing to be distracted.

'Yes. He had a few convictions for petty theft, that sort of thing. All of them took place in and around Szabadka and Palics.'

Anna hesitated before continuing. 'He might have been involved in some kind of people smuggling – maybe as a contact between the smugglers and the refugees. Are you looking into that?'

'There was one conviction for smuggling, but I'm not on that case. Things like that are generally dealt with by the Central Criminal Police and Interpol. Local police only help if they can.'

'Do you know anything about it?'

'The people smuggling? I know it's on the increase – because of the huge number of refugees, of course. Soon there will be more of them here than there are inhabitants in Kanizsa. It's only a matter of time before something explodes.'

'A bomb?'

'It was a figure of speech. People are on edge. Some are on a short fuse.'

'They're no trouble. The refugees, that is. Or are they? They haven't bothered me once since I've been here, if you don't count the annoyance that the world is such a shitty place that people have to flee their homes in fear of their lives.'

'They make a mess. And lots of people are afraid of them, call them ISIS terrorists.'

'Jesus Christ, how stupid can people be?'

'You never know, amongst all those people, there might be a few terrorists.'

'Sure. But isn't terrorism exactly what the others are trying to escape?'

'People take comfort in the fact that the refugees aren't staying here. They're just travelling through on their way into the EU.'

'What crimes were on Lakatos's record?'

'Pickpocketing, shoplifting. One count of assault, but he was only arrested on suspicion. In the end he was cleared of all charges. Interestingly, the assault case was the only connection I could find to Kanizsa.'

'In what way?'

'The guy they eventually convicted was from round here. Lakatos had been with him – the two of them had been out drinking together – but Lakatos didn't touch the victim. Even the victim confirmed that.'

'So who was the Kanizsa man they convicted.'

'Orsós Gyula was his name.'

'Orsós? Not Judit's husband?'

'The very same. He's currently serving a thirteen-month sentence for common assault.'

'So Judit's husband and Sándor knew each other?'

'Seems that way.'

'That means Judit must have known him too. And Dzsenifer. That woman lied to my face.'

'They're like that, the gypsies.'

'Don't you start,' Anna sighed.

'Sorry, I don't really think that. Who's Dzsenifer?'

Anna explained how she'd found the girl and what she told her. The wine had robbed her of her natural caution, made her trusting and open. Besides, Péter had helped her so much, Anna could think of no reason why she shouldn't tell him everything. He listened intently and was about to ask her something when his phone rang. He apologised and stepped inside to answer it.

The storm was coming closer and bringing the rain with it. The night was finally cooling down. Anna watched as swollen raindrops drummed against the roses in the garden. A frog leapt across the lawn.

Péter came back out to the patio and lit a cigarette. His expression was taut.

'Who was it?' asked Anna.

'Nobody. Nothing important.'

Anna didn't want to pry any further, though she could see that Péter's good humour had vanished. He sat down, calmly smoking his cigarette.

'Let's forget about investigations and gypsies and handbag thieves for a moment and concentrate on finishing off this bottle,' he said.

'What will we do then?'

'Then I think I'll investigate you for a change.'

JUNE 12th

'ANNA! Time to get up!' Her mother's voice calling from downstairs almost burst Anna's ears.

She rolled stiffly on to her other side and tried to open her swollen eyes. A throbbing pain was hammering at her head, and in her dry mouth she could still taste the night before. Or rather, it wasn't the night before at all. Anna had only come home a few hours ago.

'It'll soon be time to go to church,' her mother shouted up the stairs. 'Don't you feel well?'

'Hmmm…' Anna mumbled in response and dragged herself out of bed. The room seemed to swirl, and Anna felt weak. She staggered downstairs, her legs still shaky.

'Dear girl, what a sight,' her mother laughed. 'I take it the wine tasting was a success?'

'Hmmm,' said Anna.

'Have a cup of coffee, take a shower and you'll be right as rain.'

'Do I have to come?' Anna asked as though she was still a child.

Her mother replied as she would to a child. 'Yes.'

'But I don't want to see anyone. I can't. I feel dreadful.'

'Nonsense! If you're a hero in the evening, you have to be a hero in the morning, too.'

Anna did as she was told, took some ibuprofen, gulped down a cup of coffee and ate a banana, then went into the shower and stood beneath the cool water long enough that her grotty hangover began to ease.

Returning to the kitchen, she ate the omelette her mother had prepared and felt herself gradually coming back to life.

'Feel better?' her mother asked.

'A little.'

'There, what did I tell you? And try to lay off the cigarettes today. They'll only make you feel worse,' her mother continued to lecture her.

'I don't want any. Ugh, the mere thought.'

Anna watched her mother clear away the breakfast things and wondered about how best to bring up what she'd heard at the wedding. She knew her mother would get upset. But the matter was so important, Anna was prepared to risk it.

Very carefully, she began. 'Mum, there's something I want to talk to you about.'

'What's that?'

'At the gypsy wedding I heard something about Dad's death.'

Her mother's breezy movements tensed, her happy smile froze for a moment. 'Let's talk about it later, once we've come back from Totovo Selo. We'll talk this evening.'

'No, we'll talk now. An old Roma gentleman told me that the man convicted of Dad's murder wasn't the real killer, that somebody else did it. Could there be any truth in that?'

'I don't know and I don't want to know. Your father is dead, that's all that matters to me. And that's the end of it. It's been quite a job taking care of everything without a husband's help and support – leaving as a refugee, living in Finland, that cold, hostile country where neighbours don't even say hello to one another.'

'Did you really hate it in Finland?' Anna was surprised at her own question.

'Yes, I hated it. People told me the long winter months would be the most gruelling, all that darkness and wind and snow and ice. But for me the worst was the summer. I hated the fact that it never got warm at all.'

'It gets warm there too, Mum.'

'A few days in the year there might be something you could call warm. What kind of summer is that? It's nothing at all. I felt cheated, taunted. I hated that apartment and that house. I hated Koivuharju.'

Anna was speechless. She'd never realised that this was how her mother had thought of their life in Finland. In fact it had never crossed her mind. Mum was just Mum. A stoic, a survivor. Dinner was always at the same time each evening; we all had to go to sleep on time; we made sure our homework was done, and Mum had never complained or looked unhappy. As far as Anna was concerned, everything had been fine. She wanted to talk more about it, to find out all about her mother's experiences of Finland, but at the same time she was disappointed that her mother flatly refused to discuss the subject of her father. She always managed to steer the conversation in another direction.

'This is all very interesting, but now you're changing the subject,' she said. 'I asked about Dad.'

'We have to go now or we'll be late,' said her mother. 'Come on, get yourself dressed.'

THE CHURCH SERVICE WAS HELD at the local community centre, in one of the smaller rooms, whose primary function Anna couldn't quite figure out. Kanizsa was predominantly Catholic, and the congregation of the Reformed Church in the town and surrounding area was so small that there was no need to build a separate church.

In the room were gathered a total of nine people, including the priest, Anna and her mother. The service was austere and simple. A few hymns, a prayer, a short sermon – and that was it. No liturgy, no communion, not even a cross on the table that served as an altar. A white tablecloth had at least been draped over the table on which was displayed a vase with yellow and red flowers. Molnár László spoke in a monotonous and almost pompous voice, and Anna couldn't bring herself to listen properly. Instead she stared through the window at the glorious weather outside; the temperature was getting warmer by the day. She watched the blurred blue sky and a flock of pigeons that swooped through the air, from the roof of the community centre and back again. When the priest asked those present to join him in prayer, Anna clasped her hands together and lowered her head but didn't mutter along with the canonical words. She said her own prayer instead.

Heavenly Father, or whoever you are, look after that little Romani girl. Look after Réka, József and their baby, and forgive me for what I did to my own. Let Ákos be happy. Amen.

The congregation sang a final hymn, and, with that, the service was over. Despite the dull throb in her head and the fact that she'd only had a few hours' sleep, Anna felt surprisingly well. Perhaps I could do this more often, she thought – go to church. It wouldn't do me any harm.

László chatted with the members of his small congregation for a while. Anna heard them discussing something about an upcoming charitable event. A clothes collection for the refugees. Food packages for families with children.

Once the priest had done his duties, Anna and her mother set off for his place in Totovo Selo. They had decided to take their own car. So you don't have to drive us home, her mother had told László when he offered them a lift. Anna realised she was still well over the limit and shouldn't get behind the wheel. What the hell, she thought; when in Rome. She was grateful for the powerful air conditioning in her small rented car, which dried the droplets of sweat on her forehead and seemed to wipe away the last of her morning grogginess.

The garden at the vicarage was swarming with stray cats. They scampered into hiding as Anna and her mother walked across the yard. Her mother explained that László had always liked cats and that one of his many callings in life was to feed the strays. The sun was beating down, and the priest's wife, Ágnes, showed the guests to the shade of the covered terrace, where drinks had already been laid out on the table, Anna poured herself a glass of lemonade. Its sharp, citrus tang fizzed in her mouth.

'How has your holiday been going?' asked the priest's wife.

'Very nicely, thank you.'

Anna's mother scoffed. 'Very nicely? Apparently it's nice to spend all your free time working.'

'What have you been working on?' László enquired instantly, and Anna recalled how strange she'd found the man's questions when they'd met outside Békavár.

'I've just been looking into the theft of my handbag, that's all,' said Anna, trying to play it down as much as possible.

'I heard about that,' said Ágnes, aghast. 'The man died. Do we know what happened to him?'

'He drowned. It was an accident,' said Anna. She could sense both László and her mother staring at her pointedly.

'Yes, that's right. How terrible,' said Ágnes.

'Were you at the wine fair when it happened?' asked Anna.

'You went there, didn't you dear?' said Ágnes, and László nodded.

'I was supposed to meet Nagy Béla but I couldn't find him. I arrived too late, and Béla must have left.'

'Did you see the incident?' Anna asked, trying to keep her tone casual.

The priest hesitated for a moment.

'There was some commotion going on as I arrived. That must have been the moment he snatched the bag. I couldn't find Béla anywhere, so I sent him a text message, but he didn't answer and I left straight away. Why do you ask?'

'There are a few details I'd like to clear up, that's all. I'm a slave to my work,' said Anna.

'Anna,' her mother cautioned her.

'That's right, you're a police officer. Just like your father,' said Ágnes and gave Anna an irritating tap on the thigh.

Anna instinctively jerked her leg to one side and noticed her mother's disparaging look. Am I supposed to let myself be groped by complete strangers just so you don't feel embarrassed? Anna thought angrily, but forced herself to give a reluctant smile.

'Come on inside, Mária, and I'll show you the embroidery I've been working on,' said Ágnes, standing up.

'How lovely,' her mother replied. The look she gave Anna was clear: do not ask anything else about this case. Please try and behave properly, this once.

The women went indoors, leaving Anna alone with László.

A scrawny grey cat pattered towards them and started meowing at their feet. It began rubbing its head against the priest's bare ankles. László stood up and fetched it some food. The clatter as László shook food into the bowl attracted the rest of the cats that had been hiding in the garden. They ate greedily, glancing warily at Anna as they did so.

'Your father was a good man,' László said eventually, breaking the awkward silence.

'So it seems. Were you living in the area when he died?'

The priest looked at her intensely. 'Why do you ask?'

'I just wondered. People always ask where you were when Kennedy died, don't they? Or Princess Diana.'

'I was in Kanizsa when I heard the news. I came straight over to your house. Do you remember?'

Again Anna tried to think back to that day. The weeping, the shouting, the silence. She vaguely remembered people coming and going, but she couldn't recall seeing the priest. She shook her head.

'I was told they convicted and executed the wrong man for my father's murder,' said Anna.

'Who told you that?' László's expression tightened and the furrows on his brow deepened.

'I heard some talk about it. Probably just a rumour.'

'Who have you been discussing this with?' he asked. He was clearly agitated and began gripping tufts of his thinning grey hair in rapid, edgy movements.

'Nobody.'

'Good. Don't talk to anyone about it. There's no point spreading rumours like that.'

Anna was taken aback by the priest's reaction; it was at once dismissive and curious, agitated and reserved. Her police officer's instinct was triggered; she wanted to ask this strange man what else he knew about the matter. But just then her mother and the priest's wife came back outside. Anna thought her mother seemed a bit too fulsome in her praise of Ágnes's embroidery.

'Have some more lemonade, Anna,' said Ágnes.

'Thank you. I heard at the church that you donate clothes to the refugees.'

'That's right. We collect the clothes – and money too; we use it to buy water and hygiene products for them,' Ágnes explained.

'How do you get it all to the people that need it?'

'I visit Szabadka once or twice a week. I take everything to the camp,' said László.

'I'd like to help too, if I can. It bugs me when I see all those people wandering around and I don't know what to do.'

'It's just awful,' said her mother. 'Women and small children too.'

'Could I join you?' Anna asked László. 'When are you going there next?'

'In the next few days. But I warn you, it's grim there, truly shocking. I'm not sure whether…'

'Of course Anna can join you if she wants to,' said Ágnes.

'It won't be a fun day out,' said László.

'I don't expect it to be. But it would be nice to help people, seeing as I'm here anyway.'

'Well done, Anna, that's the spirit,' said the priest's wife. 'We should always help those in need. You've been a refugee yourself, you know what it's like.'

Do I? thought Anna. I haven't had to walk thousands of kilometres or cross an ocean in a leaking tin can. I haven't had to cross borders illegally, get myself in debt to smugglers and be entirely at their mercy. I haven't had to live in camps in inhumane conditions. What do I know about any of this? The reception centre where we lived in Munkkisaari was probably heaven compared to the forests outside Szabadka. I've been damn lucky – privileged in fact. I have an old home and a new home, a job and an apartment. I have experienced what it's like to feel different, an outsider, homeless in a way, but I've never thought of myself as a refugee, not even when the local kids taunted me about it at school.

'What are you thinking about, dear?' asked her mother.

Anna snapped back to reality. Everyone was staring at her.

'Nothing really. Just lost in thought.'

'Anna went to the wine tasting at the new vineyard last night. I think she tasted a little too much,' her mother explained.

'Good for you, Anna,' said Ágnes. 'Life isn't worth living if you don't drink some good wine every now and then.'

Anna smiled. The priest's wife seemed nice. Much nicer than her agitated husband.

'Have you ever seen any skinheads in Kanizsa?' she asked.

'They're no problem. Just kids. The difficulties are elsewhere,' said László.

'Where?'

'In people's minds and opinions. The far-right have stoked resentment here, just like they have in Hungary. It's brainwashing, if you ask me.'

'Do we have to talk about this subject again?' Ágnes said, trying to intervene. But the priest was now in full flow.

'The Hungarian government churns out xenophobic propaganda from every media outlet, and there's no way we can avoid it over here. The Serbian authorities scrutinise anyone trying to cross the border, but the media is free to send out whatever crap they like. You know, yesterday I heard that a local policeman robbed some of the refugees. Can you believe that? Even the police are taking advantage of the situation.'

'That's enough talk about all these horrible matters,' Ágnes said, clearly deciding to lay down the law. 'I can't bear listening to it any longer. Anna, tell us about your life in Finland. Do you have a husband over there?'

I thought we were supposed to stop talking about horrible matters, thought Anna. She ignored the question and started telling them about the kind of things that always seemed to interest people: the Finnish weather; the cost of living. When László began asking her about the church in Finland, Anna had to admit she knew very little about it. She hadn't gone to confirmation camp, and since the end-of-term services at school she hadn't even gone to church. I'm a hardened heathen, she thought.

***

As they drove home through the endless fields, Anna started to crave a cigarette. Despite her mother's nagging, she pulled the car over to the verge, stepped out into the heat, lit a cigarette and checked her phone for messages. The wheat fields shimmered in the gentle breeze, carrying the faint smell of ripening grain. A flock of dark birds – starlings, perhaps – flew overhead in a large, dotted swarm. Réka had sent her a message.

I've got some important information. Call when you get home. I'll come straight round.

Anna pulled the smoke deep into her lungs, felt her heart beating intensely from the combined effects of the hangover, the nicotine and the contents of the message. The birds had disappeared, the sky above was cloudless. Below it, the oil rigs that punctuated the skyline looked like nodding dinosaurs as they slowly pumped black gold from deep within the earth. The hypnotic movements of their silhouettes fractured the vast horizon, making the landscape look almost apocalyptic. Here the sky is never so bright that it hurts your eyes, thought Anna. Or am I the only one with a hazy gauze hanging in front of my eyes? Am I missing something important? Is there something I can't see? She thought of Judit's premonition. And Péter.

'I RUMMAGED THROUGH some old newspaper articles, like I promised,' Réka said. 'Well, I didn't really rummage at all. All I did was search the name Lakatos Sándor, and bingo – it came up straight away.'

Réka had come round as soon as Anna and her mother had returned to Kanizsa. They were sitting on Anna's unmade bed, the door locked, whispering like schoolgirls.

'Tell me,' said Anna impatiently.

'The guy that was convicted for your father's murder was called Lakatos.'

'You've got to be kidding,' Anna said in Finnish.

A whirl of thoughts spun in Anna's mind, catching at the various threads that had hung loose ever since her arrival in Serbia and drawing them into a great ball of wool, so tangled, she couldn't find a single end, let alone start unravelling it. What was this all about? Anna felt as though she no longer understood anything at all. Powerlessness, confusion and fatigue pressed down on her shoulders, blurring her vision.

'Of course, it's a fairly common surname, but still … Remember, I did wonder whether the theft had something to do with you,' said Réka.

'At the wedding there was an old man who said the wrong man was convicted of my father's murder.'

'What? Surely not! Wait a minute, you mean this Lakatos wasn't the real killer?'

'Right. And now another Lakatos has stolen my bag – and ended up dead. It's quite a coincidence. But I can't begin to fathom how the two cases can be linked. Besides, what I heard about my father's death was surely nothing but hearsay. I tried to bring it up with my mother this morning, but she wouldn't say anything. Surely she would have told me if there was anything suspicious about the original conviction, wouldn't she?'

Réka thought about this.

'I don't know,' she answered eventually. 'I really don't. I guess she would have said something. Has she ever talked about what happened to your father?'

'No. Never.'

'You're going to have to ask her again.'

'I know.'

'And you should ask Kovács Gábor too. After all, he used to work with your father and he probably knows a lot about what went on.'

'But I've got to find out who killed Sándor, too. I haven't got much time left for that either.'

'Maybe it's the same person,' said Réka.

'If it is, Sándor's killer must be pretty old by now.'

'Didn't the gypsy girl say that?'

Anna looked up at the primitive investigation notes she'd taped to the wall, at the grey-haired man she'd drawn in the middle without eyes or a mouth, and a terrifying scenario began to take shape in her mind.

Dzsenifer had indeed said the man was old, but it hadn't occurred to Anna that he could be so elderly. Could he be her father's age? Would she have to tape a photograph of her father to the wall too? The thought wrenched at her stomach. There wasn't time for all this. She felt almost like giving up. The case was too messy, so twisted and knotted that she would never have enough resources to unravel it. The worst of it was that she could no longer see the case laid out in front of her. Instead she felt it inside her, heavy as a steel ball.

'There's something else too,' said Réka.

Anna wondered whether she even wanted to hear it.

'The fisherman, Nagy Béla, was somehow involved in the case of a boat-load of refugees drowning in the Tisza.'

'No!' Anna shouted.

'The charges against him were eventually dropped. I don't know exactly what happened, but I got the impression Béla was involved with the smuggling going on round here.'

'It's hard to imagine Béla having anything to do with it,' said Anna, 'but it's true that most people smugglers have to know the local area like the back of their hand. They're nearly always truck drivers, taxi drivers, fishermen.'

'We know that Lakatos was involved in smuggling the refugees. Could Béla have something to do with it too?'

'I suppose I'll have to ask him directly,' Anna sighed.

'How can you ask him something like that? What if ... what if he's the killer?'

'I am a police officer, remember. I know how to ask people questions. And I know how to take care of myself. Besides, I really don't believe Béla is the killer. He wouldn't have taken me out on the river if he was.'

'Still, be careful. I'll pull everything I can that was written about your father's case,' said Réka.

'This is beginning to seem impossible. I'm tired,' said Anna.

'Can you ask that lover-boy of yours to dig out the old case files about your father's death?'

'He's not my lover-boy.'

'Well, what is he then?' Réka scoffed.

'Nothing. I'm going to have to give this a lot of thought,' replied Anna, swiftly changing the subject.

'Do that. But I'm convinced that two dead men, both called Lakatos, can't be a coincidence. I knew the handbag theft had something to do with you.' Réka was almost triumphant.

Once Réka had gone, Anna remained in her room for a long time, deep in thought. She stared at the papers taped to the wall so hard that they began to look as hazy as her thoughts. Threads dangled here and there, but if she was ever going to make sense of this she needed to know which of them she should pull at, and in what order.

She stood up, quietly went downstairs and pulled the old photograph album from the lower shelf in the bookcase. Its thick plastic sleeves were filled with yellowed, out-of-focus photographs from a time when the Fekete family was still intact. One of the photographs was of her father laughing – a close-up, taken from below. Anna had been told she had taken the photograph herself the first time she'd been allowed to use the camera. She carefully slipped the photograph from its sleeve and went back to her room. She attached the photograph to the wall, next to the faceless drawing of the grey-haired man.

It now looked as though her father was laughing at her makeshift investigation. Not belittling, not mocking, but supporting her, encouraging her. Anna could almost hear her father talking to her.

'Point up here and look carefully. Good. What a clever girl.'

AS SHE PICKED UP HER PACE and lengthened her stride, Anna felt a sharp twinge in her lungs and she knew it was because of all the smoking and drinking she'd been doing in recent days. Péter had called her and said he wouldn't be able to join Anna for a run because his son, Sámuel, was spending the night at his house. Anna was disappointed. To her irritation she'd even felt something approaching jealousy.

Before setting out she'd tried to talk to her mother about what she'd heard and what Réka had found out, but all her mother had said was that people had said various things at the time but it had all happened a long time ago and she didn't believe any of the rumours. Her father had been shot and died, and that was that. Nobody and nothing could change that fact any more.

But Anna had pushed the matter: What if the real killer is walking free, alive, right here among us? she had asked. That would be almost unbearable. It would be a stain on her father's name. He was a man who always wanted to do the right thing, to be honest, to uphold the law, unlike so many of his colleagues. At that point her mother had stopped to think, and Anna thought she might finally have pulled the right thread, but then her mother had simply said it had all happened far too long ago. And that Anna must not under any circumstances start raking it up again.

Now, as she ran, Anna tried once again to remember the day her father had died, but all she could recall were vague half-images. Her mother wailing on the rug in the hallway. Áron trying but failing to lift her up and carry her to the sofa. Ákos … where had Ákos been? Anna couldn't place him that day. Maybe her brother had been off somewhere with his friends, drinking. Did she dare ask her mother about it yet again? She was already beside herself from Anna's questions. Perhaps she thought Anna didn't realise how much talking about her father's death opened up old wounds; wounds that might never heal properly. But Anna had noticed the effect her questions had. Her mother had tried to remain calm, but the slight tensing of her shoulders, the way her face seemed to freeze, wax-like and expressionless, the few deep breaths, had all revealed how distressing she found the subject. Anna had even heard her mother go out to the patio for a cigarette once she had gone back to her room. Her mother – a woman who never smoked. No, there was no point in trying to bring this up again.

She'd been running for almost an hour, trying to make sense of her muddled thoughts. With each step she began plotting a plan of action. First, talk to Kovács Gábor and all her father's other old friends – Nagy Béla, Remete Mihály and Molnár László – about her father's death. Find out who had testified at the trial. She'd have to talk to Judit too. Why had the woman lied about her husband? And how was Judit's husband linked to Lakatos Sándor?

What else could she do? As Réka had suggested, she could ask Péter to get hold of the old case files. It wouldn't be easy because she didn't want to get Péter into trouble. Then there was the people smuggling. Anna suddenly realised she was mixed up in a case more complicated than she could ever have imagined.

Once she reached Békavár she turned back towards the town. She was jogging slowly downhill, lost in thought, not paying particular attention to the car behind her. It had appeared in the yard outside Békavár and had driven along the breakwater to the intersection of the road and the pathway as soon as Anna had run past. The car had waited a while on the breakwater, as if surveying its surroundings. There was nobody else out and about.

Anna only noticed the car when its motor roared and it began accelerating. The noise startled her; she looked behind her, stumbled on a crack in the pavement and hit her knee so hard that she cried out in pain. She saw the car hurtling towards her and managed to roll out of the way just in time. The car continued on its way, its wheels screeching, and disappeared as it headed into the town.

Anna lay on the ground gasping for breath. Her heart was

pounding so hard that it felt as though it might burst out of her chest. A thick trail of blood was trickling from her knee, but the rush of adrenaline from the fright smothered the pain. She hadn't had time to see what kind of car it was. She couldn't even say what colour it was, because as it approached her it had looked like nothing but two enormous floodlights, a monster's glaring eyes. A few more centimetres, millimetres, even, and the monster would have crushed her.

⁂

All night Anna's thoughts kept returning to the car, so that she couldn't get to sleep. Was it a black car? What size was it? But all she could see were the dazzling lights heading straight towards her, and again she felt the fear and her heart racing. Had someone tried to kill her? Or was the purpose simply to frighten her? A sudden encounter with a speeding car didn't seem like an accident. Nobody would drive that recklessly unless it was intentional.

Maybe it was just kids playing around, she tried to tell herself. A group of drunken boys would be sitting somewhere, laughing at the terrified look on her face. After a few drinks this silly, dangerous game probably seemed like a hilarious prank. That must be it, thought Anna though she had barely convinced herself. Still, she decided not to tell anyone about what had happened; she didn't want to worry her mother or her friends.

Just as Anna was finally about to fall asleep, her phone rang.

It was Rambo.

Dzsenifer had disappeared into thin air, and nobody knew where she was.

JUNE 13th

'WHY DID YOU LIE to me?'

Anna and Judit were walking through the sweltering town towards the old cemetery. The heat was already radiating from the asphalt and the whitewashed walls of the houses, making the air humid and uncomfortable. Judit didn't feign surprise or pretend she didn't understand.

'I was ashamed,' she said. 'Because you're with the police, and everything else.'

'Everything else?'

'You live abroad, you're sophisticated, smart, rich – all kinds of things I can barely dream about. The fact that you came to the house and talked to me, treated me like a human being. It was somehow so … I just didn't want to spoil it.'

Anna didn't know what to say. She smiled cautiously at Judit.

'I understand the bit about the police,' she said eventually. 'It can't be easy to tell a police officer that your husband is a convicted criminal.'

'Yes, though I must admit those other things felt even more overwhelming. You know, I rarely ever get to feel anything other than worthless. There aren't many people in this town who are openly racist, but sometimes it feels as though silent contempt hurts far more than the shouting and name-calling. Sometimes I wonder whether I exist at all, whether I'm nothing more than an unpleasant smell in the air.'

'It must be difficult,' said Anna, though she knew it sounded trite. She wanted to change the subject.

'Your husband knew Lakatos Sándor. Did you know him too? Are you somehow involved in everything that's been going on here?'

Judit didn't answer straight away. They crossed the railway tracks and sat down for a moment in the shade of the cemetery walls. Judit had a bottle of water in her bag and offered Anna a sip.

'It's all so complicated. I was frightened. I still am.'

'Of what?' asked Anna.

'I've tried to ask the cards, but they won't tell me anything.'

Anna felt like telling the woman to forget her stupid cards and start talking. Forget the *tiszavirág* and the worlds we can't see, she wanted to say, and tell me in your own words what you know about the reality right here before our eyes. But she didn't want to pressure her. Judit wasn't the kind of person who would open up if Anna grilled her.

The stone wall felt cool against Anna's back. She pressed her head against its rough surface and closed her eyes. I have all the time in the world she told herself. I mustn't rush anything just because I'll soon have to leave. Everything will resolve itself. All of a sudden everything will work out; the mists will clear, the sky will turn bright and the truth will be revealed, and I will be free of this burden. I have to forget about time, to stop running against it. An inexplicable calm descended around her and for the first time in weeks she breathed freely. It only lasted for a moment.

'Something happened the night you turned up at my window,' said Judit. 'Dzsenifer was at our house.'

'I guessed as much,' said Anna.

'The girl was petrified. I hid her in the kitchen cupboard and told her to be quiet. Then you appeared in the street shouting. Once you'd left I tried to ask the girl what she'd done, but she wouldn't tell me. Then she dashed out of the house, and I haven't seen her since.'

'How do you know each other? What's the connection between your husband, Sándor and Dzsenifer?'

'It was Sándor that beat up that man. My husband took the blame for it, and now he's doing time.'

'Why?'

'Because Sándor had a lot of good business deals coming up. He said he'd give us half the money if my husband did the time so he could continue working. My husband was unemployed. He was planning to go to the West to beg – to Germany or Belgium. So we all thought this might be the best solution. Sándor could continue with whatever it was he was up to; my husband would take the rap for the assault – the sentence was only just over a year long; we'd get the money and we'd be able to visit him in prison. If he'd gone abroad, we wouldn't have seen him for at least six months. Who knows, he might even have stayed there.'

The gate to the cemetery clanged open and shut, and Anna watched an old woman move slowly across the railway tracks, her visit to a loved one's grave now over. Anna wiped her brow.

'Do you know anything about what happened to my father?'

'No. Why would I know about him?'

Anna told Judit everything she'd heard. The woman listened intently, occasionally nodding her head. Again Anna had the distinct, unnerving sensation that Judit was reading her thoughts.

'That's right, now I remember,' said Judit when Anna had finished the story. 'Sándor once mentioned that one of his relatives had been executed for a murder he didn't commit.'

'Did he ever talk about who the real killer might have been?'

'No, at least not to me.'

'Is there any way you could find out the names of the witnesses who testified that the accused couldn't have killed my father?'

'I don't see why not. I'm happy to ask around for you,' said Judit.

'And now Sándor is dead too. After stealing my handbag.'

'Nothing happens by chance,' said Judit, staring into the distance.

'I'm terribly worried about Dzsenifer.' Anna paused. 'She's disappeared again.'

'I swear to you she's not at my place this time. I lied before because I thought I was protecting her. It was a stupid thing to do.'

'I don't have time to do everything. Could you ask around about Dzsenifer too? Try to find out where she's hiding? I'm sure that girl saw her brother being killed. I'm worried she might be in danger.'

'What should I do if I find her?'

'Send her as far away as possible, somewhere she'll be safe. And don't tell anyone where she's gone, not even me. But do let me know she's safe and sound.'

'Poor child. She has nobody now. When we find her, and I want to believe we will find her, I'm going to take her in and she can live with us.'

Judit's words moved Anna. She cursed herself for letting her stay with Rambo; for not taking the girl with her. It was an incredibly stupid mistake. If something happened to her, Anna would never forgive herself.

'That would be wonderful. Could you really do that?'

'I'm sure it wouldn't be a problem.'

'We will find her. I want to believe it too.'

'There's something else I saw, too,' said Judit.

'In the cards?'

'No, in our street, the night when you turned up. It was after you'd gone.'

'What was it?'

'A man walked past our house shortly after you had left. I went out to the yard for a cigarette and tried to calm the dog down. That's when I heard the footsteps. I could swear he stopped just outside our gate and stood there for a moment before continuing on his way. It was terrifying. I was frightened to death.'

'Did you get a look at him?'

'Only from behind, and only a glimpse. I didn't dare move until the footsteps were further away. He was a big man, tall. Later I thought it might just have been a passer-by, but what if it was the …? Good God!'

'Dzsenifer told me the man who strangled Sándor was tall. Would you recognise the man if you saw him again?'

'I don't know. There was nothing remarkable about him. He was just a normal, everyday man.'

'What about the dog? Didn't it run up to the gate and start barking?'

'No. That's the funny thing. But it heard the footsteps too. Its ears pricked and it looked towards the gate but didn't make a sound. Perhaps it's because I was stroking it at the time. Or maybe…'

'Or maybe what?'

'It might not have been a living person.'

'Nonsense, Judit!'

'I've seen dead people before. There wouldn't be anything out of the ordinary about it at all.'

'Listen, you either saw the murderer, who was looking for Sándor, or you saw a neighbour on his way home. I don't want to hear any more about dead people or cards or anything else like that. My head is already spinning from everything that's been going on without all this supernatural hocus-pocus. Agreed?'

'Very well,' said Judit.

'Let's lay these flowers, shall we? And when you hear anything, let me know immediately. If anyone can testify that Lakatos didn't kill my father, I must find out who they are.'

'I REMEMBER THAT DAY WELL,' Nagy Béla sighed. 'Far too well. I heard the news the next morning. Somebody telephoned to say Fekete István was dead. Who was it? It was Mihály. That's right, Remete Mihály. Do you know him?'

Anna nodded.

'My wife and I drove straight over to your house. We were worried about your mother. And about you children, too, of course. My wife packed some food, as she imagined your mother would be in no fit state to cook for you. You women are like that – you think of these things.'

Anna gave a cheerless smile. 'What happened to my father?'

'How much do you know about it already?'

'All I know is that he was shot while working on an investigation, that the killer was caught, tried, found guilty, and eventually executed. Nobody wanted to tell me any details back then because I was so young. As I grew up I didn't want to ask.'

'But now you want to know,' Béla muttered to himself. 'It's perfectly understandable, of course. At some point we all want to know our family history.'

Anna sipped the *pálinka* that the fisherman had poured for them both. It burned her throat so much that Anna had to stop herself wincing.

'Your father was investigating a case involving the mafia. He'd found out something important about what they were up to. The people he was dealing with were involved in international drug and weapons trafficking. They'd amassed a substantial sum of money from the sale of drugs, and the money was due to be smuggled out of the country and into the West. He'd gone off by himself that evening. That's the bit I never understood. Your father was a risk taker, but he wasn't stupid. Why did he go out to that old farm by himself? He must have assumed there wouldn't be anyone there.

But criminals like that never leave anything unguarded. The place was full of weapons, assault rifles, pistols – you name it. There was enough to equip a small army.'

'What about the money?'

'I don't think they ever found the money. But I'm not sure about that. You'll have to ask Gábor. He probably knows all about it.'

'I would have asked him, but he didn't answer my call.'

'He was planning on going shopping in Szeged today. I spoke to him on the phone last night about the tailback at the border crossing. You can spend hours queuing, apparently.'

'Dad would never have gone anywhere by himself,' said Anna quietly.

'That's the strange thing. Anyway, the mafia had a guy on guard, a local gypsy, and he shot your father.'

'How did the police catch up with him?'

'They arrested him at his home the very next day. The murder weapon was found in his garden, exactly where he'd hidden it.'

'If he was a professional criminal, that was a pretty amateurish mistake,' said Anna.

'I don't know anything about that. But it's a good job they caught the bastard.'

'Who was he?'

'Some man living over in Velebit.'

'I heard a rumour that he might not have been the man that killed my father.'

The fisherman looked at Anna long and hard with his bright-blue eyes, then lit a cigarette and offered one to Anna.

'You shouldn't believe everything you hear round here,' he said and poured them both another glass of *pálinka*.

'Still, I want to find out whether there's any truth in it.'

'I can't imagine there is. And after all these years it's pointless trying to find out.'

'The statute of limitations doesn't apply to murder. The case will never grow old,' said Anna defiantly.

'No, but you will. You need to let things go and live your life – and I hope it's a longer one than your father had.'

Anna took a sip of *pálinka* and drew on her cigarette before asking her next question.

'Do you know anything about the smuggling of refugees along the river?'

Nagy Béla scowled at Anna, clearly displeased at the change of subject.

'No. Why would I?'

'You told me yourself you're on the river every day and that you notice everything that goes on there.'

'No one's being "smuggled" or "trafficked". People just use the river to cross the border. It's much easier than by road, as long as they don't end up in Ásotthalom.'

'Why is that?'

'The mayor there is crazy, a real neo-Nazi. He doesn't like refugees. Not that many people round here like them either.'

'It seems the man who stole my handbag was somehow involved in smuggling refugees along the river,' said Anna.

The fisherman was silent for a moment and lowered his blue eyes. He seems agitated, thought Anna. He's lying or hiding something.

'Maybe,' he said eventually. 'But I don't know anything about stuff like that. And now I have to be getting out to the river. If you'd like some more *pálinka*, ask my wife to come and join you.'

'No, thank you,' Anna replied.

Together they walked out to the gate. The elderly fisherman looked worried, almost angry, but still he hugged Anna as they said goodbye. As he did so, Anna noticed a grey hair on his shoulder, and something flashed into her mind.

'I should never have shown you where the body was found,' said Béla as he opened the latch on the gate. 'And I regret showing you that photograph, too. You shouldn't dig into this case anymore.'

Anna couldn't decide whether this was a warning or a threat.

ANNA WALKED ALONG the sunny side of Fő utca. She wanted to soak up every last ray of sunshine before returning to the unpredictable summer weather in northern Finland.

She had to travel to Belgrade to get a new passport before it was too late, but the thought of making the long trip by herself felt dismal. Should I ask Réka to join me? she wondered. Her entire holiday was ruined. I haven't been able to spend quality time with anyone – not Réka, my mother or Ákos. Then there was Péter. Anna reluctantly admitted to herself that she was particularly keen to spend more time with Péter. On the spur of the moment she texted him. *Any chance of joining me for a little road trip the day after tomorrow?* The response came immediately. *I'll switch my day off with Milo. He owes me a favour. Where are we going?*

Anna smiled. Something warm and pleasant bubbled inside her. She told Péter what it was about and he replied straightaway: *Sounds great!*

Putting her phone away, Anna noticed a familiar figure standing at the edge of the road, loading up his car. The man was filling his car boot with bottles of water wrapped in plastic; they were piled up on the pavement next to black bin liners filled with clothes.

'Hi,' Anna shouted. 'Are you taking that lot to the camp right now?'

Molnár László stretched his back and wiped the sweat from his forehead. He didn't look pleased to see her.

'I could join you if you like,' said Anna as she approached.

'I'm sorry, I'd love to take you with me, but I don't think there's room in the car.'

Anna peered inside the old Renault and saw that the passenger seat was empty. The back seat was filled with bulging plastic bags.

'Why don't you want me to come along? It seems like you don't want my help.'

'Well, it's great that you want to help but...'

'But what?'

'It's nothing. Come on. We can stuff those bags of clothes in at your feet and hopefully you'll have enough room. I just thought it might be too cramped in the car and you wouldn't be comfortable. The air conditioning doesn't work properly either, I'm afraid.'

'Great. Thank you,' said Anna. 'The cramped car and the heat don't bother me.'

At first glance, the abandoned brick factory on the outskirts of Szabadka didn't look like a refugee camp at all. It was just a large, bleak, barren warehouse surrounded by grass scorched in the heat. From a distance the place looked deserted, but as Anna and the priest drove closer, the more clearly they saw the human presence. Litter was strewn across the forecourt. Here and there people were sitting hunched against the decaying walls. Anna guessed there would be far more people inside the building, sheltering from the sunshine during the day and the thunderstorms at night.

'There are more refugees in the woods over there,' László said, pointing to the tangle of trees and bushes behind the brick factory. 'They're the lucky ones: they've got tents.'

When the priest parked the car in the factory forecourt, people began streaming out of the building's doorless openings. Some greeted the priest like an old friend, some kept their distance and stood further off. Two small children ran on to the forecourt, soon followed by an exhausted-looking woman in tattered clothes, a scarf tied tightly round her head.

With a sense of routine the priest began handing out bottles of water. A quiet queue of thirsty people began forming in front of the car.

'Start sorting out the clothes,' the priest said to Anna. 'Put men's, women's and children's clothes in their own piles over there by the wall. Then people can fetch what they need.'

Anna got to work. She lifted the bags out of the car and began emptying them. The children came up to her and watched as she worked. Anna fetched them water bottles. She saw a flicker of a smile on the face of a woman standing in a nearby doorway.

Shorts, T-shirts, skirts, trousers, shoes. Anna looked at the feet of the men standing in the water queue. Many of them had no shoes at all; their feet were swollen and covered in sores. They should get a doctor out here, she thought.

In one of the bags she found a pretty, dark-blue skirt embroidered with golden thread. Anna showed it to the woman standing in the doorway, watching her children. The woman took a cautious step towards her, then backed off again.

'Come,' said Anna. 'This might fit you.'

One of the older children said something to their mother in what sounded like Arabic. The woman smiled and ventured closer to Anna. She warily picked up the skirt and stood looking in turn at the skirt and then at Anna.

'*Beautiful*,' said Anna in English.

'*Yes*,' the woman replied. '*Thank you*.'

Then the woman said something to her children and they all disappeared back inside the warehouse.

'I'd like to take a look inside,' Anna shouted to the priest, but then noticed that he had disappeared. The water bottles had all been taken from the boot of the car and the queue of people had dispersed too.

Anna looked around, but the priest was nowhere to be seen. She left the piles of clothes and stepped inside the warehouse.

Inside the hangar-like warehouse the air was cool and almost bearable. Steel girders jutted up from the concrete floor as though the building had been left unfinished. Perhaps the place had been empty for so long that it had begun to return to its constituent parts, to disintegrate layer by layer.

People lay on the floor among piles of junk and rubbish. Anna felt the sceptical gaze of their dark eyes on her body. The woman to whom Anna had given the skirt was watching from a corner. She pointed towards a ladder leading to a hatch into the upper floor of the building.

Anna climbed up the ladder. Peering through the hatch, she saw the priest talking to three young men. The men all had what looked like brand new smartphones, which they were tapping and swiping as the priest whispered something to them. Numbers. One of the men repeated what the priest had told him. And, as he did so Anna quickly took out her own phone, and typed the numbers into the memory. Then she quietly climbed down the ladder and went back outside to the piles of clothes. They had all disappeared. Two young men were standing in their place.

'*Where are you from?*' she asked the boys in English. They looked barely out of school.

'*Iraq*,' said one of them. His chin was covered in a thin, downy beard. One of his front teeth was missing. He was wearing a baseball cap bearing the logo of a multinational company.

'*Have you seen this man?*'

Anna showed them a photograph of Lakatos Sándor, but the boys shook their dark heads and explained in broken English that they'd only arrived yesterday. The boy with the cap pointed to a man sitting by the wall.

'*He might know. He's been here longer.*'

Anna approached the man and showed him the photograph. The man nodded and said something in Arabic. Anna asked the boys to interpret for her and discovered that Lakatos Sándor, who people at the camp knew only as Fox, had promised to arrange transport into Hungary for the man and a few of his relatives. He'd taken the man's money and disappeared. The car he'd promised never turned up. Now the man was out of money. Now he planned on walking into Hungary but said he was tired. He showed Anna his swollen calf. You should rest a while, she told him. Anna tried to give the man all the cash she had, just short of four thousand dinars, but he pushed her hand away.

'*No, no*,' he said, ashamed.

'*Please, it isn't much*,' Anna implored, because it truly wasn't a huge sum of money.

Eventually the man wiped his eyes, swallowed his tears and agreed to take the money.

The priest appeared, shook hands with the men standing around Anna and said he would pray for them.

'Are you ready? We should get going,' he said to Anna.

'What were you doing upstairs a moment ago?' Anna asked as they got into the car.

'I was talking to a couple of new arrivals and wished them God's blessing. What about you? What were you talking to those boys about?'

'I was asking them about my handbag thief. Apparently he'd been here, organising transportation for the refugees and looking for new customers.'

'Really? I can't say it surprises me,' said the priest as he steered the car out of the forecourt. 'Lots of people are making a quick buck at the expense of these refugees.'

'His name was Lakatos. Have you ever come across that name before?'

'It's a common gypsy surname. I can't think of anyone in particular, though.'

'No one at all?'

László looked at Anna for so long that Anna was worried they might end up in a ditch.

For the rest of the journey home he didn't say another word. Why do I get the impression that all my father's grey-haired old friends seem to know something? Or that they sense something, at least? Why won't they open up? Is it because I'm not asking the right questions? Or am I just imagining this?

The grass verge was dotted with blood-red poppy flowers. They made Anna think of Dzsenifer and her skirt. Uneasy thoughts and worries about the girl's well-being weighed Anna down. She felt as though there was something she had missed. Something simple yet crucially important, something that would unravel this mess in an instant.

As they drove back towards the town, they saw groups of refugees trudging along the road. There were more than there had been a week ago, far more. Anna winced as she thought of the cows that wandered the fields around Velebit. At least they had shelter every night.

WAS THIS PERHAPS ONE OF THE BEST evenings of my life? wondered Anna as she went to bed later that night. She had forgotten all about numbers, about refugees and about unsolved murders. After dinner the whole family had sat on the patio chatting and drinking wine. They'd talked about everything under the sun: good books; the local Kanizsa gossip; the Finnish lakes; Kata's new pole-dancing hobby; the pig at her mother's friend's house that dug up onion bulbs and demanded to be scratched whenever someone walked into the yard. Nobody brought up difficult, painful subjects. Not because they deliberately wanted to avoid them but because they simply didn't occur to anyone on that gentle, warm summer's evening. Ákos drank tea. Kata's children had been put to bed in Áron's old room. They'd been a little shy at first, sneaking glances at Anna, cautious but curious. But with a little encouragement from Ákos and Kata they soon relaxed and started chattering and giggling. Their funny comments and questions seemed to make the evening even more pleasant. Children can actually be quite wonderful, thought Anna, and couldn't remember the last time she'd felt so at ease.

But another reality awaited her in her bedroom. The night beyond her window was pitch black, and an unfamiliar star had risen into the sky. Anna stared at the fragments of the investigation she'd taped to the wall. Her laughing father looked at her from beside the faceless, grey-haired man. Anna had taken a thick felt pen, written the series of numbers she'd heard from the priest on a piece of paper and attached it to the wall, but now she couldn't concentrate properly. The wine and tiredness kept pressing her eyelids shut and she didn't want to let go of the elated emotions that the dinner she'd shared with her family had given her. But she knew she had to carry on. She would not give up. She went to the bathroom and took a quick, cold shower, which invigorated her just enough for her to get back to work for a while.

She tried to make sense of the numbers by imagining dots and spaces between them. After weighing up all the possibilities she could think of, she was almost certain that the beginning of the series represented a date and a time. 61423. Could that be tomorrow evening at eleven?

She let the internet make sense of the rest of the numbers. The results were startling, but fitted the picture perfectly. Coordinates. The GPS on her telephone placed a red dot only a few kilometres from her house – on the banks of the Tisza between Kanizsa and the small village of Martonos.

JUNE 14th

ANNA MET KOVÁCS GÁBOR in a café on Fő utca. Gábor was already sitting on the terrace drinking his coffee when Anna arrived. She apologised for being late and allowed the policeman to order her a cappuccino and a mineral water. Sitting at the next table were four dark-haired young men having an animated conversation in Arabic and fiddling with their smartphones. Anna noted their brand-new estate car and fashionable T-shirts. They will be the talk of the town, she thought.

Anna and Gábor exchanged the compulsory pleasantries and talked about the weather and the flowering of the Tisza, which everyone in town was awaiting impatiently. Gábor told her that people came from abroad to marvel at the swarms of insects. 'Though it looks like this year the audience will consist mostly of Syrians and that lot,' he said and nodded towards the group of young men. 'That's if they have any interest in such things.'

To her relief, Anna noted that there was no hint of disgust or scorn in his voice. Anna's first impression of a stiff and somewhat arrogant man, old-fashioned and with unflinching opinions, was beginning to change. Gábor planned on taking his boat out on the Tisza as soon as word came that the flowering had started.

'It's so beautiful out there, it's quite moving,' he said, almost dreamily. 'But there was something important you wanted to talk about,' he continued.

'Yes. I've been thinking a lot about my father's death. It's really bugging me. I'd like you to tell me everything there is to know about it.'

'Why is it suddenly bugging you now?' asked Gábor, a little confused.

Anna wondered whether to mention the rumours she'd heard; she decided against it.

'It probably has something to do with finding my roots. At some point we all want to know more about our family history, don't we?' said Anna.

'That's true enough. My wife and I have started looking into our own family history. We've been reconstructing our family trees for years, and you wouldn't believe the interesting things that have come up. For instance, my wife's great-grandfather on her mother's side was a general in the Austro-Hungarian army, and nobody knew anything about it. We went to Vienna to look through the old archives and found—'

'Did you investigate my father's death?' Anna interrupted him. She had no interest in the Kovács family's aristocratic ancestors and she didn't want to waste her time talking about them.

Gábor gave a sad, wistful smile. 'No. I wanted to, but I was recused because I was far too close to your father. Besides, I was in shock. To tell the truth I was utterly devastated. Beside myself.'

'I heard there was a substantial sum of money found at the place where he was shot. What happened to that money?'

Gábor thought back for a moment. 'The state confiscated it. It belonged to the mafia.'

'So you were both looking into the case?'

'Yes; or rather we were both involved in the larger investigation. It was a big case.'

'What happened then?'

'A few mid-level and grassroots operatives were eventually sentenced. The big fish got away. Typically.'

'Who shot my father?'

'One of those gypsy rats. Lakatos János was his name. He'd got himself mixed up with the mafia crowd. He was a small-time crook – already had a few convictions for theft. One of the police's old acquaintances, you might say. It took us all a bit by surprise that small fry like him was involved in such a high-profile case. You don't normally see the gypsies working together with the white mafia.'

'What were you doing that evening?'

'I was afraid you might ask that, Anna. It's plagued me for years.' Gábor looked pained. He squeezed the napkin in his hand. Anna stared at the liver spots on his weather-beaten hands and waited for him to continue.

'I was supposed to be with him that evening.'

'Really? What happened?'

'I didn't know what he was planning. He hadn't told anyone.'

Anna could see the man was trying in vain to hold back his emotions. A large tear rolled down his wrinkled cheek; he wiped it away immediately.

'I'm sorry,' said Gábor unable to prevent a sob.

The young men at the next table turned to look.

'I … I didn't know he'd gone out there. If only I'd … Damn it. I was at the station, writing up case reports in my office. It was a quiet night and I had a backlog of paperwork to get done. Your father disappeared while I was sitting there and I didn't notice a thing.'

Gábor blew his nose and dried his eyes. He drew a series of deep breaths to steady himself, took a gulp of coffee and continued.

'Back then the mafia wielded a lot of power round here, and, like I said, we were investigating one branch of their operations – in this case, dodgy building work. At some point István turned a bit mysterious. He wouldn't tell me everything he knew or suspected. At first I didn't think anything of it – he wasn't the most talkative guy to start with and he liked to investigate things by himself. But later on, after he'd died, I began to wonder what was really going on. I heard rumours but I didn't want to believe them. I still don't want to believe them.'

'Such as what?' Anna was getting restless. She could sense that she would soon hear something vitally important.

'I probably shouldn't talk about it. They were just rumours. There was never any evidence.'

'Tell me. I want to hear everything, even rumours.'

'Very well. There was a rumour at the time that someone close to him – close to us, that is – was involved with the mafia. That would explain why he didn't tell me what he was doing.'

'Was the chief of police working here back then?' Anna asked immediately.

A pained expression flashed across Gábor's face.

'Yes, although he wasn't the chief back then. But I simply can't believe … No, Anna. Now you're letting your imagination get the better of you. He was a low-level traffic cop at that time.'

'Where is the farm where this happened? I want to see it,' said Anna.

'Are you sure that's wise?'

'No, but I want to see the place all the same.'

'Do you want me to come with you?'

'No, but thank you for the offer. Does anyone live there nowadays?'

'Not to my knowledge. I think it's been empty ever since…' Gábor again tried to hold back his tears and stared far into the distance. 'If only István had told me what he was up to.'

'You might have been shot too if you'd been there.'

'Or I might have been able to save his life. Can you imagine what it's been like, having to live with that thought? And to see you here now, a poor fatherless girl?'

'How do I get to the farm?'

Gábor sighed. 'Anna, are you absolutely sure you want to do this? If you ask me, you're just torturing yourself.'

'I'm not sure of anything any longer. Although I do know that I want to understand my past…'

Gábor explained how to get to the farmstead. Anna was confident she would find it, even though there was no marked road, just a dirt track leading up to the house, as was the case with so many farms out in the *puszta*. The farmland between Velebit and Kanizsa was immense, but Anna had walked round that area so many times with Réka, she could just about picture where the farm was. Maybe it's not wise to go out there, thought Anna, but I have to see the place where my father spent his final moments.

AT FIRST ANNA COULDN'T FIND the farmstead. She drove slowly along the tracks that scored the *puszta*, admiring the monotonous countryside that opened up around her almost like a lunar landscape.

Eventually she had to stop at a small farm to ask for directions. A group of shaggy dogs – a black puli and two small brown terriers – came bounding up to the car and informed the people indoors that someone had appeared in the yard. A small, old man stepped into the garden, lit a cigarette and looked warily at Anna and her white rented car. A few geese waddled across the garden, pecking the ground for something to eat, harassed by a clutch of chickens. Anna explained what she was doing, and the man told her that the farm she was looking for was two kilometres away and that it was empty.

'Are you going to buy it?' he asked her.

'Maybe, but I want to see it first,' Anna replied.

'It's only on the market for ten thousand.'

'Do you know who owns it?'

'A rich man in Szabadka, apparently. An artist, he is, or something like that. Never visits the place. I can find his name in case you want to get in touch.'

'Thank you, that would be kind. Has he always owned the farm?'

'No. If I remember rightly, he bought it sometime in the late 1990s.'

'I've been looking for a farm for a long time, a summer place for me and my family. I imagine it needs a lot of work,' said Anna, surprised at how easily she lied through her teeth.

'It's been empty for a good while now. But as far as I know it's still in pretty good shape. It's still standing, that's something.'

'I heard that some terrible things happened there once,' said Anna.

'You mean the policeman's murder? That was decades ago.'

'Did you live here back then?'

'Yes, and I remember the day it happened very well. We heard on the news that shots had been fired. My wife was frantic. She was still wanting to keep the doors locked for weeks after.'

'Did you hear the shot? Or did you see anything that evening?'

'I didn't hear anything; we live a bit too far away. But I saw the headlights of two cars driving across the *puszta*.'

'What cars were they?'

'First, I saw one set of lights heading towards the farm and soon after that another set. It caught my attention because we see so little traffic out this way. It was quiet back then. Still is. The road to the farm runs along there.' The man pointed to the fields far off to the west. 'In the dark you can see any headlights quite clearly.'

Anna thanked the man, agreed that she'd stop on her way back to pick up the name of the farm's owner and drove off in the direction the man had shown her. Before long she found the farmstead in precisely the location where the farmer had said.

The farmhouse itself was stunning. Its white roughcast had begun to crumble in places, but the roof was in one piece and all the windows were intact. In the yard stood two large outhouses and a cowshed, which was in the worst condition of all the buildings; it was about to collapse.

Anna tried the front door of the farmhouse, but it was locked. She walked round the building, looking in through every window. The house was empty. It contained five rooms, arranged one leading into the next, and had thick wooden floorboards and decorative rafters on the ceiling. It was beautiful.

Anna took some photographs, then went to examine the outhouses. It was in one of these buildings that her father had died, here that he'd been shot to death. How had it happened? Anna didn't know whether her father had been killed by a single, carefully aimed bullet, or by a random volley of machine-gun fire. Did he have time to register that he was about to die? Had he suffered? Did he lie there in agony? Why did he come out here by himself? I would never do something like that, she thought. Though I'm here by myself now. The now-familiar, uneasy shivers ran the length of her arms, even though the air was stiflingly hot. She'd learnt that this meant she could be in danger.

The doors were locked with thick chains and padlocks, but a small window behind one of the outhouses was broken and there was just enough room for Anna to squeeze through the gap. It was dark and cool inside the building, almost cold, like walking into a stone church on a hot day. The broken window cast a thin strip of light on the concrete floor, and the air was thick with decades of dust. All around her was junk covered in cobwebs and dirt; farming machinery, spare parts, boxes and pieces of wood were all piled up along the far wall, but other than that the space was empty. Is this where it had happened?

A scratching sound came from the corner. A large rat pattered along the wall, its nose twitching. Anna gave a start and the rat darted into hiding. Once her eyes had become accustomed to the darkness, she went through the building, opening up some of the boxes and peering beneath and behind the bits of machinery, as though she were looking for something – perhaps a shadow, perhaps a memory hidden between the dark walls – something that had stayed behind to haunt her. She found nothing. The building remained silent. Anna sat down on the rough concrete floor, her back to the small window, the faint light trying to force its way inside and disrupt the quiet, motionless atmosphere of the room. She lay down and stretched herself out, the cool of the concrete against her back, the smell of damp and mould covering her as she closed her eyes. The rustling of the rat had stopped. Outside she could hear the sound of faint birdsong. Her thoughts scurried fleetingly here and there. She would have to go to the river that evening, she thought, and felt as though she didn't have the energy, that all she wanted was to lie here and sleep.

The beep of her phone brought her back to reality. She couldn't say how long she'd lain there. Her back felt cold and numbed. She'd received a text message. A shiver made the fair hairs on her arms stand on end. Judit's message contained two names: Farkas Lajos and Bakró Bertalan. One was serving a life sentence in the Szabadka town jail, the other had been dead for years.

AT TEN O'CLOCK ANNA heard a boat approaching. It was pitch dark. Anna was crouching in the thicket along the riverbank, some distance from the spot the GPS had shown her, trying not to swipe away the colony of mosquitoes that was swarming around her, hungry for her blood. The sound of the motor stopped, and Anna heard the boat glide along the river right in front of her. Someone switched on a torch. In its beam of light Anna saw a rope flying across the water and landing only a few metres from her feet. Someone got out of the boat with a groan. The man coughed, cleared his throat, spat in the mud. Anna recognised those sounds. Without a thought for the consequences she stood up and walked out of the bushes.

'Good evening. What a surprise to see you here,' she said.

Nagy Béla was so startled that he dropped the torch. It rolled along the sloping riverbank and plopped into the water. Darkness surrounded them.

'Christ alive, I could have had a heart attack,' the fisherman snapped. 'What the hell are you doing here?'

'I was going to ask you the same thing,' Anna replied.

'I don't need to explain my business to you.'

'Really? Not even if I suspect your business might have something to do with the death of Lakatos Sándor?'

'So that's the name of your handbag thief?'

'Don't play innocent with me. I know Lakatos was involved in smuggling refugees along the river and so are you, as is our dear friend Molnár László.'

'He been talking, has he? So the Good Samaritan couldn't keep his damn mouth shut after all.'

'I heard him talking to a group of young men who I imagine will be arriving here shortly. And Béla, I am armed, so there's no point trying anything funny. Did you kill Lakatos Sándor?'

'Of course I didn't. I was at home that whole night. Ask my wife, she'll tell you. Believe me, she'd be only too pleased to see the back of me, so she has no reason to lie about it.'

'It's still a flimsy alibi. Besides, you did go to the wine fair.'

'I was only there for a few minutes. That's not a crime, is it? And would I have taken you to the place they found the body if I'd killed the guy myself? Of course I wouldn't.'

Anna mulled this over. It would certainly have been strange for the murderer to take her to the scene of the crime. But this case was already strange. It felt as though everything was just a bluff, a smokescreen, a parallel reality coming into focus behind the real world. As Judit had said, there is so much out there that we cannot see.

'Why do I think you know more about this than you're telling me?' asked Anna.

Béla coughed and spat. For a moment he reminded her of her partner, Esko Niemi.

'All right, Anna,' the fisherman said, seemingly resigned. 'I'll tell you everything I know.' He lit a cigarette, the flame illuminating his face for a few seconds, making him look almost monstrous. 'I knew who Lakatos Sándor was, but I've never actually had any dealings with him. I was shocked to find him lying there dead.'

'Why didn't you tell me his name straight away?'

Béla sighed. 'Because I'm basically a coward. I was afraid people would find out about what László and I have been up to, if they realised I knew something about the boy. László and I are working together, it's just the two of us. We don't have a boss; we don't work for any organisation.'

'You mean the mafia?'

'Whoever. The Lakatos boy was involved in illegal people smuggling, but we have absolutely nothing to do with organised crime.'

'Is there a "legal" form of people smuggling? I had no idea.'

'We don't take money for what we do. All we want to do is help people. László has seen so many people at that camp, so many poor wretches who have been abused, robbed and downright exploited, that he decided to do something about it. He came to me and we began planning how we could get people to the border by boat. Remember, I know this river better than I know my wife's body.'

'You were mentioned in the news a while ago. People drowned. And the case had something to do with what you call illegal people smuggling.'

'I had nothing to do with that. The charges were dropped because there was no evidence.'

'I believe the death of the handbag thief had something to do with my father's murder.'

By now her eyes were accustomed to the darkness, so Anna could just make out a look of shock on the fisherman's wrinkled face.

'Damn it,' he said and spat again.

'Béla, tell me everything you know. I must find out the truth before I leave.'

'I don't know the details, but I heard Lakatos was planning to blackmail someone. At first I thought it was just hearsay – you know how it is, these kinds of stories take on a life of their own – but now that you mention it…'

'Where did you hear this?'

'Let's say that, though László and I are operating on a purely humanitarian basis, we still need to know what other people in this business are up to. We don't want to step on anyone's toes, if you know what I mean. We don't want to put our own lives at risk; our charity only goes so far. But the boy had a big mouth. The night before his death he'd had too much to drink and was in the bars in Szabadka, bragging about what he was planning to do.'

'Who did he want to blackmail?'

'I've no idea. I swear.'

'Why didn't you tell me all this to start with?'

The fisherman drew his hand through the air in a swooping curve so that small sparks flew from his cigarette.

'What am I doing right now? Besides, I only heard about it yesterday.'

'Some people believe the man who killed my father is still walking free.'

'Well, as I said, when people start gossiping, things tend to get blown out of all proportion. But now I'm going to have to ask you to leave. The people I'm supposed to be transporting will be here soon.'

'How do I know you're not lying to me? Perhaps it was you who killed my father and Lakatos.'

'In that case I'd probably have killed you too,' said Béla and took a step closer to Anna. 'Now, all I ask is that you keep my little evening activities to yourself. Sure enough, you'll find the truth if you keep digging – you found your way out here, after all. Christ, you really are your father's daughter.' There was a distinct note of admiration in his voice.

'I don't believe you would do anything this risky without some form of recompense,' said Anna, dismissing his flattery.

'Let's say I take a small cut to cover my expenses – my time and the petrol. But László takes nothing; now there's a real saint if ever there was one. You're not going to go to the police, are you?'

'Would it make any difference if I did?' she asked.

Nagy Béla gave a phlegmy chuckle. 'I doubt it. They've got their fingers in this pie too, you mark my word. If nothing else, they overlook it and pretend they don't know what's going on. They look after their own. I don't mean just other officers, but the whole community.'

Anna thought of the chief of police. Did he have his finger in the pie or was he too just turning a blind eye to it?

JUNE 15th

VAJDASÁG. Heady sunlight shining from a hazy-blue, cloudless sky; sleepy villages one after the other; and fields, an endless expanse of fields. Corn, wheat and sunflowers as far as the eye could see. Péter beside her. Anna felt overwhelmed by the enormity of the landscape; she could feel herself almost bursting from the exhilaration, her spirit opening up, then both spreading across the open landscape and merging into Péter's presence beside her. His hand was resting on Anna's thigh and Anna could feel its warmth so viscerally that her other senses were heightened to their absolute peak. Any effort she made to think about what she'd found out in the course of the last few days, was lost as her thoughts disappeared into the panoramas flashing past, and melted into the warmth radiating from Péter's hand. The murder of the handbag thief was somewhere in the background, and it had something to do with her father's death, but at that moment it all felt as distant and unreal as a dream that you can no longer remember in the morning.

It was a two-hundred-kilometre journey to Belgrade, and it didn't take long before the landscape began to change. The open fields grew smaller, forests appeared on the horizon and began to grow larger the closer they came to their destination. They crossed the large bridge across the Danube, and the houses gradually appeared more frequently on either side of the motorway. Larger villages, suburbs, apartment blocks, Belgrade.

The city was lively – rundown but beautiful. They easily found their hotel in the Skadarlija district – a pedestrianised area full of cobbled roadways and attractive old houses and restaurants with terraces that spread out into the streets. They took their couple of bags to the hotel, decided to have lunch somewhere nearby then go straight to the embassy.

'Have you even heard anyone talking about my father at the police station?' Anna asked as they ordered a dish of *csevap* and salad.

'Of course I heard he was shot, but that's it. People don't talk about it anymore. When did it happen?'

'1988. I was five years old.'

'I'm sorry. It can't be easy to lose your father that young. Or when you're older, for that matter. Fathers are important,' said Péter and gently touched Anna's hand.

Anna didn't say anything. It was all she could do to hold back the tears, weeping that had been so long dormant, but was now awake and trying to force its way out of her body. She was used to the fact that she no longer had a father; she had hardened the sorrow and the bitterness into lumps she carried around within her. But it was more difficult to deal with sympathy, with understanding words, with the fact that someone wanted to comfort her because they knew exactly what she was feeling. It was unbearable and wonderful at the same time.

'Tell me more about what you've been up to these last few days. What have you found out?' asked Péter.

Anna told him about the names she'd received from Judit, her visit to the refugee camp and what she'd learned about her father's case from Béla and Gábor. She described the farmstead where her father had been shot, told Péter about what the neighbouring farmer had seen on that dreadful night decades ago. After considering the matter for a moment, she decided not to mention Béla and László's smuggling activities; she simply explained that they had vaguely known Lakatos Sándor.

Péter ate his meal of breaded catfish and fries, and seemed reflective as he listened to Anna's account.

'If I were you I wouldn't necessarily believe all the rumours about your father,' he said. 'People will always say the police have got the wrong man, whatever the crime is.'

'Maybe, but it's my father we're talking about. I want to know the truth.'

'Sometimes the truth does us no good at all.'

'I completely disagree.'

'Okay. But the truth is often relative. What might have been true for the poor guy that was executed might not be true for the judge, the witnesses, you or your father.'

'Don't split hairs,' Anna snapped. 'There is only one truth about what happened, and I intend to find out what it is.'

'In that case you're in for a busy end to your holiday. If you can call this a holiday any longer.'

'I am convinced the two deaths are related.'

'But why?'

'Both involve a man called Lakatos: the man convicted of my father's murder and the man who stole my handbag. They were related to each other.'

'The name could still be pure coincidence.'

'Could it really be coincidence that the separate deaths of two men named Lakatos were directly linked to my family?'

'You're right, it does seem strange.'

'What's more, Béla said he'd heard rumours that Sándor was planning to blackmail someone.'

'That's just a fisherman's gossip. You're a police officer; surely you know idle chit-chat should be left well alone.'

'On the contrary. As a police officer I know you should verify any piece of information, no matter how trivial. One of them might be a crucial lead. And you know it too, so don't bother pretending otherwise.'

And at that moment Anna felt she was closing in on the breakthrough. She didn't know where the feeling came from, but it was so powerful that it made her shiver.

'I want to talk to the surviving witness,' she said.

'The guy serving the life sentence?'

'Yes.'

'They won't let you visit him.'

'Maybe not, but I'm going to try my damndest to make them.'

'How exactly?'

'After going to the embassy, I'll pay Interpol a visit and get myself clearance.'

'I'm beginning to think you're a bit crazy,' said Péter with a smile.

'Why else would I be here with you?'

'Do you think we've got time to pop back to the hotel before the embassy and Interpol?'

'The hotel's just over there. We've got plenty of time,' said Anna and gently stroked Péter's cheek.

'I like you, Anna.'

I like you too, she thought, but couldn't bring herself to say it out loud.

'IT WASN'T EASY getting my hands on these, I can tell you,' said Péter.

It was early evening; the noise of the capital outside the hotel window. Cars, horns, ambulance sirens. Anna and Péter sat in the hotel room, smoking and drinking a few bottles of beer. Anna had received her new passport, finally, and visited Interpol to acquire a certificate that would help her secure an audience with a judge in Szabadka.

On the coffee table Péter placed an old cardboard folder containing yellowed sheets of paper – typewritten documents.

'I did a little digging of my own while you were at the embassy,' he said. 'I guessed the mafia investigation your father was working on was big enough that there would be a case report in the police archives here in Belgrade. 'And there it is.'

'This is incredible,' said Anna. 'How did you manage to get these papers out of the archive?'

'Well … a little money.'

'Péter! How much do I owe you?'

'Not very much. Anyway, wasn't that your original intention? To get to know me and try to milk me for information?'

'Péter, I don't … I don't know what to say. Maybe I thought something like that at first but…'

'Would you have asked me to join you on this trip if you'd thought I couldn't help with your investigation?'

'Of course I would. It's not like that.'

'Why did you ask me then?'

Anna wanted to explain to Péter that over time she'd become very fond of him; that her feelings had taken her entirely by surprise, so different were they from anything she'd experienced before; that she wanted to get to know him better, spend more time with him. She wanted to tell him that he'd awoken something within her that it was hard to put into words. But she said nothing – she couldn't find the right words.

'Tell me. Why?'

'Well, I like spending time with you,' she managed to splutter out and realised quite how lame it sounded. She raised her hand and tried to stroke Péter's cheek, but he turned away.

'I like spending time with you too,' he said after a moment. 'Actually, I've had a really amazing time with you. I can't remember the last time I've laughed this much.'

'That's what I think too.'

'Why don't you say so then? I want to know what you're thinking and feeling.'

'I just told you!' Anna snapped. 'I just said so. But I'm going back to Finland really soon. The next time I'll be here will be Christmas at the earliest. It's hard to let go in a situation like this. Do you understand? You notice you're holding back though you want something different altogether.'

Péter was silent for a moment and said he understood. He took a document from the folder and started reading it. Anna did the same. They immersed themselves in the old case file, and, though they didn't return to the previous conversation, it continued to hang between them like a heavy, dusty curtain.

'Here's something,' said Péter, handing Anna a sheet of paper. 'Your father was looking into a mafia case back in 1988.'

Anna took the photocopy and read it through, though she couldn't understand all of it. She asked Péter to translate it into Hungarian.

'Somebody in the municipal council was making sure jobs and building contracts were given to certain contractors, and that didn't please some people.'

'Gábor told me about that. And he also said my father had become secretive about details of the investigation.'

'There are dozens of pages here of interview transcripts with the managers of one of those building companies. Gábor and your father must have kept them. But the charges must have been dropped. I can't find any other documents relating to the issue.'

Péter flicked through the thick bunch of papers for a long time. Eventually he gave up.

'I can't find the court transcript. Either the case was dropped or the papers are somewhere else. Could this have something to do with your father's death? What if he'd worked out who was pulling strings for the contractors?'

'It's possible,' said Anna pensively.

'But what about the handbag thief?'

'The killer must have been at the wine fair. He saw the theft take place.'

'But why would Lakatos want to take your bag rather than anyone else's? In order to reopen the investigation into your father's murder? It doesn't make sense.'

'He didn't know who I was. It was pure chance that he chose me. But the fact that he died after stealing my bag might not be chance. If my father's killer knew that the thief was a relative of the man who had been wrongly convicted, he might have been a bit startled. Maybe Sándor was planning on blackmailing my father's killer. The killer, meanwhile, was worried that I might catch up with Sándor or that, in rifling through my handbag, Sándor would find out who I am and contact me himself. That sounds a bit more plausible.'

'Maybe,' said Péter and took Anna in his arms. 'It sounds far-fetched, but it's possible.'

'I've got something too,' said Anna, wriggled free of Péter's embrace and handed him an autopsy report.

The document gave detailed information on Fekete István's post mortem – the time of death and a short analysis of the bullet that penetrated his chest, killing him immediately.

'Anna, I'm so sorry you have to go through all this,' said Péter.

'Look who signed the autopsy report.'

'Milan Pešić.'

'The same pathologist who performed the autopsy on Lakatos

Sándor in Újvidék, though all the while the body was in the morgue in Kanizsa.'

'He must be quite old by now,' said Péter, confused.

'As old as Father Christmas.'

'What?'

'There is no pathologist by that name.'

'Wow. On the other hand, it doesn't surprise me.'

'Why is that?'

'Oh, Anna, if only you knew the kind of things you can buy round here if you have enough money.'

'Old case files and autopsy reports, apparently. This just confirms my suspicions that the same person or persons are behind both murders. Someone who knew, all those years ago, who to ask for a forged autopsy report.'

'Using the same name is quite risky. Someone else might begin to suspect that Father Christmas doesn't really exist,' said Péter and tapped his forefinger against the signature.

'Either your chief of police is embroiled in what's going on here or he's a complete idiot. It was him that gave me Sándor's autopsy report.'

Péter lit a cigarette and thought about this in silence. The smoke filling the room began to make Anna feel queasy so she opened the window. The air felt warm, like a soft pillow pressing against her face. Smothering her.

'I'm not going to start looking into his conduct, you can be sure of that,' Péter said eventually.

'I thought as much. I totally understand. I'm not going to touch it either.'

'Good! Finally, a sensible decision! You'll never find out anything about him. If he's involved in this, he'll have so much protection around him that you won't be able to get through it by yourself.'

Anna fetched her handbag, pulled out a card printed on light-yellow paper and showed it to Péter.

'But this guy might,' said Anna with a smirk.

'What's this?'

'A visit to a prison in Szabadka isn't the only thing I talked to Interpol about.'

IT WAS SO TERRIBLY HOT. Mosquitoes flew in through the cracks in the plank walls, buzzing and stinging. Dzsenifer rubbed her itchy arms against the rough surface of the wall. She was thirsty. The grey-haired man had brought her food once, taken the gag off her mouth and allowed her to eat and drink, but she couldn't remember how long ago it was. Time seemed to go so slowly. Dzsenifer drifted in and out of sleep. Sometimes light filtered through the cracks between the planks, but for the most part it was pitch dark. The mosquitoes were buzzing constantly. Dzsenifer was so thirsty she couldn't think of anything else. All she could feel was her dry throat, the old rag stuffed into her mouth and her sore, itchy arms. She tried not to think about where she was or how she could get away. She wasn't afraid of the grey-haired man coming back and she didn't think about her brother. She didn't listen to the sounds around her – there wasn't much to hear, only birdsong and every now and then the sound of barges passing on the river and sounding their horns.

The heat and thirst had made her weak. All she could do was lie on the floor of the wooden shack and dream of water. As if through the mist, she saw a woman's face, a hand holding her a bottle of water. The hand pulled the rag from her mouth, and she drank and drank. Deep inside her she knew it wasn't real. The rag was still in her mouth, it stayed put, sucking up every last droplet of spittle, but she didn't have the strength to care. Again she drifted into sleep. Or rather, she lost consciousness.

When Dzsenifer next forced her eyelids open, it was dark again. This time she heard a sound there was no mistaking. Small, bright, bell-like pattering. Somewhere near her droplets of water were falling to the ground. The sound grew stronger, reviving her will to live just as it was about to fade away. She began crawling towards the sound, felt the ropes tightening around her hands and feet each time she tugged, then relaxing as she stopped to gather her strength and listen to where the droplets were coming from.

What a sensation when the water hit her face. At first she let it drop on her cheeks and forehead, then she found a position where the drops fell directly on to the rag stuffed in her mouth. Slowly the fabric began soaking up the rain. Dzsenifer passed out again for a moment and snapped to when she realised the rag was heavy and wet and that she could suck a little bit of water from it. Thunder roared overhead, electrical silver light flared between the planks as lightning flashed across the Tisza.

For the first time in her life, Dzsenifer hoped and prayed that the thunderstorm would never end.

JUNE 16th

ANNA STEPPED INTO the dark hallway, inhaling the familiar scent of home. She closed the door as quietly as she could and locked it behind her, trying not to wake her mother. She crept into the kitchen to make some tea, wondering whether she should try to get a few hours' sleep or whether it would be best to try and stay awake. They had set off very early to get back to Kanizsa, because Péter had to work that morning. The car had sped through the brightening Vajdaság dawn: the drowsy roads, the stirring landscape; Anna relaxed after a night with Péter; Péter tired and distant; strips of cloud smudged across the sky.

On the kitchen table was an envelope. It was addressed to Anna. Who could be sending me post? she wondered and tore open the envelope. Inside was a print of a document typed up on a computer. Anna read it twice.

STOP YOUR INVESTIGATION IMMEDIATELY AND GO BACK WHERE YOU CAME FROM OR YOU'LL REGRET IT.

'What's that?' Anna heard her mother's voice behind her and was so startled that she almost dropped the sheet of paper.

She handed the letter to her mother. Her mother read it. At first her expression was one of disbelief, then panic and finally anger.

'You have to go back to Finland,' she said.

'I can't.'

'Of course you can. You've got a new passport now. Go and pack your things and tear up those disgusting papers on your wall. This minute,' her mother said.

'Have you been raking through my room?'

'I don't need to rake through anything to see what you've been up to. A picture of István on the wall, too. Imagine what it feels like to see his picture on your wall among all those papers. What have you done? I can't bear this a moment longer!'

'When did this letter arrive?'

'Yesterday, in the post.'

'It's postmarked here, in Kanizsa. I have to think about this.'

'There's nothing to think about. You're going back to Finland right now. They'll kill you too. I told you not to stick your nose into things round here. I knew this would happen! Why won't you ever listen to me?'

By now her mother was shouting at the top of her voice. Her body was trembling. The letter fell to the floor. The tea water started boiling, but neither of them moved to turn off the stove.

Ákos appeared at the door.

'What's all this racket?'

'I didn't know you were here,' said Anna.

'Well I am. I thought it would have been cool to hang out with you yesterday, but you'd already gone to Belgrade with that man of yours.'

Ákos took the kettle off the stove, poured water into three cups and sat down at the kitchen table.

'Tell me what all the shouting is about.'

'Anna's received a threatening letter,' said her mother, snatching the paper from the floor and handing it to Ákos.

'*A francba*! What the hell have you been up to? Why hasn't anybody told me what's going on?'

The day shone in through the kitchen window as it always had done, innocent and carefree, as Anna told them both everything she had found out so far. She decided, however, not to mention that someone had tried to run her over, though by now she was convinced it wasn't drunken teenagers fooling around.

When she finished her account, all three of them sat in silence, looking anxiously at one another and thinking. My family, thought Anna. My poor, truncated family – and now it's in danger of losing yet another member. How could I have done this to my mother?

'So what are you going to do now?' Ákos eventually asked, breaking the silence.

'You're going back to Finland,' said her mother.

'I can't leave this situation unresolved,' said Anna. 'Besides, I've got a warrant from Interpol that will probably allow me to interview a witness – he's serving a life sentence. All I have to do is apply for clearance from the local court. I'm planning to go to Szabadka to make the arrangements. Today.'

'You'll do no such thing.' Again her mother raised her voice. 'Have you lost your mind?'

'Mum. Surely I – we – have to know the truth about what happened to Dad and what the theft of my handbag had to do with it.'

'We don't have to do anything.'

'Would you rather Dad's killer was walking around a free man? Is that what you really want?'

'It's all just gossip,' her mother muttered.

'I might be able to believe that if it weren't for all the coincidences that seem to indicate something else altogether. I must get to the bottom of this.'

Her mother started to cry. Anna's conscience stung her like an angry wasp, but she steeled herself and brushed it aside.

'I promise I'll be careful,' she said. 'I'm a police officer. I know how to handle this.'

'So was your father,' shouted her mother and left the kitchen, slamming the door behind her.

Anna sighed. She looked out of the window at a butterfly dancing across the flowerbeds.

'I'll have to go to Szabadka soon,' she told Ákos.

'I could come with you, if that's all right.'

'What, as my bodyguard?'

'If you like. And there are a few things I want to talk about.'

'Okay. I'm going to have a shower and change. Then we'll leave.'

THE JUDGE WAS A SMALL, stout man who clearly enjoyed fatty food and plenty of it. He had red, chubby cheeks, and his double chin wobbled every time he took a breath. Anna imagined him roasting whole pigs on a spit, licking the melted fat from his fingers and happily smacking his lips. More importantly, though, he seemed like a decent, friendly man.

Anna showed the judge the document she'd received from Interpol, explained in detail why she wanted to meet Farkas Lajos, and even managed to force out a few convincing tears as she talked about how much she missed her father. Anna's strategy was not to put too much emphasis on the possibility of a wrongful conviction but to stress that she was a grieving daughter who wanted to come to terms with her tragic past. To her surprise she saw that her plan seemed to be working. The judge asked her a few clarifying questions, and expressed his sympathy and condolences in such lavish terms that Anna didn't understand a thing and Ákos had to interpret for her. Then the judge explained something about visiting protocol at the prison and wrote Anna a warrant allowing her to see Farkas Lajos. The meeting would take place the following day between two and three in the afternoon, and there would be no guard. Anna and Farkas would be alone together.

'You understand this is all highly irregular,' the judge explained. 'If you weren't a police officer and if your father hadn't been a police officer, I couldn't possibly allow this,' he stressed. 'I trust your professionalism and I hope this will give you peace of mind.

Anna thanked him, took the warrant, placed it carefully in a plastic envelope and put it in her bag. She couldn't go back to Finland yet, despite her mother's worries. The threatening letter only proved that she'd found something that had been kept carefully hidden for a very long time. Now all she could do was wait for her meeting with the prisoner the following day.

After they left the judge, Anna and Ákos visited the Roma shantytown, asking after Dzsenifer, but nobody had seen her. Rambo was lying in his shack, clearly drunk. His clothes looked dirtier than before and the room smelled of rotting leftover food. Anna noted Ákos's expression as the man slurred his words. She was certain that Ákos saw himself in Rambo and she hoped the image would leave a lasting impression on her brother and prevent him ever going back to his former life.

As they were leaving the shantytown, Ákos suggested they have lunch in Szabadka; Anna was more than happy to agree. They went back into the town centre and found a cosy Italian restaurant along one of the pedestrian streets with a good antipasto and salad selection. Anna's mouth watered as she read the menu. She'd already had enough of white bread and fatty food. It was a sign that some part of her was already yearning to go back to Finland.

Ákos talked about anything and everything, the conversation twisting and turning like a plane waiting to land, as he waited excitedly for his food. Anna ordered *insalata mista con pollo*, Ákos took a pizza. They tucked in, chatting about the weather, the incredible heat wave of the last few weeks, which would dry out the wheat fields if it continued. Then they talked about the price of food in Finland and Serbia; Ákos's old friends and what they were up to these days; the widowed old lady next door; their mother's habit of washing the dishes with a kitchen broom, which disgusted them both; and eventually, finally, Ákos mentioned Kata. He looked so happy, so healthy and glowing. Anna didn't have to ask; she knew the answer already.

'Are you planning to stay here?' she said nonetheless.

'That's what Kata and I have been talking about. I think it's the most sensible solution, at this stage at least. We don't want her kids to have to switch language all of a sudden. It's a tough process, as you know only too well. And they'd be too far away from their father.'

Anna felt like saying she understood perfectly well, there was no need to explain any further, but she remained silent and let Ákos finish speaking. He talked about Kata's good job, about how it would probably do him a world of good to get away from the old Koivuharju gang, about how a guy in Szeged had already promised him a bit of casual work. Once Ákos had finished, Anna finally spoke.

'What about me?'

Ákos stood up from his chair, took a few steps to her side of the table and wrapped his arms around her. Anna could feel the tears running down her cheeks and did nothing to try and stop them.

'Anna, you've always been a fighter,' said Ákos. 'You can pull through anything in the world. I've always envied that about you.'

'You envy me? How can an older brother envy his little sister?'

'Easily, if he's got a sister like you. You're smart, good-looking and in damn good shape. And you haven't got any problems.'

'Me, no problems? If only you knew…'

'I mean the kind of problems I've had. I really think it'll be easier for me to stay away from them here. To remain sober.'

'I'm not really a fighter, you know. And I'm going to miss you.'

'I know, I'm going to miss you too. At least we've got Skype and Viber and all that. And there are cheap flights these days too.'

'You can never afford a plane ticket, no matter how cheap they are.'

'Then it's a good thing you can, isn't it?' said Ákos and laughed happily.

After lunch they wandered round the streets of Szabadka, admiring the beautiful old buildings like tourists. The idyll was broken only by the sight of the refugees lying in the parks. Clothes were hung out to dry on the branches of the trees, people lay asleep on the park benches. And yet the atmosphere was surprisingly calm. The locals were leaving the strangers in peace.

Anna bought a few souvenirs to take back to work: packets of cookies and several bags of melt-in-your-mouth Kiki caramels, which she used to eat as a child. Back then this country was still called Yugoslavia, she thought. Wars had broken out, people had fled from their homes and died, but Kiki caramels had remained unchanged.

Back in Kanizsa, she felt a peculiar sadness as she packed the caramels away in her suitcase. Would the refugees of today ever be able to experience the tastes and smells of their childhood again?

JUNE 17th

THE SZABADKA PRISON was situated in the centre of the town, at the end of a busy pedestrian street next to the train station. A school of some description seemed to be operating out of the part of the prison facing the street. Réka recalled that only a while ago there had been a bank in that spot. Anna was amused at the thought of a bank and prison sharing the same building.

An announcement crackled over the station's loudspeakers: the intercity train from Belgrade would shortly be arriving at platform three. The prisoners must hear the announcements too. Anna looked at the bars across the windows and the heavy iron door that she would soon step through. Réka said she would wait in a nearby café.

Anna took the steep steps up to the door and pressed the buzzer. An intercom buzzed and a voice asked who was there and what business they were on. Anna replied, the voice asked her to wait a moment, and, before long, the iron door began to swing open like the entrance to Ali Baba's cave. Two guards, a man and a woman, stood waiting in the small, brightly lit entrance hall. Anna showed them the warrant signed by the judge, her identification card and her police badge. The female officer asked Anna to empty her pockets and walk through a metal detector. After that she gave Anna's body a thorough scan with a small monitor and frisked her by hand through her clothes. The male guard spoke into a walkie-talkie and Anna heard that she had been granted permission to enter the prison.

First, the guards escorted Anna to the office of the prison governor. The room featured a large bookcase, three filing cabinets and a desk with neat piles of papers placed between a computer and a penholder. The governor looked through Anna's paperwork, asked a few questions in English – not Serbian or Hungarian, she noticed – and informed the guards that Anna and the prisoner could be taken to the interview room.

Farkas Lajos stared past Anna into the distance. He seemed frozen. He was skinny and pale, his face was gaunt and his eyes didn't betray the slightest flicker of emotion. Anna felt as though she was looking into the eyes of a dead man. She'd planned all her questions in advance, but suddenly she seemed unable to say anything. The man looked like the living dead. How do you talk to someone like that?

'What?' the man asked abruptly and stared at Anna with his black, lifeless eyes as though he saw nothing at all. As though he didn't want to see anything; as though he couldn't bear it if he did.

'My name is Fekete Anna. I'm the daughter of Fekete István. Do you remember him?'

'Remember? What's that? Things like memories lose their meaning in here. Think about it too much and you'll go mad.'

'How long have you been in here?'

'A long time. Ever since your father died. Almost.'

'Why? What did you do?'

'They said I robbed three banks and assaulted a guard.'

'Did you rob the banks?'

The man suddenly gave a hollow, harrowing laugh. 'What does it matter? Here I am and I'm going to stay here for a long time yet.'

'But you remember my father, is that right?'

'Never met him.'

'But you testified that Lakatos didn't shoot him.'

'We weren't asked to testify to anything.'

'What happened that night?'

'And why the fuck should I tell you that? Anyway, I can't remember.'

'I … I have to know what happened.'

'Knowing things, remembering things, it's all meaningless when you're cooped up in a padded cell a few metres across without seeing anyone for forty years.'

'I don't live in a place like that.'

'You know, there's nothing in my cell. Nothing at all. No table, no chair, not even a bed. There's a hole in the floor to shit in. Nothing else.'

'Do you sleep on the floor?'

'They bring me a mattress at night and take it away in the morning.'

'Surely they let you into the yard sometimes?'

'One hour a day. By myself.'

'Do you have anything to read? A radio? A television?'

The man looked at Anna as though she was stupid.

'Nothing,' he said.

'What do you do all day?'

'Nothing.'

'How do…? How can you cope?'

'You can't. A death sentence would have been better than this. But they wanted to be like a modern European country, so they got rid of the death penalty, because it's supposed to be barbaric. Now they give us life sentences in these fucking padded cells, alone for forty years. That's the worst of it, to be alone the whole time. Alone with your own thoughts. Though they soon disappear too.'

'What happened that evening?'

'What evening?'

'The evening when you and Lakatos were together and my father was shot somewhere else.'

'Do you believe that?'

'I want to hear your version.'

'And what are you going to do with it? Do you think you can help me?'

'To be honest I'm more interested in helping myself. And a little girl who has disappeared. Her surname is Lakatos too.'

Something flickered in Farkas Lajos's eyes.

So you're not completely emotionless after all, thought Anna.

'How come they let you in here?' he asked. 'They don't let just anybody come in.'

'I work for the police in Finland, so they granted me special permission.'

'Ah, a fucking cop.'

'That's right.'

'A foreign cop. They like kissing the foreign cops' arses. Do you want to know what they do to me in here?'

'I'm not sure.'

'They decide I've been behaving badly. So they tie me by my hands and feet to a metal ring on the floor, inside the padding. And there I sit until they decide I can behave myself properly.'

'How long do you sit like that?'

'Days, weeks, months, who's counting? What's the date today?'

Anna told him the date and he began to laugh. He rubbed the thin grey hair on his head and rocked back and forth.

There was a knock at the door and the guard looked inside.

'Ten minutes,' he said and disappeared again.

'We were sitting at my place playing cards that night and drinking a bottle of hooch. Me, Lakatos and Bakró. We didn't leave the house all evening. Then the next morning the cops turned up and took Lakatos away. Nobody listened to me and Bakró. They said we were so drunk we couldn't have remembered whether Lakatos had slipped out or not. But it wasn't true. We weren't that drunk. Then they found the gun in Lakatos's yard. In the trash. And it turned out it was the same gun that was used to shoot Fekete.'

'Where did you live back then?'

'In Velebit.'

'Quite close to the farmhouse where it happened?'

'Yeah.'

'Was there a car?'

'Where?'

'Did you have one, or did Lakatos? Was there a car in the yard?'

'None of us had a car. Lakatos had a horse.'

'Where did he live at the time?'

'In Velebit too. Almost next door.'

'A neighbour who lived near the farmhouse remembers seeing two sets of headlights passing by that evening.'

'It was the murderer, for sure, heading for the farm. When they found the gun, that was the end of it. They took Lakatos away and we hardly saw him after that. Me and Bakró tried talking to the police, said we'd testify, but they wouldn't listen to us.'

'Have you any idea who the real killer might have been?'

'No, but it couldn't have been just anyone. You don't put an innocent man away for nothing. Not even a gypsy.'

'Was there any talk about it at the time? Rumours about a miscarriage of justice? Someone must have suspected something.'

'Folk said all kinds of things – that somebody was paid a large sum of money, that it was mafia cash, a bribe or something like that. The guy that shot your father became a rich man.'

'Did you know that Bakró has died?'

The man grimaced, revealing his rotten teeth. 'I didn't know, but it's not surprising. Says a lot, doesn't it? Lakatos and Bakró are dead and I'm going to spend the rest of my life rotting away in here.'

'Time's up,' the guard shouted from the door and Anna stood up. She thanked the man and felt a great sorrow that she couldn't reach out her hand and touch him.

The guards led Farkas Lajos out of the room, then fetched Anna and escorted her out of the building.

The iron door slammed shut behind her.

The sun was shining. Anna lit a cigarette and didn't know what to do.

THE ATTIC IN ANNA'S childhood home wasn't the typical frightening, airless space covered in cobwebs. Small windows at the start of the roof let daylight flow inside and fluorescent lamps lit up every last corner. Boxes of old possessions were neatly stacked, some in shelving units, some in orderly rows on the floor. Her mother had always been good at this – maintaining order and taming chaos – but the fact that such organisation continued unhindered into the attic space never ceased to astonish Anna.

Anna was different – she usually grabbed clothes from the line and threw them into the wardrobe without much thought for orderliness. But neither did she have excess stuff packed and hidden away at the back of her cupboards or in her basement storage space. If she had something she didn't need, she gave it away – though that happened rarely, as she had never been one to acquire things for the sake of it and didn't enjoy shopping. So the amount of stuff hoarded in her mother's attic took Anna by surprise. Why keep all this? Why had these things been acquired in the first place?

Now, however, she was grateful for her mother's sense of organisation and for the fact that each box was carefully labelled. She wanted to stop at the box marked BOYS' TOYS and see what her brothers had played with when they were children, but decided to leave it for a later date. She was sure that Áron's miniature cars and teddy bears would have derailed her search and set off a wave of nostalgia, which right now she didn't have time for. Instead she was thrilled to find her father's old microscope – she might yet have use for that.

She easily located her father's papers, but there were lots of them and they weren't in as systematic an order as the rest of the attic. It took Anna almost an hour to find the right year – 1988, her father's last. Sweat trickled down her back as she put the handwritten notebooks in order; the attic had stored the heat of the previous weeks and the hot air was thick and almost tangible. She gathered the pile of papers under her arm and went downstairs into her room.

As Anna already knew, her father had been involved in an extensive investigation into the operations of the local mafia. She had read through all the old reports in the police case file and wanted to compare them to her father's private notes. Something in the reports had bothered her, something that didn't tally with what she had seen and heard, but she couldn't put her finger on what it was. She hoped to find the answer in her father's papers.

Most of the mafia's criminal activity was concentrated in Belgrade and Prishtina, but its arms had reached into northern Yugoslavia too, as far as Szabadka, Kanizsa and other towns along the border. The investigation was not only about fraudulent building contracts but also involved smuggling. Drugs and even people and guns were being illegally transported across the border into Western Europe. Nothing new there, thought Anna. Whatever the cargo, it went by the same routes, the same methods, and more than likely involved some of the same people: there were bribes, kickbacks, embezzlement and deceit; corruption in the highest echelons of politics, the police force and the customs service.

Her father's notes were scanty and not very detailed. He never mentioned any names. These notebooks must have served as a way of helping him work through his thoughts, Anna pondered. These were private comments that were never intended to form part of any official documentation. Anna thought she remembered the way her father would retreat out to the patio with a beer and a cigarette to think over the day's events and write down things that came to mind in his notebooks. A criminal investigator even in his spare time. Like father like daughter.

One annotation caught Anna's attention: *I think someone is deliberately hindering the investigation*, wrote her father in October 1988. *Someone is leaking information, perhaps working directly for the criminals. Find out who it might be.*

Then, a few pages later, an entry for the following month: *How can someone do this job without getting their hands dirty, if a good friend turns out to be a rotten apple? Where should our loyalties lie? With the state, the party, the cause or the person? Should we remain loyal to our friends? What should I do now?*

Why had he gone to the farmhouse by himself? If he was expecting to run into the entirety of the Yugoslavian mafia, surely no policeman would be so reckless, so downright crazy as to walk right into the lion's den by himself.

That was unless he thought he was going to meet a friend – someone he could trust after all. Had her father gone there to try and talk to this friend, to convince him to leave the criminal activity behind and get back on the straight and narrow? Her father must have known who or what he was expecting to encounter at the farmhouse. He must have deemed the situation safe, otherwise he wouldn't have gone.

Who would he have trusted so unquestioningly?

At the end of the notebook were eleven empty pages. Anna flicked through them carefully, hoping against hope that some kind of mysterious, invisible code might appear and reveal what her father might have written had he returned from the farm that night.

On the final page there was a name. Underlined.

Remete Mihály.

JUNE 3rd

He went to the wine fair like everybody else in town that evening, drank a few glasses of wine and chatted with lots of people, because he was known throughout the town and people expected it of him. Nothing out of the ordinary, just the same old perpetual small talk that for some unfathomable reason seemed to be a requirement for all of humanity – people diligently engaging in it in every corner of the world and at every opportunity, as though talking about real things was something to be avoided at all costs, like a dangerous, contagious disease. Small talk was like a protective shield. It meant there was no need to engage properly, to reveal what you were really thinking, what was really happening. It was theatre, and on some level everyone knew this; and yet at the same time it strengthened the bonds between people, was the foundation of so much social interaction.

He would have continued exchanging this meaningless chit-chat late into the night if the incident hadn't happened. Fekete Anna's handbag changed everything. He believed in some form of fate – he always had. And for a brief moment, as the gypsy barged into Anna, grabbed her handbag from the chair and scarpered, he felt that this was meant to be, that it was written in the stars. Lies always strive towards the light; they yearn to be revealed. But the feeling lasted only a second, perhaps two. After that came a sense of panic. If the thief had been any other gypsy in the world, he would have been fine. But it was Lakatos Sándor, Lakatos János's great-nephew, who claimed to know things about the past, about the one case he thought he'd buried long ago. And now Sándor said he needed money to put his sister through school. He'd tried to dismiss the boy's claims outright. This gypsy kid couldn't have any hard evidence; if there had been any he would have been locked up long ago. The boy must have heard local gossip and decided to try his luck. But the theft changed everything. He had to act fast, without a plan, without making preparations. Anna and Sándor must never be allowed to meet. That was a risk he simply could not take. Ever.

As a commotion ensued at the fair, he slipped away unnoticed, walking briskly through the shadows in the direction the thief had run, chased by Anna and her friends. He carefully crossed the intersection in the black spot that the CCTV cameras missed so that he wouldn't be seen. He darted down towards the darkened streets of Kőrös, where he saw the bag thief running ahead of him and turning right, either back towards the town or heading down to the Tisza. A cold sweat trickled down his neck. Damn the jumped-up little brat. Nobody was going to threaten him. Nobody was going to tell him what to do. And nobody was going to undermine his upstanding reputation, especially not a tinker, a crook, almost a kid.

He followed Sándor far along the riverbank. At last the thief came to a stop. He quietly said the boy's name, and when the kid turned he saw the fear and exhaustion on his young face.

'You?' the boy said in astonishment. 'How did you find your way out here? Did you bring the cash?'

He stepped closer to the boy, with a quick swipe of the hand knocked him to the mud, jumped on him and grabbed his throat. The boy fought back; he was young and strong. He felt the boy's muscular body struggling and writhing beneath him. But he had decades of experience on his side. Calmly he squeezed his fingers tighter and tighter round the boy's throat, using his weight to press the boy's body hard against the mud. He felt the boy's breathing becoming sporadic; he struggled less and less, and eventually stopped moving altogether. To make absolutely sure he continued pressing down on the boy's throat and counted slowly to a hundred.

Once he was satisfied that the boy was dead, he gripped him by the wrists and hauled the body to the water's edge. His first thought was to push the little shit into the river, but he realised that the body would be found more quickly in the water than it would on the riverbank. Nobody moved around in these bushes. The river, on the other hand, had a busy traffic of fishermen and people roaring up and down on water-scooters and sailing boats. With any luck nobody would ever find the body.

Scanning the scrub with his torch, he quickly examined the area to make sure he hadn't left any trace of himself – a dislodged button or something similar. He wasn't at all worried. He just had to carefully plan what happened next, that was all. He could no longer afford panicked reactions, he thought, just as he heard a branch snapping nearby and saw something disappear through the bushes.

JUNE 18th

THE HOUSE LOOKED EVERY BIT as ridiculous as it had the first time she'd visited. Pompous and tasteless.

Anna rang the bell. The gates opened with a click. Remete Mihály appeared at the front door and shouted something to one side. A haggard old man with a pair of garden shears appeared at the corner of the house. Mihály said something to the man, who placed his shears on the patio and left as Anna and Péter stepped inside.

'Hello. What brings you here?' asked Mihály, looking quizzically at Péter, who was in civilian clothes. 'Aren't you the new police officer from Újvidék?'

'Vajda Péter, *jó napot.* I wouldn't say I'm particularly new. I've lived here for years.'

'Doesn't time fly? Well, come on inside. Would you like some coffee? *Pálinka*?'

'No, thank you,' said Anna, and Péter shook his head.

'I'll get straight to the point,' said Anna taking a bunch papers from her bag.

Mihály looked at them nervously and poured himself a glass of *pálinka.*

'You are involved with the mafia,' said Anna, calmly, 'or at least you were involved with them at the time my father was killed. He was investigating a case in which you were implicated.'

Mihály didn't respond.

'When the boy who stole my handbag died on the night of the wine fair, at first it seemed like an accident. However, I've discovered that his death wasn't an accident after all. He was murdered.'

'Really?' Mihály gasped.

'Yes. Strangled. By a man with grey hair.'

Mihály raised a hand and touched his own hair. He looked frightened now.

'Pretty soon my unofficial investigation brought me back to the case of my father's death. It turns out that the deaths of the handbag thief and my father are linked to one another. In the local Roma community there are still rumours that an innocent man was convicted of my father's murder. It's thought that a Roma man by the name of Lakatos János was framed for the murder. Lakatos was also the name of the handbag thief.'

Anna paused. But Mihály still didn't speak.

'You were at the wine fair and you saw who took my bag,' Anna continued. 'Bad luck, wasn't it, that it was Lakatos. I found your name in my father's personal notes on the original investigation. My father wouldn't have gone out to that farmhouse alone unless he knew who or what would be waiting for him. He would never have put himself at risk like that. But it seems a man can't even trust his friends. You … you disgust me.'

Péter touched Anna's forearm. *Control yourself*, the touch said.

Mihály leafed through the notes with tears in his eyes and poured himself another *pálinka*.

'I … I knew something was wrong,' he spluttered.

Then a wave of sobs wrenched his body. He buried his head in his hands and wept like a child.

'But I didn't kill your father,' he said at last. 'I am – or rather I was once involved with the mafia. But that was a long time ago. I've left it all behind. I couldn't do it any longer. I abused my position in the city council in a few instances – building contracts, that sort of thing, and I was paid very well for it. But, believe me, I was just a tiny cog in the mafia's enormous machine. Then your father started looking into what was going on, and I realised I was behaving like a despicable crook. I was afraid it would all come out. But I was serious about politics. I still am. I had ideals and values. I didn't want to tarnish my reputation.'

'Back then you were a trusted comrade of the Communist Party. Now you operate on the far right. It seems your values change with the wind,' said Anna, her voice dripping with contempt.

'That's another story,' said Mihály, almost in a whisper. 'Please let me explain.'

'Start talking.'

'When your father died I realised what kind of organisation I'd been working for. Over a period of time I gradually began to distance myself from them. You could say that the war saved me. Amid all the chaos and upheaval I managed to sever my ties with the organisation without any problems. Under normal circumstances I doubt that would have been possible. They keep their own on a short leash, as I'm sure you know.'

Remete paused for a moment, swallowed and took a deep breath before continuing.

'There was something strange about your father's death. I've heard the rumours too. All these years I've been carrying the guilt around inside. What if I hadn't used my influence to offer those construction contracts? What if I wasn't such a money-grabbing bastard? Would your father's investigation have caused the same chain of reactions, led to the same fate? Would he still be alive today?'

Mihály wiped his tears and blew his nose.

'But I didn't kill him or the thief,' he said plainly.

'Can you prove it?' said Péter.

'I wasn't in Kanizsa when István died. I wasn't even in Vajdaság.'

Mihály went into his office. Péter moved his hand to his hip, ready to pull out his gun and shoot. A moment later Mihály returned carrying a large newspaper cutting.

'At the time I was on a three-day trip to Prishtina in Kosovo. It was a party meeting.'

Anna and Péter looked at the image from the *Večernje novosti* newspaper in which a young Remete Mihály stood smiling with a group of men in dark suits. At the top of the page was the date; it matched perfectly: 25th November 1988.

'Very well. But what about the wine fair? What did you do after that? After my bag was stolen?' asked Anna.

Mihály looked reluctant to answer and nervously sipped his fruit liquor.

'You'd be advised to tell us the truth,' Péter said in a quietly encouraging tone. Anna was surprised that Péter had remained so calm throughout the interview.

'I had a meeting,' said Mihály.

'Where? With whom?'

'At the party office. I went there as soon as the commotion over the theft had calmed down. I was there for several hours, almost until morning.'

'Who were you there with? Can anyone verify your account?'

Mihály listed the names of five men. 'You can ask all of them. I was there with them.'

'You can be sure we will. What were you doing?'

'It was a meeting of the party's youth wing. In other words we were drinking a lot. These are the same boys you've already been asking about, Anna. The ones who shave their heads. I've always believed politics needs to reach out to the younger generation. They are the future.'

'And you need voters. So you attract them by plying skinheads with free booze, is that right?' Anna asked in disgust.

She was disappointed. Mihály was so unpleasant that she'd hoped he was the one behind all of this, that the mist would finally clear. Now everything was as blurred as before.

'Come on, Anna,' said Péter. 'Let's go.'

A THIRSTY HORNET CIRCLED above a rapidly evaporating puddle, like a helicopter preparing to land. There had been a heavy thunderstorm the night before, and here and there obstinate puddles glinted in the dips in the asphalt where the sun hadn't yet succeeded in drying them out. Anna walked home, her thoughts heavy and oppressive. She didn't answer her mother's greetings but headed for her room and went straight to bed.

Anna had gone to Péter's place after the meeting with Remete; they had made love, Péter had massaged Anna's knotted shoulders, played music quietly and held Anna in his arms so gently that she eventually drifted off to sleep. Never before had Anna been able to relax so completely with someone, felt such a natural connection with another person that she'd taken a nap in his arms. When Anna eventually woke up an hour later, Péter made some coffee and dropped the bombshell right amid the cups and croissants.

His wife and children were moving back home.

Anna hadn't asked anything more. She just nodded. That's nice, she said and calmly finished her coffee. Péter handed her a memory stick with material from the CCTV cameras in town – he'd finally been able to get hold of it but had forgotten to mention it when Anna had urgently asked him to come with her to Remete's place.

Anna had thanked him and left without saying goodbye. Péter had tried to stop her. Let's talk this through, he implored her, saying Anna was important to him, that he didn't want to let her leave that way. But Anna shrugged herself free of his arms. She forced herself to walk out of the house as if nothing had happened, though she wanted to bolt out of the door. She wanted to shout and run, to slam the door so hard that the frame came off and splinters flew from the wood. Instead she walked calmly until she couldn't be seen from any of Péter's windows or from the yard. Then she broke into a sprint, ran through the town to the banks of the Tisza and walked along the riverbank until she was utterly exhausted.

Now she lay in bed staring at the ceiling. Anxiety gripped her chest, crushing it tightly, but still she lit a cigarette. She smoked two cigarettes back to back. Ash fell on the sheets, leaving black marks. There came a knock at the door and her mother peered inside.

'Goodness, it's smoky in here,' said her mother and sat down at the end of the bed. 'What's the matter now?'

'It's nothing,' Anna replied and stubbed her cigarette out in an empty water bottle.

'I can see something's up. Tell Mum all about it and it'll feel better.'

Anna looked into her mother's troubled, concerned eyes, and she could no longer hold back. The sobbing started as a pathetic whimpering and eventually burst forth in a primal roar.

Anna's mother stroked her hair for a long time and Anna curled up against her mother's thighs, making them wet with tears.

'I could come to Finland for Christmas this year,' said her mother, once Anna's sobs had subsided. 'That would make a change. But only if you don't mind.'

'That would be nice. I never want to come here again.'

'When you were a teenager, I secretly dreamed that I'd be able to experience a moment like this with you again.'

'A moment with me bawling my eyes out?'

'I didn't want to see you suffering, of course – don't get me wrong. But matters of the heart like this; something that would let me show you that I'm here to support you and protect you. I felt so helpless, so estranged from you all those years, when all I wanted to do was help you find your own path in life.'

'I knew that without the heartbreak.'

'Sweet, sweet Anna. We all get through heartbreak. Eventually,' her mother said, and stroked Anna's hair again.

Anna closed her eyes. She felt like a little child who needs nothing more than a hug and someone to look after them, and the feeling wasn't at all unpleasant.

IT WAS LATE IN THE EVENING by the time Réka arrived at Anna's house to look through the CCTV footage Péter had given them.

Anna had talked to her mother for hours. About Ákos, Áron and their father. Her mother had been astonishingly frank and talked with almost heartbreaking intensity about the pain of her losses; a pain that, as the years had passed, had turned into a dull, wistful longing. She talked about how worried she'd been about Anna and how happy she was that, despite all their misfortunes, Anna had made a success of her life, studied and got a job, settled in her new country. Anna told her about life in Finland, about the loneliness and the sense of rootlessness. She talked about her ambitions, about how much she enjoyed her job and wanted to do the best she could. Her mother seemed to understand. Neither of them mentioned the issue of starting a family. That aside, Anna felt as though she'd never been this close to her mother before. Eventually her mother said what Anna had been hoping to hear: that she too wanted to know the truth about what really happened all those years ago.

There were three CCTV cameras in Kanizsa. One at the town hall and two at the corner of the school, facing the intersection at Karadjordje utca, so that approaching cars appeared in one camera and left the crossing in the other. In all probability the handbag thief, followed shortly by Anna and Ernő, should be visible in the latter two cameras. Anna nervously pushed the memory stick into the computer and clicked the file open. The footage was every bit as blurred as that of any security camera she'd seen before. These cameras were designed to follow traffic, not people. The intersection by the school was busy and there were plenty of traffic collisions. Anna wound the video forward to Friday evening. Réka sipped a Coca-Cola.

'Isn't that unhealthy for the baby?' asked Anna.

'Yes. And for me. But I can't take the heat a moment longer without some. What am I going to do in August when my stomach is bigger and the temperature is even higher? At least now I can still sleep at night. By then the nights will be so humid I'll feel like pulling my own skin off.'

Anna wasn't listening. She was concentrating on watching the tapes. The lights of approaching cars moved in jolts, as if the camera had taken photographs instead of rolling footage. The cars disappeared from one camera and their rear lights appeared in the next, then disappeared again just as quickly. New cars appeared, and Anna caught a glimpse of a few pedestrians walking along the edge of the screen. There was very little traffic that night.

Then things started to happen. Anna gave a start as Réka shrieked at the computer.

'Look! Someone's running over there.'

'It's Lakatos Sándor.'

At the corner of the screen a man had appeared – wearing a dark hoodie and with a bag in his hand. It was Anna's handbag. In sporadic, edgy movements he ran across the street without looking behind him and disappeared beyond the reach of the camera. A second, two perhaps, and the street was empty again. A minute went by, a minute that felt like an eternity, and then Anna's image appeared on the screen. Ernő was there too, but the camera angle cut him out of the screen. Anna was waving her hands and feverishly explaining something, she took off her shoes, ran across the street and vanished.

Anna stopped the video and wound it back to the point where Lakatos appeared. They watched the incident three times. Anna was becoming increasingly frustrated.

'This is no use,' she sighed.

'Quiet,' Réka scolded, stopped the video, wound it back and started it again. 'Look. Someone arrives at the crossing after you.'

A shadow had appeared on the pavement.

'And now another car.'

A brown car pulled up at the intersection, stopped to let a pedestrian cross the road, jolted into motion again and disappeared from sight just as its rear lights came into view in the other camera.

'Who was that crossing the street?' asked Réka.

'It could have been anyone.'

'Why did we only see the shadow?'

'I don't know.'

'It's as though he knew that's where the cameras were positioned.'

'I imagine quite a few people know about them.'

'Yes, but they don't deliberately avoid them.'

They watched the sequence of events over and over, and Anna too became convinced that the person casting the shadow was avoiding the cameras, and doing it so skilfully that he crossed the road without showing even the briefest glimpse of himself.

'The car's registration number is visible in this frame,' said Réka. 'Maybe the driver might remember who crossed the road? I'll find out who the car belongs to.'

'Great,' said Anna wearily.

'Is everything all right? You seem sad.'

'It's nothing.'

'I can see something's bothering you,' Réka said, pushing the point.

'Péter's wife is moving back.'

'Oh, Anna, I'm sorry.'

'There's no need. It's probably for the best. Nothing would have come of it, with me in Finland and him here. Anyway, he has a son. The kid is probably thrilled that his mum and dad are getting back together.'

'You really fell for him, didn't you?'

'It seems that way. But you know what?'

'What?'

'I just remembered that Molnár László has an old Renault just like the one we've just seen. I was sitting in it only a few days ago. And would you believe he's involved in people smuggling? Nagy Béla claims he does it out of pure charity, but perhaps he's not quite as righteous as he makes out.'

'László is a priest,' said Réka suspiciously.

'And? He wouldn't be the first shepherd to turn into a wolf. Either he saw Lakatos's murderer or he *is* the murderer.'

'*Úr Isten*,' Réka gasped.

'I must go and talk to him,' said Anna.

'Should I come with you?'

'It's probably best if you don't. It's safest if nobody knows you've been helping me.'

'I'm scared,' said Réka. 'You've even received threats. What if it's him?'

Anna thought about the matter.

'Perhaps I'll have to swallow my pride and call Péter, ask him to watch my back. He has a police weapon, after all.'

'Do it, Anna. József and I want you to be the godmother to the baby. You're my best friend, my oldest friend, and I want us to end up in the same old folk's home together. Don't do anything stupid. Agreed?'

Anna promised and hugged her friend.

JUNE 19th

ANNA MET UP WITH Molnár László first thing in the morning. They had agreed that Anna and Péter would come to the rectory, which was situated in a small building in the courtyard of a house on Ady Endre utca. Péter had seemed thrilled at Anna's phone call and agreed to help her as much as she needed. He said he wanted them to remain friends. Anna had heard the sound of his little boy in the background. And the voice of a woman asking him who was calling. Anna decided not to tell him what she thought of friendship between former lovers. She still needed Péter, but this time only for protection. She tried to convince herself this was the case.

The cherry tree outside the house was heavy with ripe fruit. Or should cherries be classified as berries? Anna wondered. László was waiting for them in the street. He'd already made them coffee. For Anna this was her second cup of the morning of the strong, Turkish coffee that made her heart race and her mind restless if she drank even a little too much of it.

'I've been examining the town's CCTV cameras from the night when my bag was stolen,' Anna began. This time, too, she had decided to skip the meaningless chit-chat and get straight to the point.

'Really? Does the video show anything?'

'Maybe. Your car can be seen crossing the intersection in front of the school shortly after I ran past, chasing the thief.'

'Well, that's no surprise. I was probably on my way to the wine fair. Besides, I probably drive past those cameras a hundred times a day when I'm in Kanizsa.'

'I think it's quite suspicious that you were at the wine fair and drove off in the same direction the thief and I were running. What's more, I've found out that you knew Lakatos and that you are involved in some form of people smuggling, just like he was.'

'Where did you hear that?'

'I heard you giving coordinates to the young men at the refugee camp. I caught our friend Béla red-handed,' said Anna. Don't play stupid, she thought. You expect me to believe he didn't tell you about this?

László looked at Péter, who sat drinking his coffee as if he wasn't listening to the conversation.

'Is that why he's here?' asked the priest. 'To arrest me? You'll never be able to bring charges against me for smuggling. I have never taken a penny for it. Besides, many people in the police force are doing the same thing. Even the chief of police. Well, he doesn't actually get his hands dirty, but he turns a blind eye to the activities of some of his officers. Makes sure the investigations don't lead to his own station. That's why he doesn't put a stop to what we're doing. He's afraid of anything that might turn heads further up the chain of command.'

'That's all very interesting,' said Anna, and decided to call the telephone number on the back of the card from Interpol as soon as this meeting was over.

'But people smuggling isn't the reason we're here,' she continued. 'I believe that you murdered Lakatos Sándor.'

László stared at Anna for a moment. 'I heard you talking about the autopsy in Békavár. I guessed it must have something to do with the theft of your handbag. So I arranged for you to visit the body in the chapel. Yes, that was me. I would hardly have done that if I'd been guilty of the murder, would I? I have the keys to the chapel and I knew it was where the body was being stored.'

Anna tried not to show her surprise. She needed a moment to take in what she'd just heard. The priest must have been telling the truth, because otherwise he couldn't have known about Anna's nocturnal adventure in the cemetery.

'Why didn't you tell me directly? Why the secrecy?'

László stood up so suddenly that Anna almost knocked over her coffee cup with fright. Péter was ready to pull out his weapon.

'Because this is all so difficult for me!' László shouted. 'Damn it, this is all so bloody terrible! That's why!'

Anna and Péter held their breath and waited for the priest to calm down. He paced back and forth to the door a few times before eventually sitting down at the table again.

'I don't know what happened to that gypsy boy,' he continued. 'But I have my suspicions. Later on, when you mentioned the name Lakatos, the pieces of the jigsaw fell into place. I've had strong suspicions right from the start.'

'From the start?'

'From the time of your father's death.'

'What do you mean?' asked Anna. Her mouth was suddenly dry and she felt dizzy. Part of her didn't want to hear what the priest said next.

'Lakatos János was sentenced to death for your father's murder. I was the only person who saw him before the sentence was carried out. I don't know why he picked me – as far as I know he was a Catholic. Perhaps I was the only priest who agreed to visit him. I truly do not know. Be that as it may, he told me he had been drinking somewhere nearby on the night of the murder and that someone had framed him.'

'I heard that too. Tell me what you suspect.'

'When I drove to the intersection on the night of the wine fair, someone crossed the road in front of me. A pedestrian. Did you see him on the tapes?'

'Yes, but I couldn't identify the man. I was going to ask you about him.'

'Well, I did identify him.'

'Who was it?'

'It hurts to say it out loud because I don't want to believe he has anything to do with the death of the thief or of your father. It simply cannot be. He is … he is a good man. My friend.'

'Remete Mihály?'

The priest looked out at the cherry tree outside the window and attempted a smile. 'No, not him.'

'For Christ's sake, tell me. Sándor's little sister Dzsenifer is missing – she's probably dead too by now. I've been threatened, and someone even tried to kill me. You must tell me what you know.'

László sighed and looked at Anna, his eyes moist with sadness.

'It was Gábor who crossed the road that night,' he said. 'And that's not all.'

ANNA LOCKED HER BEDROOM DOOR, looked at the chaos of notes and photographs taped to her wall and spoke to it defiantly: I'm going to crack you now, she said.

Molnár László had told her he was certain he'd seen Gábor driving back from Velebit on the night of her father's murder, just as he had been coming from Totovo Selo. At first he hadn't paid the matter any attention, but later on he heard that Gábor claimed to have been at his office in the police station all night. Anna explained that a possible sighting didn't amount to anything at all, and the priest said that was precisely why he had never spoken about this to anyone. But when he saw Gábor at the crossing on the night of the theft and later heard what had happened to Sándor, it was as though the decades had flashed before his eyes. Why was Gábor yet again near the spot where a murder had taken place? Why did the bag thief have the same surname as the man convicted of István's murder? Was it coincidence? How had Gábor afforded to pay his children's university fees and trips abroad, even though inflation in Yugoslavia had eaten up everybody's savings?

Anna took her collection of plastic bags out of her desk drawer. She believed that László was telling the truth, but there was still one matter she needed to confirm. One of these grey-haired men might be guilty of, or at least indirectly involved in, the two deaths. Nobody seemed to have a decent alibi for the night of the wine fair; everybody had something to do with the mafia; everybody seemed to be hiding something and worried about their reputation. If there was one thing she had learned about her former homeland, it was that nothing is necessarily the way it appears.

The hairs. The named re-sealable plastic bags were in a row next to the microscope. Anna thought of all those Hungarian greetings and courtesies. She loathed them so much, but they could prove very useful in a criminal investigation. Kisses on the cheek and hugs with the fisherman, the politician, the priest and the policeman – long enough for her to snatch a loose hair or two from their shoulders. It was at László's house that Anna had finally completed her collection. With Péter's help she had originally planned on arranging a DNA test on all the hairs, but there wasn't time for that now.

It is incredible that something as mundane as a strand of hair can be so different in every person, she thought. The structure, colour and surface patterns all differed significantly, even in these grey-haired old men. Not a lot, but clearly enough that a simple microscope was enough to show her which of the four samples most resembled the hair that Anna had found at the site of the bag thief's murder. A DNA test would verify the matter later, but using just her eyes and a microscope, the result was clear and reliable.

She read through one of the old case files one last time. All the pieces of the puzzle finally fitted together. She looked at her investigation taped to the wall and saw the familiar face of the grey-haired man. She called Réka first, then Péter.

'I KNOW IT WAS YOU. There's no point trying to threaten me or do anything stupid. Réka has already been to the police station and now she's on her way to the offices of *Magyar Szó* to write up the story. Vajda Péter also knows everything. You can't get out of this.'

Kovács Gábor was sitting at his bare desk and staring past Anna with empty eyes at the cherry tree growing almost flush against the window.

'You can't prove anything,' he said quietly.

Anna showed him the plastic bag containing the few grey hairs. 'You really believe that? Guess where I found these. And guess who they belong to.'

'I went to the site of the murder, wanted to examine it for myself. That's not a serious crime.'

'You said earlier that you didn't visit the site.'

'I didn't dare admit it while my boss was listening. He wouldn't like a retired old man like me sticking his nose into his cases.'

'We have a witness who saw you running from the wine fair and pursuing Lakatos Sándor. The same witness saw you behind the wheel of your car near the farm where my father was shot on the night he died, though you claim you were at the station all night. Twice in the wrong place at the wrong time. How do you explain that?'

Gábor said nothing.

'Add to that the fact that you've lied to me about other things, too. You told me the state confiscated the mafia's money found at the farm where my father died. That's not true. I've read every report that was ever written about that case. The money disappeared, and no trace of it was ever found. I know you took it that evening. After you shot my father.'

'I'll kill you,' said Gábor feebly.

'You already tried that once without much success.'

'That was just supposed to scare you.'

'Everybody knows what you've done. There's no point trying to get out of it.'

Gábor turned to face Anna. His expression was frozen, wax-like. Again he was silent.

'Have you killed Dzsenifer too? Tell me where she is, or do you want her death on your conscience too?'

'What's that?'

'Excuse me?'

'A conscience. I haven't had one of those for years.'

'How could you? My father's closest friend.'

Anna felt like spitting in the man's face, lunging at him, tearing that revolting look from his face.

'My mother told me you helped her financially, looked after the house while we were in Finland. How … how could you bring yourself to do it? You two-faced piece of filth,' Anna shouted. 'You destroyed our family, ruined my whole childhood. Do you understand? I've had to live without a father, all because of your greed, your reputation and your honour. My mother has had to live without her husband. And let's not forget Ákos and Áron. Would Áron have ever gone to war if he'd had a father at home to prevent him? Have you ever thought about any of this?'

Gábor didn't lower his head, didn't show any sign of shame or regret. Perhaps that was a good thing – Anna didn't think she would have been able to bear Gábor's remorse; she might have attacked him physically. She was happy she wasn't in Finland now and that she wasn't operating in an official capacity. If she'd been carrying her weapon, she would have shot him there and then, without words, without warning. She thought of Farkas Lajos in his padded cell and felt an overwhelming sense of satisfaction at the thought that this despicable murderer would soon be the Roma man's neighbour.

'Where is the girl? Is she still alive?' Anna asked once again.

'I couldn't do it,' Gábor said, so quietly that Anna couldn't hear him properly.

'What? Speak up, man!' Anna shouted.

At that Gábor cracked. He began to sob.

'I've ruined everything. But I couldn't kill the girl with my bare hands. I left her there. I don't know if she's still alive.'

'Where did you leave her?'

Spluttering with emotion Gábor told her where he'd taken Dzsenifer.

'The police are on their way here, so don't try any tricks,' said Anna and bolted out of the room, out of the building, and on to the street. She called an ambulance, then turned left at the end of the street, where she bumped into a group of schoolchildren. Then she ran all the way to the banks of the Tisza.

She didn't hear the shot that ended Kovács Gábor's life.

THE TISZA HAD BEGUN flowering that morning. The news had spread through the town like wildfire – posters went up, felt-tip markings giving the specific time when a string quartet would float down the river on a pontoon, playing Handel and Bartók. People had already begun to gather along the riverbanks, the *bogrács* ovens were already warming, and the first swarms of insects were already fluttering above the water.

The blossoming was growing by the time Anna reached the river, which by now was full of boats and celebrating people. There were so many insects that it looked as though a cloud had descended on the Tisza, a rippling, living cloud made up of millions of shimmering spots. The insects forming that cloud would die as the day progressed and fall into the water, a delicious meal for the fish and birds. Anna had learned as a child that the Tisza flowers floating on the surface of the river were already dead, that, as long as they were alive, they remained in the air.

Music could be heard from further upstream. It was a surreal moment for the people waiting along the bank – when the pontoon glided slowly down the river, the beautiful music growing louder all the while. Everyone fell silent as this astonishing piece of theatre took place; they wanted to enjoy every minute of it, as the insects danced in time with the music. Even the children were quiet.

Anna barged past the people in front of her and tried to run through the crowds as quickly as she could. She accidentally knocked a little boy to the ground. The boy started crying and an angry father shouted insults at Anna.

Behind Békavár and the playing fields was an area where the local kids used to hang out. Nowadays there was nothing but overgrown grass and a ramshackle wooden hut, which had once been used to store spare parts for boat motors. Anna sprinted towards it and began kicking at the door, which was fastened with a large padlock. The rotten boards gave way easily. Splinters flew up as Anna's foot finally punched through the wood. She enlarged the gap by pulling at the planks until it was big enough for her to clamber inside.

Dzsenifer was lying on the floor. She seemed lifeless, didn't move. Anna tore the rag from the girl's mouth, put two fingers on her throat and checked her pulse. The pontoon was approaching, engulfed in the cloud of insects, and the music grew louder. Two violins, viola and cello. The flotilla of boats turned off their motors. Music filled the air. Anna felt a light pulse in Dzsenifer's veins, a faint flow of air at her nostrils. The music was drowned out by the wail of sirens.

NOVEMBER 24th, 1988

Everything was supposed to be clean and simple. All he was supposed to do was visit the farmhouse; the owners lived elsewhere and only visited their farm in the summer months to grow vegetables to keep them through the winter. The money was stashed in one of the manure stores behind the main building. The farm was out in the puszta, *in the middle of nowhere. The door to the storehouse had been left open. Nobody lived nearby, everything should have gone as planned.*

There was a lot of money, in US dollars and Deutschmarks. The Yugoslavian dinar wasn't a good currency; inflation had eaten up much of its value and people were saying there was still worse to come. An account had been opened at a Swiss bank and the money was to be deposited in Belgrade three weeks later.

The weakest part of the plan was how to get to the farm. Nobody must see him or his car going out there. Still, he had to drive out of the town to reach the puszta, *and that almost certainly meant being spotted. The drawback of living in a small town. That was why they had decided that the money would change hands late in the evening – but not so late that the sight of his car would arouse suspicion. He chose the normal route out of town, and only one acquaintance walked past, drunk, on his way home from Három csöcs. The man didn't raise his hand or greet him. Good. Perhaps nobody would see him after all.*

Once outside the town he no longer took the direct route to the farm but drove all the way round Orombhegyes and from there took the back roads to Velebit, then the dirt tracks to the puszta, *and further on towards the farm.*

He stopped by the fence running round the farm and sat in his car for a while, looking at his surroundings. Nothing. Nobody. Somewhere in the distance he could see the solitary light of another farmhouse, like a far-off star in the night sky. He stepped out of the car, didn't close the door, listened for a moment then walked briskly to the gate, which had been left unlocked for him. The hinges gave a piercing creak as he pushed it open. A large bird flew up from a tree in the yard. He could hear his heartbeat getting faster. He took a deep breath. Silence enveloped him once again.

He walked behind the main building and headed to the storehouse, stepped inside its low-slung door and started looking. He'd been told that the bag with the money would be behind the sacks of manure. There were many rows of sacks and he had to look behind each one of them. He began to the left of the door. There was nothing behind the first row, the second or the third. Then he got lucky. He sighed with relief and gripped the large sports bag, pulled it out from behind the sacks of manure and switched on his torch. He undid the zip. What he saw startled him. The bag was stuffed full of large banknotes. He was a rich man. Christ, with this money he could live comfortably for the rest of his life; send his children to good universities abroad and renovate the house to put a stop to his wife's nagging. He wouldn't do anything over the top – nothing ostentatious, nothing that would make people suspicious. No expensive cars, no swimming pools, at least not immediately, not all at once. One thing at a time. There was no hurry. He had the rest of his life.

At that moment the lights in the manure store flickered on.

Fekete István was standing in the doorway looking at him, his eyes full of disappointment, his expression one of revulsion.

Instinctively he reached to his hip, pulled his gun and fired.

He saw the surprise in István's face, the terror; heard the muffled pop as his gun fired through the silencer; watched the bullet pierce his friend's chest, almost in slow motion; saw the dark blood spew forth and soak the fabric of his shirt; watched István fall to the ground almost without a sound. All he heard was the thud. His friend died in the blink of an eye.

Good shot, was his first thought. The man didn't suffer, there was no need for a second bullet. His next thought almost choked him. He had killed his friend and colleague, a father of three children, perhaps the only honest cop in the region. This is going to be hell, he thought. I'll have to cover my tracks, make them lead far away from myself. What happened here must never come to light. Otherwise my reputation will be destroyed and my life will be lost.

He picked up the sports bag and left.

He hatched his plan as he drove through the desolate puszta, *watching the dark night sky. He drove towards Velebit, where he knew a few petty criminals lived.*

EPILOGUE
JUNE 5th

THE BUS'S LARGE WINDOW felt cool against the woman's forehead. The empty landscape extended before her, sweltering in the heat – the fields raising ears of wheat to the sky, praying for rain, but there was air conditioning in the bus and she felt light. She closed her eyes and succumbed to the exhaustion. It consumed her whole body, one limb, one muscle at a time. Her feet relaxed first – they were covered in painful, festering blisters – then her buttocks, her stomach, her arms. Her eyelids fell shut heavily, as though they were weighted down, but she didn't fall asleep. Her mind was still alert. It would take a long while before that could finally rest.

She had bought the passport from a scruffy little girl who turned up at the camp one morning. The girl reminded her of a stray cat, her hair was so tangled and the look in her fearful eyes so wild. The girl approached her as if they'd agreed it in advance. There weren't many women at the camp and even fewer women like her – with no children to look after, with no one.

The passport didn't cost much. She still had a decent sum of money left. A nest egg. A new start. Flashbacks from the camp in Turkey darted before her eyes; then the fishing boat; the merciless waves that battered the boat to pieces and dragged its miserable passengers into the water. The images tried to push their way into her thoughts – she felt her thighs tensing yet again – but she managed to push the memories aside and focus on her destination. Where that would be, she couldn't say. The main thing was that she was safe now, and that she no longer needed to walk.

She had left the camp as soon as she'd bought the passport, sensing instantly that this was her chance. A Finnish passport would help her out of here. It was the best passport in the world. She had to act fast and hope that the passport hadn't yet been reported missing, that they wouldn't stop her at the border and send her back to that filthy camp, where hundreds of lustful men stared at her hungrily.

She had stepped on the first bus heading for Budapest. From there she would continue directly to Germany, perhaps by train. She'd cross that bridge later.

The border crossing passed without any difficulty. Two customs officials entered the bus, checked everybody's papers, asked if they had anything to declare, rummaged through a few people's bags. She remained calm by imagining she was the woman whose passport she was carrying, on her way home. A stern customs official checked the stamp showing she had entered the country, gave the photograph a cursory glance, stamped her out of the country and handed back the passport. She could easily have been the woman in the photograph. She was the same age, had the same dark hair, the same brown eyes. Passport photographs were always a bit out of focus, and luckily it seemed that attention to detail wasn't one of this customs official's strongest qualities.

And here she was. She opened her eyes and smiled. The reflection in the window smiled back at her. She took out her mobile phone and sent her mother a message. She pictured the message travelling in a matter of seconds the thousands of kilometres it had taken her months to cross, imagined it reaching her mother, somewhere far away amid the ruins, the weeping and the hunger. Right now her mother would hear a beep, she'd take the phone in her withered hands and read the message.

All fine. I'm finally free.

ACKNOWLEDGEMENTS

I would like to take this opportunity to thank Mikko for all the expert advice about police work. Thank you also to all my friends living in Serbia.

My gratitude also goes to everyone at the Otava Publishing Company, particularly Leenastiina Kakko, and to Aleksi Pöyry, my patient and encouraging editor.

Thank you to the indefatigable Karen Sullivan at Orenda Books and to translator David Hackston for all their hard work in bringing my work to an English-speaking public.